CALL TO QUARTERS

HONOR RACONTEUR

A GÆLDORCRÆFT FORCES NOVEL

RACONTEUR HOUSE

Published by Raconteur House
Antioch, TN

CALL TO QUARTERS
A Gældercræft Forces Novel

A Raconteur House book/ published by arrangement with the author

PRINTING HISTORY
Raconteur House mass-market edition/September 2016

ISBN: 978-1537540979

For information address:
Raconteur House
3425 Daisy Trail
Antioch, TN, 37013

www.raconteurhouse.com

THE ADVENT MAGE CYCLE

Book One: *Jaunten*
Book Two: *Magus*
Book Three: *Advent*
Book Four: *Balancer*

ADVENT MAGE NOVELS
Advent Mage Compendium
The Dragon's Mage
The Lost Mage

Warlords Rising
Warlords Ascending*

SINGLE TITLES

Special Forces 01

The Midnight Quest

Kingslayer

THE ARTIFACTOR SERIES

The Child Prince
The Dreamer's Curse
The Scofflaw Magician
The Canard Case *

DEEPWOODS SAGA

Deepwoods
Blackstone
Fallen Ward

Origins

KINGMAKERS

Arrows of Change
Arrows of Promise

GÆLDERCRÆFT FORCES

Call to Quarters

*Upcoming

As long as one keeps searching, the answers come.

- Joan Baez

—As explained in chapter 2, in 1857 a massive earthquake rocked California along the San Andreas Fault. This would not be the only massive earthquake to shake California because of that fault line.

In 2008, it was noted by several experts that the San Andreas Fault was "locked, loaded, and ready" for another large earthquake. Simulations showed what the effects would be but they anticipated that the effects would spread south, covering the area between Los Angeles and San Diego. Because the San Andreas fault system is the boundary between the Pacific Plate and the North American Plate, the conclusion experts reached was that while the cities were in danger of being shaken up, the plates were moving horizontally past one another, so that no part of California was in danger of falling into the ocean.

These calculations proved to be incorrect in 2021 when the cities of Los Angeles and Santa Barbara abruptly cracked from the mainland. Experts are still not sure if the San Andreas Fault was entirely the cause or if this was a continuation of the mantle pieces breaking off that they had already witnessed in Virginia in 2011. Regardless, both seaboard cities wrenched free entirely and started sinking into the ocean at a steady rate.

Panic was widespread, but there was no way to escape from either Los Angeles or Santa Barbara except by boat or plane.

A national emergency was immediately placed in effect, and the Gældorcræft Forces were on scene before the dust even settled. In a herculean effort that has never since been rivaled, the entirety of the Forces took both cities on and, through magic and willpower, kept them from sinking entirely. Engineers and architects were called in, and a system was hastily cobbled together to support the cities. A network of generators and buoyancy machines were attached to the cities. One head engineer observed that if they had been given the task before the cities actually broke off, it would have taken several years to manage this. As it was, in two short weeks, the system was online.

Perhaps because of the haste in which the system was set up, it was not perfect, and it could not keep the cities completely above the water. The Gældorcræft Forces decided to rearrange their organization, and established exactly thirty-six teams dedicated to keeping both Los Angeles and Santa Barbara afloat. Between their tireless efforts and the network of generators and buoyancy machines, the seaboard cities were stabilized enough to live on.

There is still a movement in the government that suggests relocating the inhabitants of both cities as some legislators feel that the resources needed to keep the cities afloat is a waste and could be put to better use elsewhere. So far this movement has gained no traction.

Excerpt from The History of California Earthquakes
Written by Bryce Moon 2026

GROUND ZERO

"ADAMS, Brian," a burly looking sergeant barked out.

"Oh, another male Mægencræft, that's rare. I thought Teddy was the only one here at boot camp," Tye commented. She raised up in her seat a little to take a better look at the person called. There were two rows of seats between them, so it took her a second to get a clear look. "How did we miss seeing him?"

"Easy," Sam answered, not even glancing up from the packet in her hands. "He was in a different group than us and he's male. We wouldn't see him in the dorms." Flicking a finger against the file she demanded, "They don't really expect us to read through this whole thing before we leave camp, do they?"

"No," Noriko assured her, "we're expected to read through it before we reach our assigned station."

"Phew. About had a heart attack." Sam finally looked up and peered ahead. "Why are we testing our levels, anyway? After this much schooling they surely know by now."

One would think. Noriko was also a little puzzled by this. When a child tested positive for either Dwolcræft or Mægencræft talents, they were immediately tested for general power levels before even being put in school. Then, throughout their schooling, they were tested on a religious basis. Not just because they were growing, either. Ranking was only in part based on power level— knowledge and visualization skills also played heavily into it. The more information that they knew, the more magic they could wield. Or to be more accurate, that a Dwolcræft could wield. A Mægencræft was a conduit that channeled energy to her partner. They couldn't actively use that magical power themselves.

More's the pity. Noriko sometimes lamented that she was born a Mægencræft. Out of her family of six, it was only she and Haru that were Mægencræftas. Takako, Kyou, Shigure, and Ryou were Dwolcræftas. It looked like they would all join the Gældorcræft Forces too. Their parents lamented over this, as they had chosen the civilian side of things and were both teachers, so naturally they wanted at least one child to follow in their footsteps. But none of them were inclined to do so. Even the youngest, Haru, wanted to be actively in service.

Even now she wasn't sure what it was about being part of the Force that had drawn her to sign up. It wasn't the lure of being in uniform.

Well, they had a uniform of sorts, if one could call the red windbreakers and tan cargo pants a 'uniform.' Maybe it was the unpredictability of the job. On the civilian side, her options were limited to building or teaching, and both of those had steady routines. Noriko didn't really want a set schedule that remained the same day to day. She wanted something outside the norm. Being part of the GF was the perfect way to do that as they supplemented the police and fire stations, often having office space inside police stations. Criminal activities, fires, natural disasters—they were expected to help with all of it.

Hopefully she wouldn't end up in the middle of nowhere, where nothing ever happened. Not that she wanted to be in a hotbed of trouble, either, but somewhere in the middle would be nice.

Sam was still going through the packet they'd been handed. "There's forms in here to apply to the legal department, medical department, tech department, or for active service. I thought we'd made our choices clear before even coming to camp?"

"They don't have enough people signing up for either legal or medical," Noriko explained, her eyes actively trained forward. A hologram display slowly cycled through names, and more than trusting her ears to hear above the chattering crowd around them, she watched it, waiting for her own name to appear. "Although I can't figure out what the incentive would be to join the other departments. Legal and medical both require more schooling than active service."

"Probably why most people choose active service instead," Tye observed. "Shame they don't have a culinary section. I'd be all over that."

Noriko privately seconded that as Tye was an amazing cook. But she understood why things were organized the way they were. The Gældorcræft Forces were a paramilitary organization run by the government. They had all of the benefits, cons, and quirks of many other government organizations because of this. They were unique in one thing only: they were mostly in charge of themselves. The power they handled had unique elements to it that were undetectable by modern science, and so the average human could feel the effects of it but could not discern it directly. Medical treatment had to be given by a fellow Mægencræft and Dwolcræft. Trials, too, had to be handled inside the GF. It made some people nervous, to have the guardians guard themselves, but there was little way around the problem.

"Arashi, Noriko." Her name popped up in bold black lettering on the hologram even as the caller boomed out her name.

"My turn." She stood with a certain level of nervousness.

"You'll do fine," Sam assured her. "We'll meet up on the other side. Don't take off without us, okay?"

"I won't," she assured both of her friends before marching straight for the evaluator, an older woman that looked like a very well-preserved sixty. The name tag on her windbreaker read "Barrett." Noriko went into parade rest and greeted, "Instructor Barrett."

The instructor had been speed reading Noriko's chart through her holograph shades, but at this greeting focused in. "Miss Arashi. Your English is impeccable."

"Born in the United States, ma'am." Used to this reaction, it didn't bother her. She might have been the first generation born here, but she looked fresh off the boat. It was her parents who had accents, although they spoke English very well, and knew the United States like the backs of their hands after living in there for twenty years.

"I see." The instructor went back to reading and she frowned at the chart.

Noriko mentally groaned. She knew exactly where the woman's eyes had stopped reading even if she couldn't see the holograph display. She'd had this problem before when listing out her three preferences in stations. Just because she was 5'3" and a hundred pounds soaking wet didn't mean she was weak. She *could* handle more than routine work. After semi-raising five siblings, she knew that for a fact.

This time there were no questions—instead Barrett continued to scroll. "Test scores are excellent, congratulations for passing fourth in your class."

"Thank you, ma'am."

"Visualization skills are above average as well, I see. Let's test your power level." Barrett waved a hand to the testing apparatus behind her.

To this day Noriko couldn't shake the feeling that she was being tested by a giant thermometer. There was a giant hollow ball at the base, then a clear glass tube that went straight up for about ten feet. Each foot was marked clearly with a level in bold black numbers. The gauge rested at the very base, Level 10, and it was entirely up to her to get it toward the upper levels. The scale went all the way up to a one, although it was extremely rare to have a Level 1 Dwolcræft or Mægencræft. They had to be able to use a megamerlin of power to attain that rank, a near impossible feat for a human being to attain.

"Begin."

Noriko drew up every bit of power from the ley line under her feet. In this particular section of North Carolina, there were many fault lines and, as a result, any number of ley lines to choose from. The earthen energy that flowed between the fault lines ran warm and pure. The one directly below her was particularly strong and felt strangely a little sticky. Or was that just because of the humidity today? It felt akin to tugging liquid honey out of honeycomb.

A reporter on the news once described a Mægencræft as a walking battery, something that could draw and hold a charge of power until it was ready to be used. Especially during these tests, that's exactly what she felt like, as she drew power from the ley line and 'charged' her own aura. Once she had all that she could hold, Noriko shot it into the glass tube. It always felt strange, putting power into an object, instead of feeding it steadily to another human being. A partnering between Dwolcræftas and Mægencræftas was give and take, the Mægencræft giving what power the Dwolcræft needed to work with, the

Dwolcræft actively reaching out for that power and accepting it. Shoving it into a glass beaker like this felt alien to her and wrong.

These tests only evaluated the absolute maximum power that she could draw out in a split second, not what she could sustain. After that second, she let her connection with the ley line go. The power in the glass stayed steady, showing where her level measured at. It had shot up past the Level 10 mark and now hovered near the top, somewhere between 4 and 3. The outcome actually surprised Noriko a little, as before she had come into boot camp she had been just under a 4. Had she grown that much in just three months?

"You originally tested at a 5," Barrett noted, typing in the result with a quick hand. "But I see that it was barely a 5—you were nearly a 4 at the time. You have improved, Miss Arashi. Congratulations, we always like to see that result."

Noriko nearly beamed with pleasure. "Thank you, ma'am."

"Well. Considering these results, and your preferences, I think we can station you in a good place." Barrett unbent enough to lean forward and whisper, "And I do think that you can make it to a Level 3 in about five years. So keep up the good work."

Really? She was very glad to hear it, not only because the pay grade would be better, but because her options of choosing where to be stationed improved. "I will work hard, ma'am."

"A true Japanese response." She winked at her before drawing back. With a finger, she stabbed at the holograph display to activate a different screen before she tapped something in. "Go to the table under the blue sign over there to pick up your station assignment."

"Yes, ma'am. Thank you, ma'am." Almost bouncing in anticipation, she left the testing area and rounded the cordon before weaving her way toward the blue flag. As she went, she passed many other boot camp graduates either celebrating their station assignments or bemoaning loudly to anyone that would listen. Noriko fervently hoped she wouldn't be joining the latter group.

The table had six men manning it, all of them with holograph glasses on and stacks of envelopes in cubby holes behind them. The cubby holes were all tagged, some of them with a city and state designation, others with city and a numeric code. Noriko assumed that those were for the larger cities only, ones that had multiple stations, as she wasn't able to figure out the whole system with the peeks she was getting.

A line two deep waited before the table, so she had time to worry before it became her turn. Please, please, nowhere cold. She did not do well with cold.

The slightly harried officer at the other side looked up and demanded, "Name?"

"Arashi, Noriko," she responded instantly.

He scrolled through the screen display right in front of his eyes (although from here it looked like he was pawing at thin air), found her, then ticked it off. Turning, he went to the far right and ducked down toward the ground before pulling out a packet in a nondescript manila envelope and handing to her. "Good luck. Next!"

It was probably mean of her to open it on the spot. Noriko knew good and well that she should have waited for Sam, Tye, and Teddy, but she just couldn't contain her curiosity. Opening the top, she drew out the top sheet for a peek.

Tehachapi, Station 1.

Noriko blinked at it stupidly for a long moment. Where in the world was Tehachapi?

1ST MERLIN

AFTER three days on the job, Noriko could hardly claim she knew what she was doing, but she at least knew everyone's names. The Tehachapi Station was not a large one, nor had she expected it to be. The whole city had a population of fifty thousand, and if it weren't for the fault zone that ran right through the Tehachapi Mountains, it wouldn't warrant the three stations it boasted.

She'd initially spent her time unpacking and getting familiar with the ley lines in the immediate area. Her knowledge of them, and their quirks, would be vital later on. Hopefully much later on, although she couldn't count on that. California was famous for its earthquakes, after all.

Right now she was at her new desk, glued to the files hovering above it as she tried to memorize everything she could about this new area. The other Mægencræft, Charlotte, had given her a stack of files to go through on her first day, and she was still plowing through them. Noriko was grateful, though—they were giving her a good idea of the history of the area.

There was the sound of a computer chair rolling over and she looked up automatically to see Captain Banderas next to her. He was one of the few people in the station that didn't loom over her, being only 5'5", dark hair kept at an almost military cut, skin naturally dark because of his Hispanic heritage. Javier Banderas had proven to be kind and patient since her arrival. She liked being around him.

"Arashi. I got emailed last night, and it seems that they've finally found a partner for you."

"Did they? That was quick." And for the Gældorcræft Forces, it was. Noriko had expected it to take at least another month. "Did they give you any specifics?"

"The full file is supposedly coming today, I only got a name and a rank. Harmony Cameron Powers, D-4."

Harmony? So her new partner was a woman? "It's unusual to see a female Dwolcræft."

"I know it. But then, it's unusual to see a male Mægencræft, and your friend Stoliker is one."

True. It wasn't like it was an ironclad rule that Dwolcræftas were only males and Mægencræftas were always females, it was just that statistically that's how it normally worked out. Only 17% of Mægencræftas were males, and the ratio was about the same for female Dwolcræftas. Of course, it was also highly unusual to go through all of the education and training to be a certified Mægencræft without forming a partnership in school, but there she sat, partner-less.

"Explain to me, again, how you managed to get stationed here without a partner? I know you said that you didn't have a chance to find a partner as a teenager, but the odds of getting into your twenties without one are slim." There was no condemnation in the captain's voice, just honest curiosity.

"I'm from a very small town in Tennessee," she explained patiently. "And for whatever reason, Mægencræftas outnumbered Dwolcræftas three-to-one. It's why my friend Tye came here without a partner too." Although that had changed by day two.

"Huh. Still, you'd think that your parents or your school would have made an effort to find you guys partners."

They had. It hadn't gone well, at least not for her. "So when does she show up?"

"I'm not sure. I mean, I think she only got the notification yesterday, a few hours before I did. They give you about a week to get to station, so depending on where she's from, she might show up anytime between today or sometime next week." Banderas leaned back and regarded her frankly. "I'm not sure how good of a match you two will be, but this partnership isn't set in stone, remember that. I need my people to be in sync with each other. This isn't a job where you can set personal feelings aside and just deal."

Truly.   Dwolcræftas   depended   on Mægencræftas to give them the power that they needed in order to do magic. They couldn't store enough on their own. Because their magic power came directly from another human being, the emotions of both partners played heavily into it. Mægencræftas especially had to be careful because one error on their part and they risked doing serious damage to the Dwolcræftas. Noriko wasn't one to let emotions dictate her actions, especially where work was involved, but she appreciated the captain's sentiments. "We'll see when she gets here. Will she be in the dorms too?"

"I think so. Most land there first until they figure out where they want to live."

Noriko certainly had taken advantage of it. The station wasn't big, just a two story building for the precinct and another, separate building that served as a jailhouse. But it had a three-story apartment building that gave housing to anyone that needed it. Mostly it was the new members of the station and any single people that had found moving elsewhere to be too troublesome.

Banderas's wristwatch comm buzzed with a message. He double tapped it with a blunt index finger. "Banderas."

"Captain, your new Dwolcræft is here." Gena's voice sounded tinny through the tiny speakers. "A Cameron Powers."

"Oh? That was fast. Thanks, Gena." Banderas stood, straightening out his dark blue shirt as he moved. "Speak of the devil and she appears. She must be from nearby to get here this fast."

Noriko moved as he did, wanting to meet the woman. Just how fast had the Dwolcræft packed? It was barely afternoon after all, and she couldn't be from Tehachapi itself—Banderas would know her if she was.

The glass double doors opened and a man strode through, tall enough that he almost didn't clear the door frame. He had a surfer's build and look to him—sun bleached blond hair pulled back in a low ponytail, tanned skin, and a lackadaisical grace that spoke of natural athletic ability. He took in the cluttered office with its desks crammed together, the people inside of it, and then zeroed in on Banderas. "Captain Javier Banderas?"

Banderas's eyebrows tweaked upward before he smoothed his voice out. "That's me. You are?"

"Thought the receptionist buzzed you?" The blond's head cocked even as he made a beeline for them. "I'm Cameron Powers."

Wait. This was Harmony Powers? Noriko's jaw dropped and she mentally hiccupped. This was *so* not a female partner. What kind of parents named their son Harmony?! She blinked, making her brain move past that, and took a better look at him. Certainly good-looking enough with a slightly hippie vibe to him. He didn't appear to be nervous at all. She took him in from head to toe and was fairly impressed with what she saw on just the surface. He was indeed a D-4 to be able to radiate power like that.

"You're Cameron Powers." Banderas had a slightly doubtful face, although he was obviously trying not to.

"My first name threw you, huh." Cameron's face split in a quick grin. "Happens a lot. Everyone assume I'm a girl at first. What can I say? I was born after thirty-one hours of labor complications. Doc tried to talk my mom out of it, so did my dad, but she started threatening to sue the hospital if they didn't let her name me what she wanted to."

Banderas gave a responding smile and held out a hand. "Sounds rough. You go by Cameron, then?"

"Or Cam, pick whichever." He took the offered hand in a firm clasp before letting go.

"Cam it is, then. This is Noriko Arashi, your new partner."

Noriko shelved her surprise and offered a hand with what she trusted was a professional enough smile. "Nice to meet you."

His hand almost swallowed hers. "Hey. Nice t'meetcha, partner." Brows twitching into a frown, he paused and stared at her steadily, almost unnervingly. "Huh. Hang on." Using her hand, he pulled her into his chest and wrapped her up into a hug. She stifled a squeak and froze against him.

Not that he didn't smell nice, but seriously, what was he doing? Five seconds after he'd met her? "Um, Powers?"

"Yeah." He bent his head closer to hers, hands still strong against her back, holding her in place.

"What are you doing?" she demanded, temper rising.

"Checking something." He finally let go and she wasted no time in taking a step back. From the nonchalant expression on his face, it didn't look like he'd just been sexually harassing a woman he'd known less than a full minute. "You're supposed to be an M-4, right?"

Oh, was that what he'd been doing? Strictly speaking, they could see enough of each other that they could make a good guess what the other person's ability was. A Mægencræft's and

Dwolcræft's aura was a living thing. When they actively used their talents, their aura became very pronounced and glowed all around them like a second coat of skin. When inactive, it lay more subdued and internal. But physical touch gave them direct access to the other person's power, so it was a more accurate way of getting a measurement. Not that it excused him, he should have asked first, and why on earth had he hugged her like that? Noriko gave him an elaborate look that said she didn't appreciate being randomly pounced on. "Right."

The look did not faze him. "No way. I don't think they tested you right. "

"I'm inclined to agree, but…" The captain cleared his throat and gave Cameron a flat stare. "Powers, be more aware of your conduct. What you just did was not appropriate."

"Really?" This scolding just bounced right off, although he did shrug and tell her, "My bad."

She began to see how he'd gotten to twenty-one years old and remained without a partner. The guy was weird. As long as he could work, though, she'd put up with the weirdness. "Where are you from? We're surprised to see you this early."

"Los Angeles. Riverside, to be exact. I've been basically packed for about a week, waiting for someone to tell me where to go, so when I got the call yesterday I just threw it all in the car."

Wait, huh? "You didn't get an assignment when you graduated boot camp?" They'd assigned her on the spot.

"Well, they did," Cameron admitted with a wry smile and shrug. "And then the partner I was supposed to have got injured in a car accident on the way there. Rather than have me sit around six months waiting on her to get through rehab, they shifted my assignment to here." He reached into the messenger bag hanging over his shoulder and pulled out a slim thumb drive in a sealed case, which he handed over to Banderas. "They said this goes to the captain."

Banderas flipped it over and gave it a glance. "So it does."

Was Noriko the only one disturbed by the idea that this man was originally not supposed to be her partner but someone else's? And that the Powers-That-Be were perfectly fine playing chess with people to fit the situation?

Apparently she was, as Banderas didn't even blink. "Alright, Powers, let me introduce you to the other two people you'll be working with. This is my partner Charlie Parker."

Charlotte pushed away from her desk and strode over. She stuck a pen into the messy bun at the back of her hair as she moved, freeing up one hand, although she kept the other glued to her coffee cup. As a mother of two teenagers, it was hard enough trying to find time to sleep, but working here made it even more of a challenge. Charlotte drank coffee the way some people breathed air.

"Cameron, pleasure. I'm an M-5 although you're welcome to hug me too to make sure." She winked, flashing him a white smile. "What my husband doesn't know won't hurt him."

He shook hands, but Cameron denied, "Nah, I can tell from here they got you ranked right. Nice t'meetcha though."

"And this is Lars Torvald," Banderas continued. "He's a D-5 and who you'll be working with the most for the foreseeable future, until you get the hang of things."

Lars didn't look like a Dwolcræft, not fitting the stereotype of 'paramilitary soldier' that most people envisioned. He looked more like a young teen that had somehow escaped into this strange work world. His baby face was legendary in town. Lars was fit enough to pass the exams, but short for a man, and on the cute side. His pale skin and spiky brunette hair only made him look younger. He held out a hand to Cameron with a smile that promised mischief when the adults were no longer watching.

"Cam, welcome. I won't be the only person you work with, of course, we have one more Mægencræft on this team as well. She just stepped out to file the report for us."

"Cool. They gave us a rundown in school about what to expect but I don't think California really fits most job descriptions for Dwolcræftas. So anything you can tell me would be awesome. I'm all ears."

Well. That was a refreshingly nice response. Noriko wasn't sure what to think of him because of his interesting reaction to her, but he seemed sincere enough in his desire to learn what needed to be done. Especially here, that attitude was necessary. Cameron was right; California by nature had a very different set of needs than most places.

Banderas double tapped the phone bracelet

on his wrist. "This is Banderas." He listened intently for a moment and the whole team froze and watched with baited breath.

Noriko felt a rising sense of excitement. Was this her first real assignment on the job? So far she'd been doing nothing but reading and meeting people. She was antsy and anxious to get out and start actually working.

"Got it. Where exactly in Mountain Park? Copy that, on our way." Ending the call with a quick tap of a button, he made a circular motion with a finger. "Load up people. We got a bear stuck up a telephone pole."

...What?

She couldn't have possibly heard that right.

"Ah, boss?" Cameron's face lit up in a slow grin. "I think the joke's supposed to go 'we got a cat stuck up a tree.'"

Banderas bent a look on him although his mouth twitched. "I don't know how life is in LA, Powers, but you're in the mountains now. We don't get regular pussy cats stuck up trees. We get bears and mountain lions."

"Lions and bears, oh my," their team coordinator, Jack Torstein, deadpanned as he hefted a backpack and strode for the door.

Noriko choked on a laugh. What, the man had a sense of humor? She'd mistaken him as a breathing AI when she'd first been introduced to him.

"I," Cameron declared expansively, "am going to love this job. Okay, where's the bear?"

"Mountain Park. Powers, are you ready to work now or do you need a day?"

"My car's fully loaded and parked out front. Is it safe to leave it there? If it is, I'm game."

"Move it to the side parking lot, it's got a locked gate," Charlotte suggested. "Only fools would try to steal in front of a police station, but you never know."

Cameron didn't seem all that worried and shrugged. "I'll move it. Where do I meet you?"

"Side parking lot," Banderas answered dryly.

"That makes life easy." Whistling an airless tune, he skipped back out the door.

Noriko had only an idea of what 'essentials' were supposed to be in a kit. They'd run them through it at boot camp various times, of course, but depending on the area you were assigned to the necessities changed. She had three bottles of water, two power bars, a first aid kit, sunscreen, and an old-school radio as a backup. Hopefully that would do her for this task.

What did one need to get a bear unstuck, anyway?

They met up at the van without issue, loaded in, and headed toward the mountains. Jack was the one to punch their destination into the van's autopilot system, and since no one else even attempted to sit near the front, Noriko took it that this was one of the jobs their coordinator always did. When Banderas had said 'Mountain Park' it had not given her any indication of direction as Tehachapi was ringed by mountains on all sides. So she took note of which direction they headed— due west—with interest. It would be the first time since her arrival that she had left the town proper.

Cameron was settled in next to her, stretched

out with his ankles crossed, not at all nervous. Or at least on the surface he wasn't. Noriko was a little envious of this as she had butterflies duking it out in her stomach.

"So what kind of name is Noriko Arashi?" he asked casually. "Sounds Japanese."

"It is Japanese. I'm first generation American." Which was also why she was so short compared to most Americans. Him especially. He made her feel like a dwarf.

"Oh? Cool. Where you from?"

"Tennessee."

"From any city?"

"Not one you'd know, no." Manchester was hardly on anyone's radar unless they lived there. Noriko wasn't sure what to think about this chit-chat. Was he just trying to get to know her better? She didn't mind that, in fact it was a good idea, but they were about to work together for the first time. Wouldn't it be a better idea to ask different questions? Deciding to take lead on this, since he wasn't going to, she asked: "Before we do anything, talk to me about your comfort level," Noriko requested. "How many merlins should I be feeding you, max? Or minimum?" Saying that someone was a certain level didn't automatically mean that she knew what they were comfortable in handling. They were judged by the max amount of power they could draw in one second. But no one could sustain that kind of energy for long, and they didn't need the max amount of power for every task anyway. Sometimes they only needed a few centimerlins to complete a task. Sometimes they needed several kilomerlins. It depended on the situation, which was why she felt it proper to ask what the other person's preference was.

"I like to have enough to do the task I want without needing to think about stowing the extra."

"Good to know. What's the max you're comfortable sustaining?"

"My comfortable max is about 50 KMs. In an emergency, when it's all hit the fan, I can handle 78 KMs for about three hours before I'm tapped out."

Her eyebrows climbed into her hairline. Three hours? This statement cemented the attention of everyone in the van. Noriko couldn't blame them for openly listening in—after all they needed to know this information too, but it did make her shift a little uncomfortably to be at the center of attention. Striving to ignore it, she focused solely on Cameron. "If you can handle that many merlins of power, then why are you ranked at a four? You're a borderline three."

"Lack of experience," he said easily. "They said in five years or so I'd probably go up another level."

Oh? She'd been told something similar. Perhaps they were closer in ranking than she initially believed. "In that case, what should I start out with?"

"Gimme just a little juice."

A specific number would be nice.

"You two talk more later," Banderas requested. "We're almost there, so we need to plan out a strategy."

2ND MERLIN

BANDERAS gestured toward Lars. "I defer to our bear expert to explain the standard tactic for rescue."

For some reason Lars gave their captain a pained look. "Once, just once, that cub latched onto me. You can't let it go, can you?"

"Never," Banderas promised with an evil smile.

Cub? Noriko looked to Lizzie, Lars' partner, hoping for the full story.

"The first year we were here, we had a black bear and a cub get stuck up a telephone pole," she explained, also with a mischievous smirk on her face. "The mother bear unfortunately got shocked before we could get her down, but we got the cub to earth, and it somehow knew that it was Lars that had saved it. The cub latched onto his leg and no matter where he went, the cub tried to follow. It was completely adorable."

"For the record," Lars informed the van in

a haughty, dignified manner, nose stuck up in the air, "walking with an attached bear cub is somewhat difficult. Only those with experience can manage."

Cameron pointed to Lars and asked, "So he's Bear-man?"

Charlotte about spewed her coffee everywhere, half-strangling on a laugh. "How'd you know?"

"Oh, just a wild guess," Cameron responded airily.

"Bear-man," Jack prompted, "the strategy?"

With a resigned sigh, Lars obediently responded, "We have to be quick when we get there. The bears can get up the telephone poles no problem, but there's nothing for them to grasp so they can climb back down again. They get scared, so no amount of coaxing will get them down on their own. One set of partners needs to enclose the live electricity up there as a shield so the bear isn't shocked. Another will actually lift it down. Our third set will act as a safety net nearby if there is more than one bear. If there's a cub or something, then they'll get the other one down."

"According to the reports, it's just the one black bear," Banderas inserted smoothly. "And it's right off the main road leading up to the park, so we'll have to have someone out diverting traffic. Jack?"

"I'll do the honors."

"Good. And...here we are." Banderas turned to look out the front window as the van slowed to a stop. "Jack, pull this thing off the road, will you?"

"Certainly." Jack turned in his chair and hit

the manual override to move the van off onto the shoulder.

Far too curious to sit and wait, Noriko immediately unloaded from the van and turned, looking for the bear. It was across the street, at least fifty feet in the air, sitting on the very top and making pitiful sounds. There wasn't much room up there, and it kept shifting around, sometimes jumping a little as it got a little too close to a transformer and was zapped. The bear didn't seem to be a full grown adult, or perhaps black bears in California were on the smaller side? She'd seen them before in Tennessee and they were a good hundred pounds heavier than this version.

Although the distance and the way the sun was shining behind it might be distorting her perceptions.

Banderas craned his neck all the way back and whistled. "He would have to choose one of the taller poles to get stuck on. Alright. Charlie and I will shield him, Lars, you and Lizzie get him down. Cameron, Noriko, I'll have you on standby. Go ahead and gather up power to work with, just in case."

She took a second to grab a hair elastic out of her pocket and pull her hair up off her shoulders. It was a little windy up here—Tehachapi usually was—and she didn't want to be eating her own hair or having it blind her at the wrong moment. Noriko looked both ways before crossing, as this was a high speed highway, then jogged across. As she moved, she looked around for the ley line. She could see it glinting under the sunlight, as it turned the ground above it a muted gold. When power shone through sand, it was like looking at reflected light. Some parts shone brighter than others. There were two main ones that ran the length of the town, but they branched off in all sorts of directions. Ah, there was a good-sized stream.

The most nerve-wracking moment was always when partnering with someone for the first time. Every person was different, and of course they had their own way of wanting things done. She was never sure until actually offering a Dwolcræft power how they wanted her to shape it, how they liked to receive it, and it wasn't something that could be easily explained. A blind person would have an easier time explaining the colors of the sunset. She was convinced of that.

Especially to a man that might be her long-term partner, Noriko did not want to fumble their first partnering. Her nerves stretched thin under the psychological pressure.

Cameron reached over and smacked her lightly in the center of her shoulder blades. "Loosen up. First time never goes smooth. I am perfectly confident we'll fumble it."

Strangely, this made her laugh, although it was short. "You're not one for pep talks, I take it."

"Naw. Just fork it over," he commanded with a lopsided smile.

He wasn't taking any of this seriously. Not one iota. Blowing out a breath, she steadied her nerves as much as possible, reaching with a mental hand into the ley line. It was always rough when first drawn out, and sometimes it caught fine particles of sand and dirt as it was brought into the air. The power also didn't have any defined shape to it. It was like picking up a handful of mud— it wanted to go oozing out in every direction. Taking a second, she reshaped it into something that was easier to pass along to him and far more readily usable. Satisfied, she extended it in almost a ribbon-shaped form, pure and crisp.

For the first time in her life, the Dwolcræft partnering with her didn't just stand there like a rock and expect her to place the power squarely in his hands. All Dwolcræftas carried a little power with them, and it was with that power that Cameron reached out to receive what she offered. It was only then did she see that his preferred form was more like a funnel, as that was what his power was shaped like.

Swearing mentally, she re-shaped the power on the fly and made it more like a stream of water. It was close, but she did it just in time so that when the first tendril of her merlins reached him, it was a near perfect synchronization. The ease of the transfer was so beautifully simple that it stole her breath for a moment.

Cameron felt it too as he stopped dead and stared at her in wonder. "Wow."

Robbed of speech, she could only agree, "Wow."

This exchange was not lost on Lars, who stood nearby. "What?"

"You're really ranked wrong," Cameron informed her, but he nearly glowed with open satisfaction. "This is the easiest pairing I've ever had. Do you always reshape the power like that?"

"Of course," she responded, genuinely confused that it would be this point he focused on. "You're working with it, aren't you? Why would I channel the merlins to you raw and expect you to remake the power and harness it all at once? Doesn't that make your job harder?"

"It sure does. You're the first Mægen I've met that seems to realize that, though." He let out a soft breath of laughter, bouncing up and down on his toes. "Don't take this wrong, but I'm really glad your evaluator didn't rank you right."

"Because if I'd been ranked right, I'd never have been partnered with you?" she guessed, taking the compliment in the spirit it was meant.

"Yup." Rubbing his hands together in anticipation, he turned back to the desert at large. "You're giving me, what, 5 KMs right now?"

"About there," she agreed. "Want more?"

"Nope, that's perfect."

Noriko turned to report that they were ready but found it unnecessary. Everyone was watching them and every one of them had a smile on their faces.

"It makes me remember our first partnering," Charlotte said to Banderas, a nostalgic expression on her face.

"I don't see why," Banderas responded half-absently as he turned back to the job at hand. "We botched it badly."

For that, she smacked him on the arm.

He'd apparently expected this response, as he chuckled. "Alright, our stand-by is ready. Charlie? Thank you, that should be enough. I have the area up there shielded. Bear-man, you're up."

Lars gave another put-upon sigh at the nickname, but there was no argument from him this time.

Noriko watched with interest as he accepted power from Lizzie. Strange. She knew they'd been partners for about four years now, and yet they seemed a little rocky still. Or was that just because of how Lizzie was giving Lars power? It was filtered, certainly, and somewhat shaped, but it wasn't something that was recognizable. Lars, too, didn't actively reach out like Cameron had done, but like a typical Dwolcræft, just accepted the power that Lizzie threw at him. It seemed a somewhat inefficient partnering, but Lars had what he needed to work with. Reaching up, he snaked a line of glowing merlins around the bear. He then shaped it like a harness or a rope around the bear's belly.

At first the bear didn't seem to realize what was going on. He kept pacing the crossarms, eyes on the ground and the humans gathered around the base of the pole. But when that rope tightened around his belly, he panicked and scrambled backwards. Under their panicked eyes, he slid free of Lars's grip completely and started falling tail-first for the ground.

Swearing, Cameron threw his power forward, catching the bear not two feet from the ground. His grip was in the shape of a net, which promptly closed at the top, keeping the bear from escaping.

Noriko quickly grabbed more power from the line, refining and reshaping it so that Cameron had a steady supply coming from her to work with.

"Nice catch!" Lars complimented. He wiped a bead of sweat from his forehead. "Man, that was close. I didn't expect him to be that slippery."

"Your honorary title of Bear-man is hereby revoked," his partner joked with him. "That was terrible bear wrangling."

"At least something good came out of that," he muttered to himself.

Banderas came in closer to get a better look at the bear. "I think he's overall okay but I'm seeing some singed hair on this back leg. Let's get him to a vet for a checkup before releasing him back in the wild. Cameron, keep him trapped until the vet can get here."

"Sure thing."

Coming back to them, the captain looked at them steadily for several moments. "Your transfer of power is very smooth, very tight. I'm amazed to see it coming from your first partnering. I've got a good feeling about the two of you. I think that, for once, the Powers-That-Be might have done a good match with the two of you. But remember, if this partnership isn't working for you for whatever reason, you're allowed to change. This will not reflect badly on you. It is, in fact, somewhat rare to stay with your first partner for long. Is that understood?"

"Yes, sir," Noriko responded instantly.

Cameron gave him a shrug. "Sure, boss."

"Good."

3RD MERLIN

NORIKO reviewed her list one more time. She was supposed to pick up coffee for everyone on the team, but it had somehow grown to everyone within earshot. She'd gotten introduced to more cops than she had during her first day of orientation, all because of coffee. There was something not quite right about that.

Because Cameron owned a car, he had volunteered to be the transportation on this excursion. Not that she needed him to go along, per se. The vehicle could of course drive itself, and with its own onboard GPS function it could find the coffee shop without any input from her. But as it was his car and not hers, she could hardly tell him that he wasn't necessary for this trip.

"If you don't have a car," he asked with a glance at her, "how are you buying groceries?"

"The grocery story is only two blocks away from the apartment," she pointed out. "I can lug a bag home."

"So you're buying what you need in small doses and then carrying it all? Why would you do that when you have a partner who has a vehicle?"

Because it seemed very wrong to impose on him in any way? "I'm not the type to demand things from you just because you're my partner."

"Huh." The response was not in a happy tone. Cameron didn't like that answer.

The car slowed to take a turn, and Noriko, feeling a little awkward, turned to look outside the window. This was a section of town that she hadn't been in before. Her phone vibrated on her wrist, and she glanced to see who it was calling her. Haru. Of course it was Haru. It was always Haru at this time of the day. Hitting accept, she put him on speaker. "Haru-kun."

"Nee-chan, do you know where the AA batteries are?"

It was strange, beyond strange, but her siblings still expected her to know where everything in the house was. Despite the fact she lived over a thousand miles away. Even weirder was that she normally did. "Did you check the junk drawer in the kitchen?"

"Yeah, I looked there already."

"What about the third drawer in the china cabinet. Kaa-san hides batteries there sometimes."

"Oh really? Okay, let me check." There came the sound of rummaging, then a victorious, *Atta! "Yup, found 'em."*

"What do you need them for, anyway?"

"The remote died. Hey Nee-chan, how are things going? Did you get a partner yet?"

Cameron unabashedly leaned in closer to her to speak over her shoulder. "She sure did. Hey there."

"Hey. Who are you?"

"Name's Cameron. Who are you?"

"Haru. I'm her brother."

"Cool. You a Dwol?"

"Naw, I'm a Mægen."

"Really? Just like your sister?"

There was a distinct note of pride in Haru's voice as he boasted, *"Just like her. Although I'm more talented."*

"You are not," Noriko objected, mouth completely on automatic. "You just learned a lot by studying my textbooks. That's not the same thing; you had a head start on everyone in your class."

"Tou-san says hard work is its own talent."

"He's not wrong," Cameron assured the boy even as he grinned at her. "How old are you?"

"Fourteen. How old are you?"

"Twenty-one."

"Same age as Nee-chan, then. That's cool. We were worried when she left 'cause guys don't know how to handle her."

Noriko cleared her throat in a pointed way. "Haru."

"Ahhh...nice talking to you, Cameron. Nee-chan, call Kaa-san soon, okay? She's been whining every day since you left about missing you."

"I'll call her Sunday." Really, why were all of her siblings annoying? They loved to tell complete strangers totally useless things. She stabbed the call end button with a little more force than necessary.

Cameron grinned at her, as if he knew precisely what was going through her head. "How many siblings do you have?"

"Five. I'm the oldest."

From Cameron's wrist phone, there was a beep and then the ringtone started up. *"I'm too sexy for my shirt, too sexy for my shirt, so sexy yeah~"*

What the—? She'd never heard that song before. It sounded like a 1990s song, though, with that style.

Cameron put his Bluetooth in his ear and double tapped his wrist phone. "Hey, man. How's Mojave?" Whatever response he received made the smile abruptly drop from his face. "Yeah, that doesn't sound good. Run me through what you're seeing. Oh, yeah, that'd be a better way to do it." Cameron pulled off the dark holographic shades that hung on his front collar and slid them onto his face. "Power, on. Holo display, on. Download incoming file."

Noriko had no idea what was going on, but obviously it was at least semi-serious for Cameron to have that focused attention. What sort of file was being sent to him, that he would immediately download so he could see it with his own eyes?

"Yeah...that doesn't look good. Where exactly is this? That's perfect. Sure, I'll go take a look right now. I'll report it to my captain too. No, you did the right thing, I don't think you're overreacting. Even if you were, I'd say better safe than sorry. Don't stay in the area, okay, it'll mess you up if it's really that exposed. Naw, I've got the map you just sent, I'll find it fine. Go, go. Sure. Call you later." Cameron hung up with another touch of the finger and looked up at her, tilting his glasses down so that he could see her with an unimpeded view. "Noriko, cancel the coffee run."

"What's happened?" she demanded.

"Got a friend working in Mojave. He was driving the roads and he saw signs that there's a ley line going wonky."

Chills raced down her spine. "Is he a Dwol? Shouldn't he report this to his own superiors?"

Cameron was shaking his head before she could get the full question out. "Not a Dwol or a Mægen. He's a childhood friend—I taught him the signs of what to look for if a ley line goes sideways. He took a short video and sent it to me. Here, see for yourself."

Noriko accepted his glasses and slid them on. They felt weird, as they were much too large for her own head, so she had to hold them on with both hands. "Video, play," she commanded. The video obediently restarted at the beginning and played out. It was only fifteen seconds but those fifteen seconds felt like an hour to her. Video couldn't capture what a damaged ley line looked like magic-wise. What it could record were the effects of free-floating power. To the un-initiated, it seemed as if there was a massive heat wave in the area, but there were subtle differences— visible particles hovered in the air like massive dust motes, there were signs of surface upheaval, and some low bulging in the crust. All classic signs of a ley line that had been disrupted. Her stomach did a slow turn and her mouth went dry. This was *so* not good. "We need to get over there."

"I totally agree." Cameron tapped his wrist phone, opening the display, and then tapped their captain's icon.

It rang twice before there was a gruff, "*What, did you lose our order?*"

"Cap, I got a friend in Mojave that sent me a video just now. There's a ley line going wonky over there."

"*How wonky is wonky?*" Banderas demanded. "*And where exactly is it?*"

Noriko quietly gave the commands necessary to forward the original message to their captain. Cameron caught what she was doing and gave her a thumbs up. "Forwarding the video and GPS coordinates to you now, sir."

There was silence for a full minute as he waited for the message, opened it, and took a good look at its contents. "*That does not look good at all. You say Mojave, but I believe that's in our jurisdiction. We normally patrol that area.*"

"Oh, we do? Then, I think this one's ours."

"*I agree. Forget the coffee, meet us there.*"

"Yes, sir." Cameron ended the call with a troubled furrow to his brow. As he spoke, he spun half-around and punched in a new destination into the autopilot. "I hope he doesn't stick around to make sure we get there. Let me call him again."

Noriko waved him on, only paying half-attention as Cameron called his friend back. She took a second look at the video instead, overlapping it with a map. She could not begin to state that she knew where every ley line in this area was and what they connected to. Ley lines were rather like rivers. They connected to brooks, oceans, ponds, streams, and so forth. Sometimes they fed into something very large—their own basins of energy—sometimes they stretched so thin that there was barely a thread of power there. That was why the GF had to monitor everything they could so carefully—if a ley line had a problem, there was no telling where the backlash would go, and what area it would affect.

How had a ley line suddenly acted up without anyone noticing? That was the question plaguing her right now.

The car left the city streets entirely and went into the north section of town, toward the base of the mountains. In short order, they left most of the subdivisions as well, winding through a narrow pass and into the mountains proper, onto an old highway that seemed rather neglected, with many a crack in the pavement and weeds growing up on the shoulders. On all sides, there were the giant windmills that Tehachapi was famous for, only about half moving, collecting energy enough to light up a good section of California's seaboard. This close, the windmills made Noriko feel about the size of an ant. Strange. From the town they didn't look nearly this big.

"Not many people out here," Cameron noted in the silence of the car. "I think I see how this ley line got so bad without us noticing."

"It's probably not on regular patrol routes," Noriko agreed. "How often do you think our team comes out this way to check on things?"

"Don't know. Good question to ask, though."

Noriko made a mental note to do so. She never, ever wanted to be one of those people: the type to stick to their comfortable routines while everything outside of their bubble slowly fell apart. She wanted to take more pride in her work than that.

Because they had a head start, they were almost to their destination when the team's red van came barreling up behind them. It slowed to avoid hitting Cameron's car—on this narrow highway, there was no way to pass them—and stayed right on their tail the last mile to their destination.

There was barely a place to pull off, it was that narrow of a shoulder. The area was beyond rocky, with struggling vegetation and no sign of anything more than tumbleweeds and scrub brush within sight. As she stepped out of the car, shielding her eyes from the sun, the air hit her with almost visible force. Power permeated the air so thickly that it could have been sliced and served up on bread.

Very fortunately for Cameron's friend, he had listened and not stayed in the area. With the ley lines gushing out power like this, it would have been beyond dangerous to stay more than a few minutes. Eventually he would have felt like he was being electrocuted from every angle. The land was already reacting to the live charge, and the air sang along the top of the crevice, the hotter sections near the ley line itself either crackling or half-melting in reaction to the intense charge.

Automatically, she whirled and put her hand directly on Cameron's shoulder, channeling the magic in the air around them and feeding it directly to him. In turn, he created a shield around them both to keep them from becoming overwhelmed.

"Craaaap!" Cameron exclaimed with a tremor in his voice. "No wonder he sounded worried. It's worse in person."

Banderas unloaded first from the van, took one look at the area, and did some very creative swearing. "People, move, move, move! Lars, Lizzie, take this side, Noriko, Cameron, take the far end toward the edge of the road. There's another ley line on that end. Let's bleed power off and put it in there, balance these two out."

Noriko spun on a heel and instantly headed that direction. Now that she was past her initial shock, she saw what her captain was saying. There was another ley line almost parallel to this one that seemed drained in comparison. In fact, the way they were so off balance with each other was very strange. This close, even if they weren't directly connected, shouldn't they be more or less the same? Unless something had happened far from here that was affecting just this one line.

Cameron planted both feet shoulder-length apart and nodded to her. "Hit me."

Taking that as her cue, she drew all the power out of the air first and funneled it to him. Cameron had to drop the shield in order to accept it. He siphoned it off her, their partnership just as easy and smooth as the first time, then redirected it all toward the emptier ley line. Being in the area was beyond alarming. She felt as if she were standing in between lines of live electricity and a wrong step in any direction would get her fried.

Fighting through her unease, Noriko focused on giving Cameron the power he needed to work and drained anything in the open air before it could cause irrevocable damage. They worked like this without speaking for a solid half hour before the area calmed down.

Feeling like she could finally draw a proper breath, she redirected her attention to the heavily charged line and gingerly tapped into it. Just a light mental touch made power leap out at her, which was unnerving. Noriko actually jumped, shocked to have power hit her so hard. It kind of felt like she'd been sucker punched.

Catching her around the shoulders, Cameron leaned into her, acting like a brace. "I know it's intense, so easy, easy does it."

Gasping, a fine shiver danced along her skin, and it took serious concentration to be able to give it to Cameron. This time, it wasn't as smooth, but he didn't say a word to her about it. He just acted as a physical anchor for her and took what she could give him before directing it into the nearby ley line.

With three different pairings working on it, the ley line gradually became less unstable and lost its manic edge. Noriko took a breath, found that she no longer felt dizzy or nauseous, and carefully tried to find her own balance again. Cameron stayed put until he was sure that she was steady, and only then let go of her completely.

"Thanks," she managed, a little embarrassed that she had been overwhelmed when he hadn't.

Perhaps some of that showed on her face, as he assured her, "You took the brunt of it. Least I could do. Hey, Cap! How much more you figure needs to be transferred?"

"For you, another 5 KMs!"

That wouldn't take another minute or two, and then they would be done. Noriko was extremely grateful to hear that. She didn't want to relax her guard and have anything get messed up, so she stayed alert until the last of it was transferred and Cameron had completely disengaged from both lines. Only then did she let go entirely.

Banderas called for everyone to stop, which they all did with sighs of relief, then marched directly for Cameron. "This friend of yours, who is he?"

"Kirk Griffin, sir. He's a Highway Patrolman based in Mojave."

"So he's not a Dwol or Mægen? But he was able to spot this?"

"Childhood friend," Cameron explained, one shoulder lifted in a shrug. "I taught him to read the signs, just in case."

"That just in case paid off." Banderas relaxed enough to give Cameron an approving nod. "I'll send a formal letter of thanks to his superiors when we get back to station. He just saved our hides. I don't know what set this ley line off so badly, but if it had gone, it would have done serious damage to this and the surrounding areas. This line feeds directly into a Mojave and Rosamond ley line. It would not have been pretty."

Oh heavens, did it really? Noriko got another chill as her mind played out possible scenarios if they hadn't been able to get this line under control again. She didn't imagine that either of those towns would have come through it intact. As a student, Noriko had seen videos of ley lines that had gone berserk like this, and it was akin to a bomb going off, mixed in with an earthquake. It re-arranged whole landscapes when a ley line went south.

Banderas turned and stared hard at the ley line. "I don't understand what happened here. Charlie and I were here, what, Saturday?"

"Friday," Charlotte corrected him. "And it looked fine then. Did something happen upstream of us that set this one off?"

"If it had, we should have had some warning. That's SOP in situations like this. When we get back, let's make some phone calls. I want to know what happened." Pointing a finger at Jack, he demanded, "Generators?"

Jack held up a finger to indicate he was still tied up on the phone, then answered someone over the Bluetooth, "Yes, that's correct. Can you confirm?"

Noriko watched this interplay, but it didn't make any sense to her. "What generators?"

The whole team looked at her as if she had just asked a stupid question.

It was Charlotte who snapped her fingers. "Of course. She's not a California native, she wouldn't know."

"Ah?" Know what?

"Tehachapi supplies sixty percent of the power that goes to the coastline," Charlotte explained patiently. "All of those windmills that line the mountains? It doesn't supply just us with power, but the greater section of Los Angeles,

Riverside, Orange County, and the rest. It also supplies some of the power that we need in order to keep L.A. and Santa Barbara afloat."

"Oh," she said a little weakly. Tehachapi generated that much power?! All by itself? She'd thought it strange that a small town up in the mountains boasted three stations, but now it made perfect sense. This was literally an energy hub. Of course they would have multiple teams stationed here. "Ah, then, how many generators do we have up here?"

"Four in the main complex, but there's two other complexes, one in Sand Canyon, one in Mountain Park."

Of course. Where the other two stations were. That made perfect sense. Noriko turned to study the ley line that was still a little wobbly with entirely new eyes. If this ley line had been closer to the generators, or worse, one of the main lines that fed into the generator, what would have happened to those seaboard cities? Would they have lost the power necessary to keep them afloat? "I'm almost afraid to ask, but, in a worst case scenario..."

"We have backup generators," Lars answered with a grimace. "Unfortunately they're not enough to really keep everything afloat, especially if Tehachapi goes down completely. It's really rare, but in the history of the city, it *has* been completely calm up here a few times, where there's no wind at all. On those days, it gets a little dicey with L.A. especially. As long as the ley lines are cooperating, though, we manage. Somehow."

That was a very unnerving answer. Noriko felt

absolutely certain she was going to lose sleep over that mental image. She was never complaining about hair flying into her mouth ever again.

Jack ended the call and reassured them as a group, "Generators are fine. It didn't affect them at all."

Banderas crossed himself in a quick prayer before he circled a finger in the air, indicating they needed to wrap things up. "At least we don't have that disaster to deal with. Let's get back to station, people. Cameron, Noriko, go get our coffees. This has just turned into a long night."

4ᵀᴴ MERLIN

ON THE captain's orders they went out to do some patrolling of Williamson Road, and while they were out in the more deserted area of town, 'get some practice' in. Noriko wasn't quite sure what he was imagining they could do, out where the tumbleweeds roamed, but they obediently went.

When the whole team didn't have to move as one unit, they had smaller commuter cars available to them from the general police station pool. Taking one of those, they headed south and then east of town on Williamson Road. This late in the afternoon, the sun wasn't nearly as hot, and the coolness of the sunset was just touching the sky. It was actually easier to see ley lines at this time of day than at high noon. They glowed more brilliantly in the sand under a weaker light. Of course, her favorite time of day to look at them was in the late evening, when the sun had set.

Then it was like watching rivers of fireflies moving.

Cameron took the car off autopilot and drove them a little off the road and onto an emergency access area. "Here's good, I think."

For what? No one had yet answered that question for her. Shrugging, she put her hair up in a high pony tail in preparation. If they were going to be out in the sun for any length of time greater than fifteen minutes, she was putting on sunscreen. Noriko slid a small tube out of her windbreaker's pocket and started slathering it on any visible patch of skin.

Cameron held out a hand in a silent 'give me' motion and she obligingly squirted some into his palm. Then, without a beat, he dabbed it onto her nose.

Jerking back, she stared at him in confusion.

"You can't see your own face," he pointed out, expression teasing but gentle. "So hold still."

He did have a point. It still felt strange for someone she barely knew to touch her, but she held patiently still and let him smear the cream over her face, back of her neck, and the tips of her ears. His touch was very light and careful. "Don't you need to put some on?"

"Nope," he denied cheerfully. "I don't burn. I have enough Italian heritage in me that I just go golden."

In that moment, Noriko hated him just a little. She went tomato red at the drop of a hat.

"There, done," he pronounced, smoothing the rest of the cream over the back of his hands.

"Thank you."

"No prob."

She glanced at him from the corners of her eyes as she put the cap back on and slid the tube into her pocket. So he knew how to be thoughtful of others? Her initial impression was crumbling with every encounter they had. She still didn't quite get his sense of humor, but she was coming slowly to the conclusion that she might have judged him a bit too rashly on their first meeting.

They climbed out of the car and Noriko panned the area in slow motion. There was literally nothing out here except a few cacti, weeds, and a great deal of sand. "What are we supposed to be doing here?"

Cameron's voice dropped into the captain's register and repeated, "Just get to know the area, and use enough power to get used to each other. I don't care what you do as long as it's not destructive."

Well that left the door wide open. Granted, they'd basically been told the same thing when they'd done their initial tour of the Research Lab near the Base.

Cameron didn't seem at all confused by this indecisive order and just shrugged. "Let me study the ley lines first."

Secretly relieved at his choice, Noriko immediately bent to studying them herself. She had not wanted to randomly pull out power before knowing how the ley lines flowed and how much energy there was in them. Jerking power out rashly could have serious consequences after all.

Holoshades on, she peered toward the ground and glanced back and forth between the report she'd pulled up of the area and the ley line. "It doesn't look to have changed much."

"Or at all," Cameron agreed. He squatted down onto his haunches to get a closer look. "There's maybe a few places where it's a mite wider, by maybe an inch, but it's not enough to make much of a difference. Let's see, report says it's running at 72 KMs." Twisting, he squinted up at her. "What do you say?"

Noriko also knelt down, putting a hand directly on the ground. The sand was hot to the touch, nearly to the point of baking her bare skin, but she ignored the discomfort. "Just over 72 would be my estimate."

"That seems a little high to me," Cameron observed. "This ley line isn't a main stream, but a side branch, and they're normally regulated at about 45, right?"

"Right. Maybe we should report this?" Noriko stared down at the ley line in worry. "I don't like the idea of another one going berserk."

"Amen to that."

Noriko gave a verbal report on the matter and shot it to her captain in an email.

Cameron folded his holoshades and tilted them to rest on the top of his head before dusting off his hands. "Well then, partner, let's play in the sand."

Noriko didn't even know what he wanted to do with the power. Giving up, she tapped in and siphoned off some power before reshaping it into something that Cameron could use and funneling it his direction.

Cameron reached out as well, accepting her

offering of power like it was the most natural thing in the world to do. His hands lifted as if he was an orchestra conductor. Sand rose up at his bidding, flowing toward him before piling up in distinct patterns.

Noriko kept feeding him power, staring hard at what he was doing, as it didn't make any sense to her at first. Then she realized that putting a practical spin on his work wouldn't make sense, as it was something purely whimsical. "You're building a sand castle."

"Sure. I have all of this sand around me, what else can I do with it?" Chuckling at his own joke, he danced around to the side so that he could see what he was doing from another angle.

"And what made you think of doing a sandcastle?"

"It's one of those days where I want to be a mermaid," he explained without even a glance in her direction. His hands twirled as he built a rather elaborate tower on the corner.

Mermaids. Sandcastles. The connection failed to come together in her head. Was that explanation supposed to make sense?

Well, it didn't matter what they did, really. The point of this exercise was to get them used to giving and taking power from each other. He'd told her before that he could talk and work, so she decided to try for a conversation. "I've been checking, but it doesn't look like they know why that ley line went out of control."

"Nope, no one has any leads. Which is really strange." Cameron paused, tongue sticking out the side of his mouth as he concentrated on his battlements. "I realize we're new at this, but no one has ever reported a ley line just randomly going out of control. It's not like ley lines can spontaneously combust."

Fortunate, that, considering how many ley lines there were in the world. "There has to be a cause."

"Heck yeah. And for a buildup that fast? That powerful? It had to be something major." Cameron scratched at his chin. "Which is why everyone is so confused."

Because something that big would leave an obvious footprint, so of course they would be able to find the cause. It all sounded well in theory, but it wasn't panning out in reality. "The thing that really confuses me is why the ley line right next to it was nearly robbed of power. It was like one of them had been drained to feed into the other."

"That's exactly what it looked like. Only we didn't find any connection between the two. After experts spent two weeks looking for it, I'd think they would have found one, if it was there."

So did she. "You realize that only leaves one real possibility left, right?"

"Someone did it on purpose." Cameron paused and glanced at her, blue eyes troubled. "I know. It's what everyone is thinking, but no one seems to want to say it out loud."

Noriko had noticed that herself. The words just hovered throughout the station, there, but never given voice. "It's scary to think about. I mean, we're not talking about one person, but two in order to do that. So at least two people that are insane enough to mess with a ley line like that. How long would it take for someone to do that, I wonder?"

"Depends on how powerful they are. A few days? It's hard to say."

It was rather hard to guess when she didn't know the players involved. "Are we absolutely certain that this wasn't somehow natural? Or caused by something else? I really prefer it to be that instead of two crazy people running around making bombs out of the ley lines."

"You and me both, partner, but it doesn't look like it's natural. At least, I know several people are actively researching this, and they haven't been able to link anything to it. When they're looking that hard, I would think they'd have found it, if it could be found."

Unfortunately, he was right. Noriko let it lay and didn't try to keep the conversation going. She found it far easier to watch him build his ridiculous sand castle instead.

It was impressive, really, what he was building. It stood four stories high (in sandcastle architecture) with turrets, battlements, and even a moat with a drawbridge. She walked around the area, getting a good look at it all. Maybe she should take a picture, send it to her siblings. They'd get a kick out of seeing something like this.

"Don't step in my hole," Cameron warned her.

Hole? Stopping dead, she studied the area with a quick sweep of her eyes and realized that Cameron had only been taking sand from one spot. In fact, he'd gone quite deep, past the normal sandy topsoil and more toward the bedrock. "I'm seeing volcanic rock."

"There's lava, granite, and pegmatite, too," he informed her, still sculpting away at his castle turrets.

She stared hard at the ground, the picture slowly becoming clearer. He wasn't just playing. Oh, it looked like it, but he had obviously been paying attention as he 'mined' for materials because he knew exactly what he was unearthing. Had this whole elaborate exercise been for a purpose? To not only practice with her, but to get a better understanding of this desert landscape?

Noriko turned to study her partner. He still looked like he was about five, on a beach, playing in the sand. If one just looked at his expression, he could be dismissed as being silly. But he had never once faltered in taking power smoothly from her, and he had obviously been paying attention to the land under his feet, otherwise he wouldn't be able to rattle off what types of rocks were around them. This man was not the airhead he pretended to be.

It would behoove her to remember that.

To herself, in her native Japanese, she murmured, "*I cannot take you lightly.*"

Cameron's head came up and he hummed out in a questioning tone, "Wha'?"

Shaking her head, she said instead, "I want to take a photo."

"A commemoration photo? Great idea. After that, I guess we should head back for the office."

Noriko felt like she was baking, so escaping the desert for her nice cool office sounded good to her. She made a mental note to talk with her captain quietly at some point too and assure him that while she still didn't quite understand Cameron's sense of humor, she had no problem partnering with the man. Having someone that could connect to her like this was a rare find, and she wasn't about to let go of him.

Noriko focused on not only charging her right hand, magnetizing it, but also in keeping the power ratio with her other hand and feet. If she lost track of any of them she'd lose traction, and, even if there were a mat under her, it would be quite the fall. She was already eight or nine feet up.

Someone, at some point, had thoughtfully put a training gym together for the police and members of the Gældorcræft Forces to use. It had the usual weights, exercise machines, and so forth, but one side also had a climbing wall. For her practice purposes, the climbing wall was rather useless, but she'd grabbed the mats under them and stacked them up two deep before using the metal support beam nearby.

Half the reason she was climbing was routine, but the other half was because she needed a distraction from her own thoughts. Seeing the ley lines two weeks ago, so uneven and threatening to explode, still gave her the occasional nightmare. The ley line by itself had enough power in it to react like two tons of dynamite. If it had gone off, it would have rearranged the landscape for miles in every direction. That didn't even take into consideration how the power would have ricocheted down the connecting ley lines, setting them off as well. It would be like a very badly played game of dominoes. A destructive game at that. And if one ley line could go haywire without any obvious reason, others could too.

And that thought scared the living daylights out of her.

Yesterday she and Cameron had been given a tour of the Air Force Research Lab nearby. It was then that she saw how extensive and large all of the ley lines in California really were. The ones near the Lab were massive, like underground rivers instead of little streams. She was still questioning the wisdom of building a research facility on top of two of them. Certainly, they had their own GF team stationed there to keep a close eye on things, but—

"Whoa!"

Her concentration snapped and Noriko lost her grip, falling toward the mat. She barely had time to gasp, not to mention react, when something hard and firm caught her a foot off the floor.

She recognized the arms wrapped around her chest all too well, and the deep voice that chuckled in her ear. "What kind of crazy trust exercise was that?"

This man was bad for her heart. In the time she'd known him, he consistently showed up in her blind spot and scared the life right out of her. Not that she was going to let him know that. She took three seconds to get her breath back before saying, "Can you please stop sneaking up on me?"

"What? It's all good, I caught you, didn't I?" He set her on the floor, gently, as if that last foot to solid ground would hurt her. "You gotta tell me how you were doing that. It was like magic."

"It wasn't." She could understand why he thought it was, though. By definition, only Dwolcræftas could actually utilize magic, hence why they were called that. Turning, Noriko looked up at him. "There's just a trick to it. I let out the smallest amount of power possible through my hands and feet, right next to metal, and it magnetizes the power enough to where I can connect to the beam. But all I'm doing is connecting to and releasing power; I'm not actually doing anything with it."

"Never met a Mægen that could do that." He walked to the beam and let out a trace of power through his hand, obviously trying to duplicate what she had been doing. "Huh. It really does magnetize fast."

Oh? Her instructions had been beyond basic, but he'd figured out the exact nuance needed already? Well, he was a D-4, she really shouldn't underestimate his ability to adapt. Rankings were only partially based on power levels. Knowledge and intelligence also played into it.

He put his other hand up before releasing the first, although he didn't show any interest of going higher than that. "So you have to release your power in one hand in order to move it up. Coordinating all four limbs like that has to be tricky."

"It is."

He glanced back at her. "But you were doing it easily."

"Old exercise from my teacher in Jr. High," she admitted easily. Back then, she had sucked at it, but, over time, practice had made it easier. "He taught it to us so that we could get better at feeding multiple people power all at once. That, and he said it would be a handy escape route if we ever needed to climb a skyscraper."

That made him grin. "Like Spiderman?"

"Something like that. My teacher was fast. He could climb a steal beam like it was a ladder." She still wasn't that good at it although she improved a little bit each time. "If you came looking for me, did you need me for something?"

"Yup. Trust exercises. I want to try next."

He'd totally made that up on the spot. Noriko resisted the urge to roll her eyes. Trying to derail Cameron once he got an idea into his head was bound to give her a headache. Fine, if he wanted to try it, she'd let him. It would be a good chance for them to feel their way into their partnership in an unstressed manner. "You need to take your shoes off. I'll get you a climbing harness."

He paused with one foot in hand, perfectly balanced like a stork with a leg up. "Climbing harness? You weren't wearing one."

She gave him a flat look. "There was no one around to serve as an anchor. It would have been pretty pointless."

"Well, I don't need one either. You'll catch me."

What? She blinked at him, sure that he had to be pulling her leg. Only he didn't look like he was joking. "No. No, I won't."

"Sure you will. I caught you. That's how trust exercises work, partner, it's your turn to catch me." A glint of impish delight sparked in his eyes although he still kept a straight face on.

"Ha. Haha. You funny, funny man." Shaking her head, she went for the climbing harness. "How about I catch you as your anchor."

"I don't like that method. It's boring."

Boring? So he preferred broken bones? Because no matter how hard she tried to catch him, he'd squash her like a bug. "You'll survive."

Fortunately for her, the harnesses were already connected to a metal bar up top that could be moved from one area to the next along the climbing wall. It was just long enough to reach the metal beam, although they had the ropes at an angle. Still better than nothing, though if he did fall, he'd go sideways.

Cameron went up one limb at a time, obviously concentrating as he climbed. She watched him carefully, feeding him power in a steady if thin stream. She didn't know how to read this man. When he was open to her like this, she knew at least what his limits were magically, but trying to go off of his words or body language was challenging at best. It was like he was in code or something. But she wasn't a cryptographer.

"You're not talking," he observed, still focusing straight ahead.

Was she supposed to be? "It takes concentration to do this."

"Remember, this is harder for you than it is for me. It's natural for me. I can talk and climb at the same time until I get a good feel for this."

True, he probably didn't need to focus as intently. "You're majoring in Geology too? The captain mentioned it earlier."

Cameron reached the top and she stood firm as an anchor as he rappelled down. He hit the mats with easy grace, as if he had climbed like this a million times before. Noriko fed him enough line so that he could undo the harness and step out of it before she took it back to the hook and hung it up. Cameron leaned comfortably against the wall, feet crossed at the ankles so he could talk with her. "I am," he admitted easily. "I think that's how we both got assigned to California. I've barely started the second semester of the courses, though. How far along are you?"

"Started second course last week."

"Then I'm about two weeks ahead of you."

Wait, in order for him to do that, he would have had to start roughly the same time that she had. Having their abilities had meant more coursework for them, so it took a year longer to graduate high school, and then another year of intensive training at boot camp before they could even start college. The GF had their own online schooling system, which she had started while at boot camp, but there had been such little spare time that she hadn't made as much headway as she'd hoped.

It was not unusual for a GF member to be twenty-one and still working on a college degree. Still, she wanted it to be done sooner rather than later. Noriko had been pushing herself to get as much done as she could before getting assigned, figuring that she would lose part of her study time when she started her new job—at least until she got the hang of things. Cameron Powers struck her as many things but *driven* was not one of them. She gave him a suspicious study from the corner of her eye. "You're not one of those 'show once' people that don't need to study, are you?"

He gave her a slow, lazy blink. "Naw, I study."

Uh-huh. And pigs flew, too.

The gym door open and Lars quickly stepped through. Since Cameron's arrival, they had proven to have very similar personalities. Or at least very similar senses of humor and mischief. Noriko harbored a suspicion they actually were related, somehow.

When Lars saw them, his face fell for some reason. "Aww, is the show over already?"

Noriko gave him a blank look. "Show?"

"Yeah. Some of the guys saw you through the window, climbing one of the beams. I came to take a look." Finding them standing around chatting instead of hanging off the rafters didn't faze him for long and he crossed the room with a bounce in his stride. "Were you really climbing a beam?"

"We really were," Cameron responded. "Spidey, here, was teaching me how to do it."

"Spidey?" Noriko objected, pointing at her own nose. "I don't remember agreeing to a nickname."

"Nicknames aren't voted on, but freely given," Cameron informed her mock-seriously. The way his eyes tilted up suggested he was laughing on the inside.

"And you never, ever, escape them," Lars tacked on, in perfect agreement. "You climb something with your bare hands the first month of a job, you're going to be labeled 'Spiderman' for the rest of your time here. Right, Cam?"

"Right you are, my man. Now, you want to learn how to do it?"

"Sure, but not if you're teaching me." Without a beat of hesitation Lars turned to her with an expectant smile. "Well, Spidey? How do I do this?"

Noriko sensed a certain inevitability with that nickname. She would not be able to escape it even if she tried to shoot the two of them right now. And why were they so in sync with each other, anyway? Throwing a hand in the air, she reached for the harness. "Fine. Put this on. How many merlins are you comfortable with?"

"About 5 CMs should do for this, I think," Lars answered as he slipped his legs into the harness.

"I was using 4," Cameron offered.

"Then 4."

Noriko explained the nuts and bolts of it, which Lars tried as she explained, and then he spent a few minutes taking his hands off and on again with his feet firmly planted on the ground until he had the hang of it. He was at least more cautious than Cameron, who had brazenly gone straight up and trusted her anchoring skills. When he had the hang of it he tried going up and only slipped once with his right foot.

Reaching the top, he called down, "Ready?"

"Come on," she responded, slowly feeding the line as he rappelled back to the ground.

Landing with an expert thump, he turned

around with a grin. "That was fun."

"Isn't it, though?" Cameron agreed. "Next time, though, don't use the harness. It's more fun as a trust exercise."

Lars gave him a doubtful look. "With another guy catching me? No thanks. I will say this: Noriko, you've got good skill. In the three years I've been doing this, I haven't had such a smooth transfer of power on the first try like that. It took me and Lizzie about a month to get to that level."

Noriko privately felt that it was more because of Lizzie than anything. Why she didn't attempt to smooth out the power, or clean it, or do any refining before handing it to Lars was beyond her understanding. Wasn't that a Mægencræft's job?

"My Spidey's got great skills," Cameron agreed while sliding an arm around her shoulders and beaming like a proud older brother. "And she's pretty. It's a lethal combination."

"Hey, hey, what are you bragging about? My Lizzie is cute too, y'know."

Noriko glanced between the two of them, knowing very well they were only teasing, and felt torn between laughing and groaning. There was no way for her to take any of what they were saying seriously.

"I understand you went to Edwards already?" Lars didn't wait for any confirmation before continuing, "That's good. It's important to know the whole area. Has anyone taken you up to Red Rock Canyon? No? Maybe we can swing it by the captain as a 'necessary tour/team building' thingy."

"What are the odds we can pull that off?"

Cameron asked.

"Pretty decent, actually, Banderas is always up for a good cook-off. Let's go ask."

5TH MERLIN

"KAA-SAN," Noriko groaned into the phone, "do you realize what time it is?"

"Nine o'clock on a Sunday morning, and why aren't you up, Ri-chan?"

Clearly her mother had *not* read the email Noriko had sent last night. Noriko gave a dramatic flop back into her bed. "Kaa-san, I have second shift. That means I don't get home until about 1 a.m."

"You still got eight hours of sleep, what you complaining about?"

Noriko gave up. Why did she even try to argue with a woman that only required four hours of sleep a night?

"Well? How is your first week at work going?"

Between moving, getting a new partner, and facing a rogue ley line, Noriko hadn't had a chance to really process it on an emotional level yet. So her own words surprised her a little. "I think

I've landed in a good place. The people here are kind with good personalities, and so far the work seems interesting."

"You've done something already?"

"Um, just a little? Tehachapi seems quiet for the most part, but apparently when something does happen, it's major and affects the whole town. My new partner and I went into the desert with our team. There was an unstable ley line that we managed to get to in the nick of time."

"Ehhh? That sounds quite serious. How did it happen?"

"We're not quite sure yet. We can't find a cause for it, and my team captain checked that line himself not five days prior to it going, and it was stable then. Having a ley line suddenly flare up like that has us all agitated." Noriko didn't need to explain why as her mother would understand the situation perfectly well. "But Captain Banderas isn't shrugging this off. He met with the other team captains and we're all now actively patrolling our areas much more than usual to make sure we don't have any other ley line problems."

"I should hope so. It sounds like he's a good captain, to be proactive about the problem like this. Haru mentioned to me that you had a partner. Really, Ri-chan, do I have to get that kind of information via your brother?"

"If you checked your email on more than a weekly basis, you wouldn't have to rely on Haru-kun," she shot back sweetly.

"You know I don't do well with emails, I want to hear my children's voices."

"Then you'll have to wait for Sunday. It's

the only day our work schedules don't overlap." Noriko leaned back in her pillows and enjoyed the give-and-take with her mother. Their relationship had always been like this, neither really giving ground to the other.

"Stop being stubborn and tell me what he's like."

Noriko took a second to think about how to explain this. "My first impression of him was strange. And I still don't really understand his sense of humor. He's nice looking, with an amazing voice, but he has this attitude...I'm not sure how to describe it. It's like nothing would ever really panic him. He's very laid back."

"Give me an example," her mother suggested. Was there a tone of worry in her voice?

"Like when we went to rescue the bear."

"Rescue a bear?" her mother repeated dubiously.

"Apparently that happens rather often out here. The black bears in this area like to climb the telephone poles and they get stuck on top. It takes a team of people to get them safely down again. We got called to the rescue the first day, and at first I didn't think Cameron was really paying attention. He wasn't even facing the right direction, really. But when the bear fell, he instantly caught it. And then he held it there for a good half hour until a vet could come. He didn't seem to mind at all—he was joking with our team while waiting."

Her mother hummed a note thoughtfully. *"So he does have a work ethic."*

"I think he has a good one. I've never seen him

slacking and he's always willing to learn. It's just that he doesn't approach anything the way that I would approach it and he's usually joking around with people while working." Honesty compelled her to confide, "My captain has now assured me twice that if I want to get a different partner, I can tell him, and he'll notify command to have me changed to someone else. But I don't think I want to. I don't always get his sense of humor but partnering with him is very easy. I don't think I've ever meshed as well with someone else."

"Not even with Sam?" she asked in surprise.

"Not even with Sam. I was kind of shocked too." It was moments like this that she blessed the fact that she was a Mægen like her mother, as she would understand what Noriko was trying to say. "With everyone else, it was like I was pouring water out onto empty ground. I was forcing myself to be the conduit directly to them as they didn't seem to know how to reach out and meet me halfway. With Cam, he not only reaches out, he shapes his own power to receive what I give him. I'm not pouring water uselessly onto the ground anymore but into a cup made to hold it."

"Ahh," her mother said in perfect understanding. *"It was like that when I met your father. I had finally met someone that knew how to receive what I could give."*

"Is that why you've stayed with him all these years?" she teased, as only a daughter could. "Despite the fact he drives you crazy?"

"I swear if that man buys one more how-to manual, I'll strangle him. Now he wants to re-do the kitchen."

"Are you going to let him try?"

"After what he did to the hallway bathroom? Arienai. The man is not a builder, I keep telling him this, but he's not at all listening."

It was an eternal struggle between her parents. Her father loved to work with his hands, but often would dive into a project he had no experience with and would quickly get in over his head. Her mother was always the one that had to pry him loose and hire professionals to straighten out the mess. It happened once a year, this routine of theirs, and Noriko was convinced that it would keep happening until the two of them ended up in a retirement home.

"Now, don't change the subject. I'm calling to make sure that everything is alright. This young man, what is his name?"

"Cameron Powers."

"Cameron Powers. He is good to you?"

"Kind and patient," if with a questionable sense of humor, "and he's easy to work with. I don't think you need to worry about me."

"I'll take your word on that for now. Your studies? You've found time to keep up with them?"

Noriko rolled her eyes. "I ask you, who is your best student?"

That had her mother chuckling. *"I do admit it's you. Have you forgotten anything? You were in such a rush to leave I was worried that you wouldn't take everything you needed."*

"I did forget a few things," Noriko admitted, "But I was able to buy them here. Right now I'm just low on furniture. The dorms here are rather nice but they basically give you a bed and a couch and that's it. I bought a small table for the living room, so I have somewhere to sit and eat, but I really should buy more things."

"Do you plan to stay in the dorms, then?"

"They're very convenient for work and the rent's cheap. Unless something happens to force me out, I think I'll stay here for a while." Tired of trying to talk while lying flat on her back, she rolled out of the bed and wandered into the kitchen. As she cooked up breakfast, she continued talking to her mother. It wasn't anything important, and yet it was at the same time. Sometimes, when this far away from home, it was nice to have a familiar voice to talk to.

Eventually she got off the phone and ate her somewhat cold breakfast. As she ate, she looked around her apartment. Furniture shopping definitely had to happen in the near future. In her immediate future, however, she had boxes to deal with. Many, many boxes.

Pointing a finger at the nearest stack, she informed them, "I refuse to acknowledge your existence until I am showered and dressed."

At that point her phone bleeped at her. Popping open the messenger, she saw an invitation from Tye addressed to her, Sam, and Teddy for lunch. "Or I can be completely irresponsible," she decided with a smile on her face.

It wasn't like the boxes were going anywhere after all.

Noriko was not an interior decorator, and she could hardly claim that she had an artistic eye, but it didn't take one to realize that the Tehachapi Police Station needed a good makeover. The station had been built in 1950 then remodeled haphazardly through the years, so it was a clash of styles without any unifying force. The dark wood counters that split the waiting area from the bullpen showed their age, the grey laminate floors were three decades newer and clashed terribly, and offsetting it all were the walls. The bright, sunny, yellow walls. Or at least they were supposed to be sunny—surely that was what the painters had intended—but the color was more glaring than anything.

Some person had had mercy on the Gældorcræft Forces, and their side of the offices were not painted yellow. If she could ignore the left side of the station, her eyes were safe, as the right side was painted an honorary GF red. Noriko hadn't done much more than stick her head into the other GF teams' offices, but the peeks she'd had suggested that the only difference between them was how the desks were configured.

Today, however, she'd come in earlier than usual to get her official badge and radio band. She couldn't immediately escape into the safety of her office, so, instead, she tilted her head to avoid that awful yellow. As she walked, she greeted the few faces she recognized, sometimes side-stepping around them if they had someone in custody. Most of the people in cuffs were sullen (no surprise) and a few glared at her. She ignored it. They were not her problem.

It was just as well the bullpen and the GF offices were separated by thick walls, as there was a lot of activity going on this afternoon. People were yelling, swearing, a few were crying, and it was enough to give her a headache just walking past it all. The sound level dropped as she gained the hallway that led back toward the IT department and Legal.

Sticking her head inside, she gave a light rap on the open door. "Hi."

A very short, petite woman with distinctly Asian features lifted her head from the computer she was typing away on. "Hello. Can I help you?"

"Hi. I'm Noriko Arashi, part of the Pathmaker Team," she introduced herself.

"Ah, yes, hi," the woman responded with a slight accent, popping out of her chair. Stretching out a hand, she said, "Khanh Chau, nice to meet you. My husband said you were supposed to come by and get a badge and radio band, is that right?"

"Yes." Khanh Chau? What nationality was that? Not Japanese, that was the only thing she was sure of. At least this woman made her feel taller, as Khanh was definitely under five feet tall.

She ducked under a desk, pulling out a plastic blue bin, and popped up again. "These are yours. If anything happens to them, just bring them back, we'll replace them."

The way she so casually assured her of this worried Noriko. Had someone already warned them how bad she was with electronics? Or perhaps it was commonplace? Not about to ask, she pasted a smile on her face instead. "I will, thanks."

The band was of course GF red again, although this set had her initials in black on it, like her phone did. She snapped it onto her wrist right next to where her phone sat, tightening it enough that it wouldn't slip around. Then she glanced at the badge. It was the magnet type so that it would attach directly to her shirt pocket's magnetic strip. There was the usual information, her picture, and a large red stripe along the bottom. To show that she was GF? She couldn't figure out what else it could mean.

Thanking the woman again, she retreated back down the hallway and into her own office. Even though she had come into work a little early, she found that almost everyone was already there.

Lizzie came in right behind her, catching the door right before it closed. "Got your badge?"

"I did," Noriko confirmed. "Explain to me why we have a radio again? That's old tech."

"Because the government does not easily update," Lizzie drawled, shrugging, although she seemed amused. "If they have a system that works, they try not to change it."

That made sense, but Noriko wasn't entirely convinced she knew how to use the thing.

A wave of disrupted power rolled through the air, visible to the naked eye. To a normal person, it would not be obvious, but every Dwolcræft and Mægencræft in the room immediately flinched from it. It was like a shockwave, one that only they could see, but the effects were obvious as it caused a temporary blackout throughout the office. The power was loose and volatile, jarred from the ley lines it was supposed to flow through, preceding a low rumble from the earth.

Jack, not being a cræfta despite belonging to the Gealdorcræft Forces, could not see or feel the power. But he certainly noticed the rumble under his feet and the two-second blackout. "What was that?" he demanded sharply.

Their captain was already out of his chair and moving for the large holograph screen on the wall. "Nothing good," he responded, looking a little grey around the edges. "It came from the base. Jack, call them now."

As their coordinator, it was Jack's responsibility to make contact for any job they took. Especially where the base was concerned. The man started moving even as Banderas left his chair, calling out the code as he did so. "Call Main Base. Torstein, Jack, code 00761."

"Calling Main Base," a canned female voice responded calmly. "Please hold while I connect your call."

Another call came through, a green phone shaking in the bottom left corner of the screen with a name scrawled above it in italics: *Main Base, Commander Hays.*

"Accept call," Jack ordered.

The phone blipped out and a man in his early fifties appeared on screen. His eyes were too wide in his pale face, GF red jacket somewhat askew as if he had slid into his chair instead of sitting in it properly. *"Torstein. I need your team NOW."*

Banderas whirled and grabbed the backpack that rested behind his desk. Taking that as a cue, Noriko snatched up her gear as well, ready to go when everyone else did.

"Commander, let me transfer your call to our team's channel so you can brief us as we drive," Jack requested.

"Excellent suggestion, do so."

Banderas barked out, "Move, people, load up. Partners sit together so we can deploy quickly when we arrive."

They moved as a unit out of the doors at a half-jog, and loaded into the same vehicle that Noriko had ridden in three days ago out to the base.

It was Jack that punched in their destination before he even sat down, then pushed the speakerphone button on the van's display module so everyone on the team heard the commander with crystal clarity. "We're on our way, Commander. What's the situation?"

"I honestly don't know the full details at this moment. There were two night tests being done up at the Lab, only one of our partners scheduled to work tonight in support. Two minutes ago, test cell 2-A blew to smithereens. I have no further information than that."

Noriko felt a wave of sickness twist her stomach. A night test gone wrong meant not only the possible loss of life to anyone working on that test cell, but also that it could set off the area below them into a backlash of energy in exactly the wrong way, setting off an earthquake. The one thing that California absolutely did not need was another earthquake.

"The Fire Department at the Lab and on Base are already responding, but...Torstein, we've

had a flu epidemic on Main Base for the past two weeks. I am desperately short on people right now. I'm sending what I can up there, but I'm putting your team in lead. You're the only full team I have at the moment."

"Understood, Commander. We will take lead."

"Team Pathmaker, keep me updated as you make progress. Especially report to me any survivors. Right now we have no idea how many people we've lost up there. Your first priority is to make sure that we're not going to get an earthquake from this. The second is to find any survivors. After that, figure out just what in heaven happened."

While Noriko believed that his priorities were exactly in the order he listed, she couldn't shake the idea that what he actually wanted was for the team to do it all at once.

"Team Pathmaker copies orders loud and clear, sir. ETA twenty minutes to arrival."

"If any of you are religious, start praying. There are good men and women up on that rock that I don't want to lose tonight. Hays, over and out."

Torstein ended the connection and looked up. "Captain?"

Banderas didn't answer him, but looked at Cameron and Noriko. "You're the strongest pairing I have, individually, but also the greenest. I'm asking you this because I need to know an honest answer. What are you not comfortable doing?"

It took strength to admit to any weakness out loud. Noriko had to wet her lips and force the words out. "Sir, I'm not good with channeling power into a machine. I tend to fry them."

"I'm good at that," Cameron stated, for once not seeming like he was either joking or flirting. "But I can't concentrate on more than two things at the same time. My Spidey taught me how to climb something without any rigging, sir, so we can go anywhere you need us to."

"Spidey?" Charlotte repeated, bemused.

"You climb a steel beam with your bare hands the first month of work," Lars repeated his words from Saturday, "you get stuck with the nickname Spiderman. Cap, I should tell you, Noriko can feed both me and Cam power at the same time. I tested her limits a little, just in case she had to do an emergency partnering with me."

Banderas demanded a confirmation from her with his eyes.

She managed a taut smile. "If you want me to feed power into multiple people at once, that I can do. Three's about my limit."

Jack let out a low whistle. "They really didn't rank you right, Noriko."

"That makes it obvious how to deploy you, then. Charlie, you and I are going to investigate the ley lines in the area and siphon off any energy we find. Let's stop an earthquake from happening if we can. We'll be working in conjunction with whoever they're able to send from Main Base." Charlotte nodded firm agreement. "Lizzie, Lars, you help those two. The control center for the test cell is in its own bunker, mostly built into the mountain. With an explosion of this size, odds are its buried. Find the survivors. Lizzie, if you find any excess energy, channel it into the nearest working generator if you can. If you can't, tell Jack, we'll put someone on it."

"Yes, Cap."

"Everyone eat before coming into work? You're all good and hydrated?" Banderas looked satisfied at their answers. "Good, good. This is going to be a long night. Because we're lead team, we won't be able to leave when our shift normally ends. Lars, Lizzie, Cameron, Noriko, when you've dug out the survivors, check in with Jack. If there's no other emergency, talk to me. We'll work in shifts on the ley lines in the area until things are back to being stable."

Even as Noriko gave an affirmative, she noted that the captain had never once suggested that the engineers and techs running the test might not have survived the explosion. Hopeful thinking on his part? Or maybe he didn't want to think about loss of life if he didn't have to. She personally hoped that people had survived. This would be her first major job, and having it end in tragedy was something she didn't care for.

The AI system in the van had been set to maximum speed, and it flew along the desert highways at nearly 120 miles an hour. Fortunately, most of the drive was straight roads. Otherwise, at that speed, they'd be taking curves on two wheels. Banderas spent most of the ride reviewing investigative procedures with Noriko and Cameron. They had taken a crash course on it in their boot camp training, but that had been over a month ago, and they had no practical experience in it, just book learning. Jack was right about their arrival time, and they came to the Lab's front gate at just under twenty minutes.

All bunched up against the gates were security vehicles, reporters and their vans, a fire truck ahead of them trying to get in without running anyone over in the process, and military personnel of different types. The gate wasn't a very large opening to begin with, so having fifty or sixty people all try to cram through at the same time made it feel like a circus. Or it would if not for the smell of burning metal that hovered in the air.

One adventurous reporter wrenched the back door open and stuck her head inside with the microphone attached to her hand. "Are the Gældorcræft Forces—" Someone grabbed her by her collar and jerked her back out before quickly slamming the door shut again.

There was no guard on duty, the gate set up for remote control, with a large screen above several different diagnostic tools and an emergency override control panel. The screen showed a young lieutenant that was crisply dressed but harried. *"Identify yourselves."*

Jack leaned out the window enough to flash the badge at one of the scanners, which gave a happy beep and a green light. "Jack Torstein, Pathmaker Team, Tehachapi Station."

"Confirmed, sir. We've been expecting you. Both Lab and Main Base's Fire Departments have gone ahead of you. We have a six-man team on site controlling entry and exit. Their squad captain is Holstein. Go through!" the gate guard ordered sharply.

Jack lost no time in obeying the command. He switched immediately over to manual override and aside from dodging a security jeep, they drove straight through, took the first road to the left, and came to an abrupt stop at a gate. Two guards were on duty there and they also checked in with everyone in the van.

Jack flashed his badge at them and introduced himself, "Jack Torstein, Coordinator for Team Pathmaker. Gentlemen, the only authorized personnel for this area are now GF from Main Base, firemen, paramedics, and whatever analyst they send to investigate this explosion. All other personnel, including Lab people, are not to enter. Clear?"

"Crystal clear, sir," one of the guards assured him with a smart salute.

Jack returned it and sat back in his seat. The gate was opened with a swipe of the card and they followed the curve in the road toward the test cell.

Explosions of this magnitude did not leave a single tidy hole. The area around them looked pockmarked, having had so many different pieces of debris torn through the landscape. It was just as well that Jack manually drove the van, as the road was not free and clear. He had to weave around smoking hunks of metal, and several times had to slow to an almost dead halt in order to maneuver around the larger pieces.

When they finally did get all the way around the bend, Noriko could see a gigantic hole in the side of the hill.

The area crawled with people in hazmat suits,

SCBA, and protective gear. Lars popped open the door only to quickly shut it again, gagging. Thick smoke and chemical residue clogged the air so much that it was beyond difficult to breathe. Noriko reached into her bag and immediately put on a face mask to help filter the air, but even though she'd reacted quickly, she still had an acrid taste in her mouth from the terrible air quality. Despite the poor visibility, she could see that a few places had been taped off with red tape, and there were water hoses and lines crisscrossing in every direction as the firemen fought pockets of fire. The largest stack of debris, near the cliff side, was in full blaze. There must have been at least five water hoses pointed directly at it and all it was doing was sizzling. She didn't even want to think of what it would take to put that out.

Everyone was better braced this time when Lars opened the door and stepped out. With the door open, Noriko could hear someone on a bullhorn shouting above the confusion, "Get me more portable lights over here! Williams, I need three over near the control bunker, we got GF people here that need to see!"

Power sparked in bursts, spider webbed along the ground, and sometimes arced in the air. The bursts were as brightly lit as firecrackers strewn across the ground, but with far more destructive power. They were nauseating to look at, and Noriko had to swallow several times to keep the contents of her stomach down. She managed to follow Cameron out readily enough, strapping on her backpack as she did so, but she had to pause when her feet actually touched ground. If looking at it was bad, actually being in contact with it was a hundred times worse.

Cameron was more than green around the gills but he managed a smile somehow. "Dying request, Spidey."

"What's that?" she gasped, still fighting her nausea.

"Don't spew on me."

Somehow the line made the situation a little more bearable and she grimaced at him. "I won't if you won't."

"Deal." He put a hand on her shoulder, grip firm but not hard, and shucked the power away from her like a mini-forcefield.

She drew on a proper breath and felt her stomach settle. "Thank you."

"Can't do that for long, so take advantage while I can." Cameron twisted his torso, looking about while still maintaining a grip on her. "Where do we even start?"

It was a good question. Despite the portable lights and the pockets of blazing fires, the lighting was beyond poor. They were, after all, on the top of a large hill in the dead of night, and whatever exterior lighting that had been up here before was nothing more than smoldering hunks of metal now. The lights and shadows flickered and reflected on the pieces, casting the area into a macabre chiaroscuro.

Jack came toward them, speaking as he did so, "We're dividing the area into zones. I'll put up flag markers so you know where the zones end. Lars, Lizzie, do you remember enough of this side of the Lab to know where the control center for the test cell was?"

Lizzie shook her head in immediate denial. It was Lars that pointed toward their left, although the frown on his face was uncertain. "Over there, I think."

"You think correctly. Four hundred feet from here, there was a slight upslope, and the control building was in there."

Noriko couldn't see a trace of it left. The area around them was so piled up with smoking rubble, remains of metal and the like that there was nothing in the topography to suggest where buildings might have been. Smoke still smoldered in the air as well, obscuring her sight, although fortunately the man with the bullhorn was making sure that portable lighting was set up in the area. The extra lighting was making things better and worse all at once. She didn't have to worry as much about tripping over things, but it was highlighting the destruction in gut-churning ways.

"Four hundred feet dead ahead?" Lars repeated, looking to Jack for confirmation. "Then we'll go in and start digging things up. Cam, you're majoring in Geology, right? You got any experience discerning rock from people?"

"Some, yeah. I interned with a Search and Rescue group last summer."

"Good, in that case, you start on the right side, I'll start on the left, and let's see if we can't dig us up some survivors."

"Remember," Jack continued, nearly vibrating in place with his need to be in about three places in one, "that the 2A block house only has the door exposed. They also have a tunnel leading out to

1A. If you can't readily find the door here, try the 1A exit."

Banderas, who stood behind him, inserted, "I will check 1A and radio in if we can reach the survivors through there. You focus on this side. We want this place cleared before the fire can spread over here."

"Roger that," Lars acknowledged with an analyst's salute.

The men led off, with Noriko and Lizzie hot in pursuit. As they climbed over the rubble, Noriko asked the other woman, "Where can I pull power from? Is it safe to take anything that's around me?"

"It's actually preferable for you to do that," Lizzie answered, pausing in between words as she focused on climbing the trickier sections. "It calms the area down, makes it less dangerous, but it's understandable if you choose to find a more stable force and channel from that. It's hard to take all of this power lying about and make it usable after all."

Certainly it would be more challenging, but Noriko preferred it over trying to take power from a ley line and channeling it to Cameron while fighting off errant sparks of power. The area was so unstable that she didn't even want to stand on it for long.

Cameron paused in front of her, offering a hand over a gap of rocks, which she thankfully took. His long limbs had no trouble crossing that kind of distance, but she would have had to find another way around without his assistance. As he pulled her into him, he asked quietly, "Which way do you wanna go? I'm good if you want to pull from a ley line."

So he'd heard that, huh? She shook her head. "Let me try to get power from our immediate area first. It's dangerous to work with power scattered around like this. If it's not usable enough for you, then I'll look for another source."

He seemed relieved at her answer and he gave her a swift smile before letting go and continuing on.

What should have taken a few minutes to walk took them nearly fifteen minutes to climb over. Lars finally lifted a hand, calling them to a halt, and signaled Cameron and Noriko with two fingers to go right. They split up, balancing their weight precariously on the shifting debris as they moved.

Navigating this potential hotbed while gleaning power from their surroundings was tricky at best, but she focused and fed a steady stream of 10 kilomerlins to Cameron. "Is that enough?"

"A little more juice, Spidey."

She gathered up more, focusing on their immediate area first, then spreading out in a spiral pattern. "Good?"

"Great. Keep that up." Cameron focused away from her, hands lifting as if he were conducting an orchestra. Rocks rose at his silent direction and shifted off to the far right, stacking up neatly into chunky pyramids. Noriko was relieved he wasn't just chucking things to the side, as that would cause an avalanche later.

Not knowing if it was safe to talk to him as he worked, she kept her mouth shut and focused on her own job. The ley line directly under them felt highly unstable but very drained, so she had high hopes that it wasn't in any danger of setting off an earthquake. It would take a while to feed more power into it and make it stable again, though. That would not be a job a single team would want to tackle, either. The line under her feet was the size of a river and it stretched out for miles in both directions. This would take dedicated personnel and time to recuperate.

"I've got people under me," Cameron announced suddenly. He stopped dead and lifted his head. "LARS!"

The other pairing wasn't far off, so they heard the shout and immediately scrambled to Cameron.

"You sense anyone?" Lars demanded as he moved, only pausing to give Lizzie a hand as she needed it.

"I've got seven down here," Cameron informed him. "At least three alive, as they're moving a little. You feel 'em?"

Lars's eyes went blind to his immediate surroundings as he used his magical sense to see below the rocks. "I feel them. I think you're wrong, though, I think we have seven alive. But I'm not sensing much air down there."

"No, they're in a small pocket," Cameron agreed. "Which makes me wonder about the tunnel."

As if in answer, Banderas's voice came in over their channel. "1A's tunnel is trapped on this side by debris. It's all on fire and we're having a hard time putting it out. What's the status over *there?"*

Lizzie put the wrist comm up to her mouth to respond, "We've got part of the door in sight, sir. It's still got a lot on top of it, though. We're sensing very little air inside. I think all of the air vents are either damaged or blocked."

"Not at all surprised. Your first priority is to get them out. Noriko, you can do three things at once, so I want you dictating notes of what you're seeing and taking pictures as they work. We need to keep some documentation of where things were for later."

"Yes, sir," she assured him even as she slung her bag around and pulled out a camera. Normally she'd take pictures with her holoshades, but, in this circumstance, she'd have to turn the camera in afterwards to preserve the chain of evidence. Besides, she wasn't convinced the holoshades had a good enough camera equipped to handle this poor lighting. "Dictated notes are fine?"

"Just fine. Ley line over here is hopping around like a frog in a hot skillet, so you manage what you can. We're not going to be available for help. Banderas, out."

They were on their own, eh? Well, Noriko wasn't too worried; Lars and Lizzie seemed very much in command of the situation. She started dictating things as quickly as she could while taking pictures at all angles. As she worked, she leant half an ear to Cameron and Lars's conversation.

"We need to get them out fast," Cameron said definitively, "Question is, do we drill a hole through first and get them air? It will buy us time."

Shifting a little to the left, Lars looked the area

over thoroughly. "Lizzie?"

Puzzled as to why he'd asked his partner for her opinion, Noriko then remembered that Lizzie had majored in Structural Engineering. Of course she would be the expert to ask in this situation. Lars was like her and Cameron, a Geology major. He wouldn't be sure what was safe to move.

Lizzie stepped back and evaluated the area for a long time before shaking her head. "It'll take an hour. At least. We better make sure they have air. Cameron, this fissure next to your right foot, can you sense how far down that goes?"

"Almost to them, why?"

"That's the most stable area right now. Where we're standing is in danger of shifting if we tamper with it in any way. Drill there first."

Noriko went back to gathering and feeding him power. Cameron would direct the flow with a hand, sometimes circling it fast to encourage her to give him more, sometimes slowing it down by reducing his winching speed. It was the perfect way for her to gauge what he needed.

Jack stood near the van with both hands cupping his mouth. "RADIO!"

Oh, whoops, had they been ignoring the radio? Noriko certainly had been treating it like background noise while they focused on the job at hand.

Lars was the first to put the radio band near his mouth. "Sorry, Jack."

"*Try not to do that again, I need to deploy people where they're needed,*" Jack responded with considerable irritation. "*Communication is key to that. Do you sense survivors up there?*"

"Yes, sir, seven distinct energies are below us."

He was too far away to read, but Jack sounded relieved. "*Get them out!*"

Lars didn't quite salute. "On it, sir!!"

Noriko prayed they could.

6TH MERLIN

THEY were not the only GF team working up on the hill. Expecting a team of six to handle a disaster of this size was unthinkable. There were four people from the Boron Station that arrived just after they did. When the new team arrived, they were dispatched to get the ley lines in the area stable. There were two main streams, one minor that branched off, and all three of them were tremulous at best. If they didn't get those streams settled soon, it would likely cause another explosion, and this time it would take what was left of the hill with it.

Aside from casting them a glance or two to check on their progress, Noriko didn't pay the people from Main Base a lot of attention. Her magical sense kept them in peripheral vision, of course, as she needed to be aware if something happened in that area. But her main concern was making sure that Cameron had the power he needed to work.

Lizzie made a frustrated sound and stopped abruptly. "Noriko. I'm having a hard time focusing on three things at once. I need to direct Cameron and Lars on what can be moved and how, but I can't seem to do that and give Lars power at the same time. Can you cover for me?"

"Of course," Noriko agreed instantly. She was surprised the woman had even tried. Just gathering up power and channeling it into something usable was taking concentration on her part. In a perfect world, Lizzie could have done both seamlessly, but this situation was as far from perfect as they could get. She was done with dictating notes and taking pictures now, as this area was hardly a virgin scene anymore. She had attention to spare now. "Lars, how much do you want?"

"What you're feeding Cameron is spot on. What is that, 13 KMs?"

"Yes." She shifted her stance so that she was more in between the men, and focused so that she could feed two constant streams of power to them. There were times, like now, that Noriko felt more like a human generator than anything.

Lizzie did stay put for a long moment, making sure that she had it covered, before moving. Ducking around, she looked at the whole area before continuing to direct the men. "Lars, this chunk here, lift it about two feet. Perfect, stop. Cameron, shift this piece out slowly. No, no, the other way. Just like that, yes. Now put it directly behind me. Lars, move yours to bracket it."

"What are we doing here, Lizzie?" her partner

asked her as he did as directed. "It sure looks like we're playing Jenga or something."

"A little, yeah," she admitted with a faint smile. "There's no room to stack things off to the side, we risk setting off an avalanche eventually. Let's just rearrange the area here enough to get people out."

That sounded like a good plan to Noriko. She'd been wondering what they were going to do with all of these heavy slabs of broken concrete. There were steel I-beams and bricks and other things that were so mangled she couldn't begin to guess what they originally were. It made for a very cluttered area.

Cameron flung up a hand. "Wait, stop. You hear that?"

They all went still. Noriko's heart flew into her throat as she heard the distinct *clang clang clang* of metal striking something hard. "I sure do."

Cameron leaned down toward the fissure and yelled, "WE HEAR YOU!"

It was barely discernable, but she thought she heard a sob of relief.

Lars came in closer and called down, "HOW MANY INJURED?"

"THREE! HURRY!" a male voice yelled back.

"Must be bad," Cameron said to the air in general.

Turning his head, Lars called down, "I NEED A MEDICAL TEAM ON STANDBY!"

The man with the bullhorn raised it to his mouth. "Did I hear a request for a medical team on standby?"

With all of the noise, even though he was a

stone's throw away, Noriko was actually impressed he'd heard Lars.

Lars didn't try to repeat himself, but instead lifted a hand high in the air and gave the man a thumbs up.

Noriko tracked movement out of the corner of her eye as a medical team poured out of the ambulance and headed for them, scrambling over the debris with equipment clutched tightly in their hands.

Cameron paid them no heed and asked, "Lizzie, how careful do we need to be for the rest of this?"

"Depends," she answered grimly. "How much can you lift at once?"

"A lot more than what I've been doing." Cameron looked up and for once there was no trace of the jokester on his face. "Lars?"

"Hey now, I'm more of a veteran than you are. You think you can outdo me, punk?" The challenge was meant to be joking but even Lars wasn't in the mood to kid around. "Give me a number."

"Sixty tons is my comfortable max," Cameron rattled out. "You?"

Lars blinked. "Sixty? Alright, if you're sure, that's what you do. Lizzie, you know my limit. Tell us what to move."

Hopping lightly to the side, Lizzie pointed. "Cameron, that beam down there, see it? From there up and to this slab just behind you. Lars, same spot down, and everything you can from where I'm standing to the slab under your feet. All at once now, ready? Three, two, one, go!"

Noriko adjusted the power flow as necessary

and fed them every bit of power they needed plus a little extra. It became more of a challenge as they demanded more kilomerlins all at once, and she drained everything within a six-foot radius for the power they needed. It also made the area safer to walk through. It was two birds with one stone, as they would soon have injured people that needed to leave the area and clearing it now was a plus in their favor.

Seeing that the medical team had reached them, she waved them to a stop and they did, hovering, bodies leaning forward as if ready to spring into action at her command. She dared not let them in any closer than this, not while hunks of concrete and metal still moved around.

Watching the men lift the slabs up was something like watching a superhero in an action movie. It seemed impossible, what they were doing, as neither of them physically touched a thing in the air. Noriko could see every thread of power they had around the slabs, netted over and around it, hoisting it upwards like an invisible crane. Under Lizzie's direction, they set it all off to the side, and only then did they release and let it all settle again. It did so with a grating, grumbling sigh.

Noriko again adjusted the stream and lowered the power she fed them. Lars was breathing a little hard, Cameron had sweat beading along his forehead, but neither man paused to catch their breath. They scrambled for the hole they had just created.

Fortunately, the hole was not deep, only eight or so feet. With the area clear, they could see the blast door. Well, what was left of it. The impact had been so severe that it left the door nearly caved in. Lars did the honors and wrenched it free, setting it off to the side and stacked on top of everything else. Cameron swung his feet over and dropped into the clearing right in front of the doorway. Noriko followed him to the edge, as she had to stay within a certain range of him; otherwise she wouldn't be able to give him any merlins of power.

The scene inside was horrifying.

Mangled computer parts and shattered chairs, all tangled up with each other, lay strewn across the room. The shockwave hadn't been severe enough to do true structural damage to the block building, but it had sent everything not bolted down flying. Dust hung thick in the air, so much so that it was almost impossible to see anything. One person had a phone on them that still worked and he had a flashlight app to light up the area. That small beam was their only illumination until Cameron flicked on the light in his baseball cap, which shed a halo of light all around.

In a merry tone, Cameron gave them a little wave of the hand. "Hello, folks. I'm Cameron Powers with the Gældorcræft Forces. I'm here to escort you off the premises. We'll do so in an orderly fashion, with the most injured first. Who's our lucky winner?"

One person snorted at his dry humor. "I think that would be Michelle. I don't know how bad, but I think some of her ribs are cracked, and she's not breathing too well."

Noriko did not like the sound of that at all. She threw her legs over the side then paused when she realized she didn't have anywhere to land. The area down below was tiny and crammed with seven bodies. It was a miracle Cameron had found a clear space. "Cameron, catch me."

Cameron's eyes lit up. "Are you finally going to do trust exercises with me?"

"You drop me and this will be the last time," she promised him firmly.

He stretched his hands out. "Come to papa."

Noriko decided to deal with him later and dropped down. He caught her, as he had before, without a second of hesitation. She patted him on the shoulder. "Nice catch. Who's Michelle?"

A woman weakly lifted her hand a few inches.

Carefully stepping over a tangle of limbs, she maneuvered her way around to the woman's side. "Let's get your ribs wrapped before we move you," she said, fighting to keep her voice level. A lifetime of looking after younger siblings and their multitude of boo-boos helped steady her nerves as she slung her pack around and pulled out bandages. "Otherwise we risk damaging things further. You, what's your name?"

"Mike," the man next to her responded. He'd had a hand on the woman, helping to prop her up. Under the bad lighting, and with the thick coat of dust on his skin, he looked like a ghastly zombie.

"I'm Noriko," she introduced herself with a brief smile. "You hurt?"

"Just scrapes and bruises," he assured her.

"Then if you'd be so kind, can you help her sit up a little more? Just like that, perfect. Let's wrap the ribs. Cameron, help the ones that can move out first."

"Can you wrap and feed me power?" he asked in faint surprise.

She shot him a Look over her shoulder.

For some reason, that made him chuckle. "I should have not questioned. Of course my Spidey can do that. Lars?"

"I've got Jack standing by!" Lars responded, already forming up power. "Someone's got to clear a better path so the paramedics can get through here, though. Can you handle getting them out?"

"Sure, go ahead."

Lars and Lizzie both immediately moved. Noriko paid Cameron enough attention to give him the power that he needed to work, listening with half an ear as he lifted people up and instructed them on where to go. Some spots were safe to walk on, others not as much.

The woman under her hands was sweating profusely, skin white with pain, and there were little tendrils of whistling in her breathing that spoke of a bruised lung. Noriko had a First Aid certification—everyone in the Forces did— but also a summer internship with Search and Rescue that gave her enough experience to know when someone needed help ASAP. This woman qualified. "Mike?"

"Yes?"

"Someone needs to get this woman's medical history down and go into the ER with her. Can you be that person?"

"You bet I can." Tapping his phone, he pulled

up a dictation app, although the holograph screen was a little fuzzy due to the dust flying about. "Michelle, tell me what I need to know."

Michelle was barely aware at this point, her body trying to suck her into unconsciousness as a way to deal with the pain. She fought it long enough to give Mike the highlights, waiting as Cameron lifted someone else out.

Cameron turned and knelt down next to them. "You ready to get outta here?"

Mike had a very worried expression on his face as he looked at his co-worker. "We need to go next."

"Yup, ready for you," Cameron assured him. "Spidey, she all wrapped up?"

"She's good, get her out." Noriko wouldn't have delayed them, but she had been afraid that lifting the woman in the air without wrapping the ribs first would exacerbate the damage. Cameron would have been able to slap a magical brace on her well enough, true, but then she would have been on top of the rubble with ribs that needed to be wrapped. It was impossible to treat her in that narrow space on top and Noriko hadn't liked the idea of her being jostled over the rough ground either. Better to wrap them down here and then move her.

Cameron was the definition of gentle as he lifted Michelle and Mike out together, using a slab of nearby concrete as a platform to elevate them to the surface. Noriko couldn't see it from her angle, but she heard the sirens of the ambulances and the different wail of the fire trucks. "Sounds like more emergency crews have arrived. Is the area clear enough for them to do that?"

"Must be, otherwise Jack wouldn't have let them in," Cameron replied. He dropped his gaze and looked around, the light perforce moving with him. "Man, what a mess. The place is well-built, though, to be able to withstand this kind of explosion. I mean, Michelle was hurt by flying equipment. The building itself is still mostly standing."

Which was a miracle. When Noriko had done the official signup with the Forces, she had been intellectually aware that her job covered a wide gamut. It wasn't just earthquakes that she was meant to guard against and prevent, but anything in the area that the police or emergency crews needed assistance with. That covered Search and Rescue, police work, firefighting, whatever was needed. She had known then that, sometimes, her work would send her harrying off to the rescue. She'd also known that no matter how fast she might work, there would be people that she couldn't save. Having everyone still alive on her first rescue mission was against the odds. She was profoundly grateful for it.

Still, seeing the damage done here and envisioning what would have happened to these poor, trapped people under a more intense explosion made a shiver go straight up her spine.

Maybe Cameron realized what she felt. He put an arm around her shoulders and urged gently, "Let's go, Spidey."

He was right. With a mental shake, she pulled herself together and gathered power, automatically channeling it to him. "You're right.

Let's go. Where's your elevator slab?"

"Up top. Lars took it from me to use so he could transport Michelle all the way to the ambulance."

The opening was just too high for them to easily climb out. Even having something to step on, to bridge part of the height, would be enough to give them the boost they needed. "Hmm, then what about that piece?"

"Too big, I think. But the one next to it should be about right." Cameron focused on the slab in question and started gingerly maneuvering it free from the corner it was leaning in.

"Noriko, Cameron, come in," Jack's voice came in crystal clear over the team's frequency. *"What's the status down there?"*

Noriko lifted the radio band strapped to her wrist up to her mouth. "We've got everyone free. There were three injured. We should be up in a min—"

Several things happened all at once, too fast for her to process or react to. The tenuous balancing act over their heads abruptly collapsed, sending every loose piece of slab and beam straight downward. Cameron jerked her in closer to him, his free hand slamming directly upwards, power rippling out in a visible wave into a dome shape. Noriko was pressed up against his chest, face buried in the curve of his neck, nerves jumping in reaction.

Everything slammed into the dome of Cameron's power in a clatter, dust flying, but it did not penetrate. There was a loud, ominous grating sound overhead as metal and stone and concrete all screeched together. Then, abruptly, silence.

With Cameron's abrupt snatch, her mask had been knocked askew, so that it was near her ear instead. A hand over her mouth, she tried not to breathe in any dust as it flew and settled around them. A few motes still got in her mouth, sending her coughing for a moment. She fought to get the mask back in place, and only then did she draw a proper breath.

"—do you read me? Come in! Noriko, Cameron, talk to me!" their captain demanded.

It was Cameron that responded, tone as lackadaisical as usual: "Hey, Cap. So, I pulled at a piece of broken slab, and I think it set everything off. My bad."

There was a collective breath of relief from the channel. Then Banderas was back, sounding calmer, although still strained. "Either of you hurt?"

"I'm not. Spidey?"

"I'm good," she assured him, still a little strangled because of the dust.

"Looks like we're both a-okay, Cap. Gotta tell ya, though, I'm not really enthusiastic about busting our way out from down here. I mean, I can try if you want—"

"Powers, you so much as twitch, and I'll suspend your butt and put you on half-pay, you copy?" Banderas growled. "Do NOT try to dig your way out of there. We will dig you out. You sit tight."

"Roger that, Cap, we'll be good little damsels in distress and wait for your rescue."

Noriko snorted at the image. If there was anything Cameron Powers was not, it was that. "Cameron, you can let go of me."

"No, really can't," he disagreed, and only then did she hear the faintest hint of strain in his voice.

She became taut as she sharpened her focus on him. This close, she could feel the flow of his power, see how he was using it, and she realized that while he had enough to keep the dome steady, it was straining his control to the max. She instantly searched out, found another power source, and channeled it to him.

He blinked at the increase of merlins and looked down at her. "How'd you know?"

"I could see it," she responded simply. "This good?"

"Exactly what I needed." There was a strange expression on his face, one of somber thoughtfulness even though the ever-present smile still lingered on his face. "Even when I grabbed you, even when all of this crap started falling, you never once faltered in giving me power. Didn't I scare you, by snatching you like that?"

"You did," she acknowledged readily. In fact, her heart was still thumping. "But if you were acting like that, then something serious was going down. And if it was, then you needed all the power you could get. Of course I couldn't risk breaking off the flow."

His smile grew, stretching from ear to ear. "They really didn't rank you right."

"That a complaint, Powers?"

"No way. Thanks to their screw-up, I got you.

Who'd complain about that?"

"You're making me blush," she drawled. He really was, too. Although statements like that made her wonder about his first intended partner, the one that he'd never gotten to work with. Did he not have any mixed feelings over that? Wonder what she would've been like? With a mental shake, she shelved the question. "I'm just glad you have such good reflexes. How'd you react that fast, anyway?"

"I sensed it start to come down. Glad I had you at hand, though, otherwise I might not have made it to you in time." Lifting his head, he listened hard for a moment. "You hear it?"

"They're clearing the rubble out fast," Noriko stated, admiringly. "I think we scared them. How much you want to bet that we're going to be in trouble for doing something reckless?"

"We weren't, though," Cameron protested.

She shook her head knowingly. "Captain's something of a worry-wart. You think that's going to save us?"

Her partner opened his mouth, paused, and closed it with frown. "Got a plan, partner?"

"I don't. But we have about ten minutes to figure one out."

7ᵀᴴ MERLIN

CAMERON'S mother might have been a hippie out of time, but she knew how to raise a gentleman. When the last of the debris was lifted off, Cameron insisted she get out first, and wouldn't budge until she was back on solid ground.

It was Lars who put a large chunk of concrete down, giving her the height she needed to climb out. He gave her a hand to brace against as she pulled herself up and through. Free of the hole, she took a look around and discovered that while they had been buried, even more help had arrived. There were lights strung up now, and huge lamps set up so that people could actually see what they were doing.

Jack was the one to greet them at the top of the rubble. Extending a hand, he helped her over the last of it. "You're looking a little grey, Noriko. Alright?"

"I'm fine," she assured him, spitting out dust and wiping her face with her palms to get the worst of it off. Only to herself would she admit her heart still raced a hundred miles an hour. She stepped over to the side, on a rare clear patch of ground, so that Cameron would have the space he needed to climb out.

From the corner of her eye, she caught sight of two men hovering near the ambulance, talking with the people they had saved. Even from here it was obvious they were a Mægencræft and Dwolcræft. "Jack, who are they?"

"The partners that are in charge of night shift up here on the hill," Jack responded as he leaned down to give Cameron a hand up. "They were on the other side when everything blew."

That didn't sound quite right to her. "Shouldn't they have been here, if there was a test?"

"SOP requires them to do a check of the area and clear out power if necessary before a test," Jack clarified patiently. "Once that's done, they're free to go patrol the rest of the area and do other duties. It's not necessary for them to stay during the duration of the test." Frowning, he glanced their direction. "Although I do wonder if it would have changed matters, if they had been here."

Cameron wiped dust from his face with an equally dirty sleeve. "We know the cause, then?"

"Not as yet. Someone will have to analyze the damage here to give us an answer. Right now it could be anything from a minor earthquake, to sabotage, to a malfunction in the engine. Or..." he trailed off and gave the area an unreadable look, "this is a ley line that went abruptly unstable."

Noriko had a hard time believing that a ley line with this many people near it could go unstable so quickly without anyone noticing. But she did take Jack's meaning. The other ley line had gone abruptly bonkers as well with no warning. They couldn't rule out the possibility of it happening here too. But that meant the cause was completely up in the air.

Their captain came to give them a once over, not just with eyes, but with hands as well. "Nothing broken? Sprained? Cut? That's a miracle."

Noriko shook her head. "Miracles have nothing to do with it. His reflexes are to thank."

Banderas gave Cameron a questioning look, getting a shrug in affirmation. "Is that right. If the two of you are still up to work? Good, we're shorthanded as it is. That must be some flu, to take out this many people from Main Base's teams. Powers, Noriko, pair up with me and Charlie. We need to do the heavy lifting for the firemen, make sure that there's no fuel lying about up here uncontained. If any of it sparks, it will make things much worse."

That sounded like a potential nightmare to Noriko. "Yes, sir."

"Lizzie, Lars, get back to cleaning up this area."

"Right-o, Cap," Lars acknowledged.

Clean-up was a nasty, nasty business. Noriko dug into it with grim determination, like everyone else around her. The firemen on scene were trained for this kind of situation, but even they seemed unnerved by the amount of damage done. She overheard several of them mutter comments to each other, usually along the lines of this being the worst they had ever seen.

Everything had to be documented before they moved it, and while they moved it. That was Noriko's job as Cameron did the actual lifting. She had a camera in one hand, a dictation program up on her holoshades, trying to clearly document where everything was. She included the time, too, although she wasn't sure if that was necessary or not. Her memory was hazy on that part of the procedure. Was it the date or the time?

A small man with thinning red hair and slightly pointed ears came over to them. He wasn't dressed like any of the relief workers—in fact he was in a black parka and jeans, glasses hooked into the front of his jacket. Maybe it was a trick of the light, but he looked rather like a leprechaun. "Captain Javier Banderas?"

Their captain stopped abruptly and carefully set the pile he had been moving back down before offering the man a hand. "That's me. You are?"

"Frank Goudie, Captain, pleasure. I'm from Industrial Forensics."

Banderas gave him a more genuine smile. "I was wondering if they would dispatch an explosions analyst tonight or wait until tomorrow. Very glad to see you, Mr. Goudie."

"I prefer to see things with my own eyes, fresh after it happens," Goudie explained. "Gives me a better sense of what's going on. Captain, as I understand it, your team was called in because the flu has laid low most of the teams on Main Base?"

"That's correct."

"They emailed me your team's profile as I was

driving in. You've got three Geology people—although I understand two are still in school—one structural engineering, one mechanical engineering, one physics major, and you yourself are retired military. Do I have all of that right?"

Banderas regarded him with some puzzlement, as if not sure where Goudie was going with all of this. "That's right, why?"

"Captain, I'll be frank, my company doesn't have any GF teams that I can pull from. Usually, in case of a disaster like this, we borrow what experts we need from the teams on base, or within that company. But right now, that's not possible. I'd prefer to keep your team on this task, if you don't mind, as you know firsthand how things looked immediately after the explosion. You've also got a good smattering of experts on your team that might help me solve this riddle. Can I formally request you?"

Rocking back on his heels, Banderas thought about this for a full second before answering bluntly, "I'd prefer to work the problem. I want to know what happened here."

Goudie looked relieved. "Then, Captain, I'll put in that formal request immediately. One question: Did anyone think to take pictures before your people dug in?"

"My coordinator, Jack Torstein, was taking pictures, as well as my Mægencræftas. I'm not sure what the quality will be, as we were in poor lighting when we first arrived."

"That's understandable, I want to take a look anyway."

Turning to her, Banderas requested, "Noriko,

can you take Mr. Goudie to Jack? Stay with them if they choose to start poking around and clear the area of power as needed."

"Yes, Cap. Ah, if I do come across some sparks, where do you want me to put the power?"

"Harness it and pass it to the next Dwol you come to," he instructed.

"Sure, Cap. What about Cameron?"

"Charlie can handle both of us, don't you worry."

She cast a glance at Cameron to make sure he was alright working with Charlotte, and he gave her a silent go ahead. Reassured, she turned to Goudie with a professional smile on her face. "I believe I saw Jack over there, Mr. Goudie."

"I'll follow you."

She went off, keeping a weather eye on their surroundings as she did, as this area wasn't clear yet. Jack wasn't in her immediate line of sight, but there were so many things blocking her view, he could still be where she'd last seen him.

"I understand that this is your third week on the job?" Goudie asked her in a conversational tone.

"Yes, sir."

"What a way to start, eh?" he gave a gentle chuckle. "If fate was kinder, you'd have an easier transition."

"If fate was kinder, this wouldn't have happened at all," she pointed out.

"Can't argue that. If memory serves, you're majoring in Geology, right? You and your partner, Harmony."

"Cameron," she corrected, waiting for his

reaction.

Confused, his steps faltered for a moment. "Is that how she prefers to be called?"

"Yes. He does."

It took a second to click, then Goudie slapped a hand against his leg. "His mother named her son *Harmony*?"

"I understand pain medications and thirty-plus hours of labor had something to do with it."

"That poor man. Cameron. I'll remember that."

"Or Cam, he's fine with either," she assured him. "You saw him standing next to Captain."

"The tall blond?" She could see it click. "Of course, why didn't I realize? Your partner would be standing next to you so the two of you could work. So that was Cameron Powers."

It begged the question, "Don't our files have pictures, sir?"

"They normally do. Several, in fact. But your files are so new that the pictures haven't been matched up to the file yet. I understand there's a bit of backlog."

Oh. No wonder the captain hadn't had a picture of Cameron at the beginning, then. "To answer your earlier question, yes, we're both Geology majors."

"I know you're new to the field, but I want your opinion. Do you think this was caused by nature?"

Noriko hesitated strongly before answering. "We had no indications that something was wrong here, sir. I came over here with Jack and Cameron six days ago, touring the area, and we studied the ley lines closely. There wasn't a buildup of power strong enough to cause even a minor quake. If it was an earthquake, then something has gone very wrong to overload this area so quickly."

Goudie gave a long 'ah' sound of understanding. "That is very interesting information. Thank you, Noriko. That does give me a better idea of what the area was like before things blew."

"Like I said, sir, my information is six days old."

"But it's also newer than my geological surveys. And I trust what you saw."

That was a point; she was giving him an expert opinion that was fresher than any report he likely had on hand. "I should also tell you, sir, that we had a ley line flare up last week for no apparent reason."

Goudie's attention sharpened on her. "How much of a flare up?"

"It was bad, sir," she admitted frankly. Just remembering it made her a little nauseous. "If we hadn't found it in time, it would have set off quite the explosion. We still have no rhyme or reason for what caused it, either."

Panning the area, she could see the wheels turn in his mind. "You think something like that happened here? The ley line abruptly flared up and caused this?"

"I don't know, sir, I just thought you should be aware of it. It's hard to imagine that a ley line could go out of control in a single day without either pairing up here on the hill noticing, but we didn't think a ley line could go loopy in just five days either. And that's what happened."

"I do see what you mean. It's very strange. I will keep that information in mind while trying to unravel the mystery."

It might not have been her place to say anything, but Noriko, for one, wanted to make sure that this man had the information he needed to figure things out. If it was an unstable ley line that had caused this, they all needed to know, too. Looking up, she spotted Jack's back just as he was rounding the end of a fire truck and called out, "JACK!"

Their coordinator doubled back and looked her direction. At her wave, he stepped carefully around the fire truck's many lines and hoses and came toward them.

"Jack, this is Mr. Frank Goudie," she introduced. "He's an explosives analyst. Sir, this is Jack Torstein, our coordinator."

"From Industrial Forensics?" Jack asked, already extending a hand.

Frank took it. "That's right."

"Very glad to see you, Mr. Goudie. I was informed you were arriving, but you made better time than I expected."

"I live in Lancaster," he explained. "I should tell you, I just spoke with Captain Banderas and he's agreed to stay on this job. I want to make a formal request to keep this team."

Jack wasn't the type to ever look surprised, but Noriko had the feeling that this was unexpected. "You don't have your own people to use, Mr. Goudie?"

"I usually borrow from Main Base in events like these. Our company isn't large enough to warrant our own GF team, you see. You've got some good people on this team and as the first responders, you know what the area looked like. I want to keep you."

"I have no problem with that. I'll send in the request as well. Ah..." he paused and looked at Noriko.

"Captain asked that I stick with both of you so you can survey the area," she informed him, hoping she was answering that silent question on his face. The man was incredibly difficult to read, even in good lighting, which this wasn't.

"That will make things safer." Jack gave her a slight nod. "Noriko, take a ten-minute break. Once we're done, we'll be doing a lot of walking around this area."

"Yes, sir." After working for several hours straight, she was ravenous. A glance at her phone showed that it was just after two in the morning. Had they really been working for nearly four hours? The time had seemed so much shorter than that.

"Noriko," Jack looked down at her, "ready to go?"

"I am, sir."

"Mr. Goudie, did anyone send you the blueprints for this place?" Jack asked.

"They did, yes, and I have them here. I believe where we're standing is near the office building."

"You are correct, sir. The test cell itself was closer to the edge of the hill, directly behind and to the left of us."

Knowing where they were going, Noriko chose to walk ahead of the men, her eyes sharply on the lookout for any stray spark of power that might be nearby. She found several, which surprised her and didn't at the same time. After all, this was a rather sizeable area for a dozen cræftas to try and clear out. Four hours were not enough time to manage it. Without a word to the men, she gathered up all of that power and carefully carted it with her. The Dwols were too far away in this moment to accept any power offering from her—she'd have to carry it with her for a little while until she could pass it on.

Something about her behavior cued Jack up and he asked, "Noriko, are there still remnants of power about?"

She paused in her tracks and gave him a nod. "There are. Please stay close to me."

Goudie gave a nervous glance at the ground. "I would have thought this area already clear."

"No sir," she corrected, "we haven't really touched this place yet. Our first priority was locating and rescuing any survivors."

"Ah, of course, I should have realized. Then the test cell is virgin ground?"

"We did have Main Base's people come over with the firemen and clear up any rocket propellant," Jack informed him. "But other than that, we didn't do much. Our first priority was clearing out an area so we could get more personnel in here."

"I'm actually glad to hear it. This will give me a chance to analyze the area without having to rely on photos. No offense, Mr. Torstein." Goudie gave him a thumbs up. "You take very nice pictures."

Was that a glint of humor in Jack's eye? "Thank you, Mr. Goudie."

Rubbing his hands together, Goudie got a

wolfish tilt to his mouth. "Well now, let's begin."

8 TH MERLIN

GOUDIE picked his way toward the edge, which in turn set Noriko on edge, and she had to restrain herself from grabbing him by the elbow and jerking him back several times. He must have caught this movement, as he stopped and smiled at her. "You are a dear, Miss Arashi. Worried about me?"

"Sir, this area hasn't been cleared," she said in protest. And it wasn't a shallow hole, either. The crater was large enough to put three vans in side by side and even from here it was clear the cliff edge section was crumbling if the wind blew on it. Nothing about this section was stable.

"The first basic step of any investigation is to go to the center of the blast, or what you think is the center, and then work your way out in a spiral pattern. From what I saw coming in, I believe the test cell is what blew, and everyone else thinks the same. I have to verify that."

In other words, she wasn't going to drag him free of this area. Noriko hadn't survived as the eldest sister of six siblings without learning a few tricks. "Mr. Goudie. I am in fact very interested in how you investigate disasters like this. We only get a crash course in investigations in boot camp. If you don't mind, will you explain to me what you're doing and what you're seeing as you go?"

"I think that's a splendid idea. This might not be the last time you walk into a scene like this after all. Here, stay in step with me."

Noriko truly was interested in what he was doing, but her aim had been for that offer, so that she could be in his personal space without seeming like a nag. She immediately took him up on it and joined him.

"Now, as I said, every scene like this must start at the epicenter, and then we work our way outwards. The effects of an explosion like this are created through several actions of rapidly occurring events. The most damaging is the initial blast wave, as it radiates out from the epicenter. It's the highly compressed air that inflicts most of the primary damage to structures and people." Goudie led them forward and pointed to an area several feet ahead. "You see that area, the one that's relatively clear? That's our epicenter."

She did indeed see what he was talking about. It was almost perfectly round, the area blown completely clear of anything but rock, with scorch marks going in deep and dark in every direction. "Do they all look like this?"

"Hmm, no it depends. Sometimes they explode above the ground more than in it, so they don't always leave gaping holes behind. But they always leave a trail of scorch marks flaring in all directions. That's the nice part—they're easy to identify, even for an amateur." He cast her a wink. "Now, what actually causes the most damage after that is from the shock waves. They will catch onto anything loose, which includes the fragments of the building itself, and blow them out at high velocity. Very damaging stuff."

Noriko panned the area with sad eyes. 'Very damaging' seemed like a gross understatement.

"The question I have," Goudie continued as he knelt to examine the area more closely, "is what was the true cause? This might be very tricky to determine. If it was an act of sabotage, say, then any remnants of a bomb might be buried or completely incinerated because of the test cell blowing up. These big engines are potentially massive bombs anyway. Under the wrong circumstances, they'll blow up without much help, so it wouldn't take a very big bomb to make it go."

Jack followed this as closely as Noriko was. "Is that your first inclination? Sabotage?"

"No, can't tell anything as of yet. Unless someone up here has found an incendiary device? Or the remains of one?"

Shaking his head, Jack denied, "Not that I'm aware of. And I made sure they understood to notify me if they did find something of that nature."

"Well, like I said, if that's the cause it might be difficult to find in all of this rubble. But I'm not sold yet that it's sabotage we're looking at.

Could be an accident. First things first, we need to sketch up the structural damage and collect any fragments we can that look like wiring, circuit boards, and the like." Goudie suited words to action by taking out an old style touch screen and a stylus. As comfortably as a police sketch artist would, he drew out the scene in front of him.

Noriko kept an eye on both men, but her main concern was making sure the area didn't have any power they could trip over. She went through it very carefully, not wanting to disturb any of Goudie's evidence, but still tried to be thorough. Their safety depended on her observation skills. The thought was more than a little nerve-wracking.

She only stepped away from them twice, heading for a nearby Dwol-Mægen pair that kindly helped her take all of the power she had gathered and divert it into the nearly drained ley line.

After Goudie finished sketching and taking pictures, he pulled out a pair of plastic gloves and snapped them on. From the same bag, he took out a large variety of evidence bags and started scrounging for anything that he deemed 'interesting.'

Her crash course had taught her at least one solid fact: don't contaminate the evidence. "Mr. Goudie, should I be wearing gloves too? I need to shift a few things, as I'm feeling residue of power just past where you're working."

He paused and glanced up at her. "That would be best, Miss Arashi, if you would. I have a spare pair?" he pulled them from a side pocket and offered them to her.

She accepted them, snapping them on, and strangely felt as if she had just joined a criminal investigative team.

Jack did not join them as they shifted carefully through the rubble, bagging anything that looked remotely electronic, but kept in communication with every team working. He did so flawlessly, never once having someone repeat a sentence or losing track of where they were. Noriko had to keep an eye on him as well as Goudie, and she admired the efficiency of how both men worked.

Goudie showed her how to tag evidence and label it. Sometimes, for a smaller piece, she borrowed a ruler from him to lay next to the object and take a picture of it before bagging and tagging it. For the larger pieces, she actually put her initials and the date on it. The rest were tagged. Noriko's handwriting was not normally neat so she tried very hard to make it legible.

The sky shifted from dark blues to steel greys and white as pre-dawn came upon them. Noriko paused and looked out over the hill. They had worked their way out of the crater and to the piles of debris scattered all around, going in an ever growing spiral outwards. From where she knelt, the view was spectacular. She could see the whole desert floor without anything obstructing her view. It almost made up for the fatigue that pulled heavily on her body.

"Noriko."

Her head snapped around, twisting to find Cameron bent over her. "Cameron. You're done?"

"For now, yeah. Cap says we've done all we can up here and wants us to go home, get some sleep."

That sounded blissful. She creaked up to her feet, catching up the pile of evidence bags that she had gathered as she moved. "Mr. Goudie?"

He stood from behind a twisted hunk of metal and waved at her. "Done for today?"

"My captain is calling us in," she explained, making her way carefully toward him. "I've checked the area three times, I believe it's safe for you to continue working."

"I'm basically done as well," he assured her, accepting the bags from her. "Ah, nicely labeled. Thank you, that was helpful. The camera?"

She'd nearly forgotten it in her sleep-deprived state. Taking it from her jacket pocket, she handed that over as well. "I dictated notes. I'll type them up and send them to you later."

"That will be fine. I'll head back after bagging all of this up. I think I need to spread all of this out on a table, take a good look at things, before I know better what to look for. Right now I just have a lot of jumbled pieces that don't seem to fit together." Goudie frowned at the area as he spoke, brows drawing together. "Miss Noriko, you're stationed in Tehachapi?"

"Yes sir, that's right."

"I'll have to see where I'm setting up shop. I'm close enough to home they might have me stay in the office. But since I requested your team's help, I might have to set up in the station. Is there room for me to do that?"

"There are empty conference rooms you can use." Well, she knew there were conference rooms, at least.

"I'll ask your coordinator before you leave." Goudie packed everything into a large bag with smooth efficiency.

"Then I'll see you later." She gave him a faint, tired smile, before turning to join up with Cameron.

Her partner waited on her, and even to the naked eye, he looked tired. Dirt had seeped into his skin and made lines on his face, aging him ten years. There wasn't a clean patch of skin or clothing anywhere on him. On a magical level, it was obvious too. Cameron's energy flow was very consistent and smooth on a normal basis. This might be the first time she had ever seen it rough. It almost stuttered, like a hiccup in the flow. She wasn't about to say any of this out loud for the simple reason that Noriko was absolutely certain she looked just as bad.

"Was it alright, working with Charlie?" she asked him as they walked toward the van.

"Meh."

His reaction made her laugh silently. "Meh?"

"It's not like partnering with you. I had to constantly tell her how much energy I needed."

Noriko's head cocked as she looked up at him. "That's normal."

Shaking his head, Cameron denied, "You don't do that. Not since the time you taught me that climbing trick of yours. You give me what I need, then double check sometimes to make sure it's enough. But always, you read me well enough to know what I need."

Well. Maybe she did, at that.

"You're spoiling me, Spidey." He gave her a

charming, boyish grin. "Keep this up, and I'll never want to let go of you."

"You're making too big a deal of this," she dismissed. "I've got more practice in reading you, is all."

"That right." Cameron's tone was clear. He didn't agree with that at all.

He was praising her for something that didn't really deserve praise. It was making her want to blush and Noriko did not believe in blushing. It was embarrassing. So she set her focus on climbing into the van. Cameron changed their positions so it was him sitting right next to the door, leaving her sitting in between him and Lizzie, which she didn't mind.

As people settled, Lizzie asked her, "You were working with the explosives analyst, right?"

"Frank Goudie is his name."

"I heard he formally requested our team to help?"

"Yes, he did. He said we've got enough expertise to be helpful in unraveling the mystery."

"I'm glad," Lizzie admitted. "Being up here really bothered me. I want to understand what happened to cause this."

She wasn't the only one. "Mr. Goudie doesn't have any theories at the moment on what happened. He said that the rocket engine in the test cell complicates things. Normally, there's something about the scene that will tell him if it was an explosive and maybe what type, but this time, because of the engine, he's not sure. Apparently they're unstable and can act like a bomb if something goes wrong."

"Oh. I didn't realize all of that. But that does make sense, it's why they're up here testing the engines to begin with. Did the two of you find any clues?"

"We found a lot of electronic fragments, and some wiring that we weren't sure how to identify, so we bagged all of that. But I'm not sure if it belonged to the test cell, the engine, or the bomb. If there was a bomb."

"The firemen think that there was a minor earthquake that happened just as they were firing up the engine for testing," Cameron informed them, slouching back in his seat. "Having the test cell go sideways is what set the engine off and caused the explosion."

Noriko twisted to look at him. His face gave no clues to how he felt about this theory. "We both were here six days ago. There wasn't a large enough buildup in the ley lines to cause an earthquake, even a minor one."

"Yeah. But we've also seen a ley line that went bonkers for no reason in a short amount of time."

That part was also true. Cameron shook his head slowly. "I don't think anything we've seen is natural. I think it was sabotage or something."

She was inclined to agree. But who would be insane enough to do something like this?

9ᵀᴴ MERLIN

NORIKO trudged up the small flight of stairs leading up to her apartment, groceries in her left arm, freeing up her right to key open the door. The day had been horrendously long, so much so that her brain felt like it would just cramp up before melting out of her ears. It felt like she had returned to her student days. Hours upon hours of working with fluctuating power, that she'd had to feed to multiple people, and then documenting everything that she'd done in the process felt like juggling six balls all at once. And she had never learned how to juggle. Were all investigations like this?

Reaching out, she put her hand flat on the screen to unlock her door. Instead of making a pleasant ding, it zapped her with a mild shock and made a sound akin to a dying airplane.

That...that was not good. She knew that sound. Swallowing hard, she tried again, but the door pad now felt a little spongy. Melted spongy. Eyes closing in a fatalistic gesture, she started praying. Then, when she couldn't take the suspense any longer, she looked at her wrist.

Her phone no longer flashed a pale light, showing that it was on. It also looked a little singed around the edges. Reaching up, she picked out the Bluetooth earpiece and looked at it carefully. Also a little singed with black around the rims of the plastic.

This was so not good. She had no way inside her apartment with the door literally melted shut, her phone was busted so she couldn't call for help, and at this hour of the morning the manager was surely home and not in the office. Her only other option for help was...wait. Didn't Cameron live on the floor above her? He'd mentioned this before. That his apartment was directly on top of hers, which was how he knew when she was home or not.

As much as she hated to impose on a man that, while technically her partner, was barely an acquaintance, she had no choice. In her sack of groceries was ice cream. In this heat, it would melt shortly and she did not want melting ice cream in her hands thankyouverymuch.

The ice cream decided her. Raising it up to rest better on her hip, she marched for the stairs.

Now came the tricky part. Knowing that Cameron was above her and knowing which door to knock on were two different things. Was he right above her? Next door to that apartment? He could hear things either way without being exactly next to her. At seven thirty in the morning, hopefully people weren't still in bed.

Marshalling her courage, she timidly knocked at the first door that was probably Cameron's.

To her utter relief, the man himself promptly opened the door. "Spidey! Hey, what's up?"

"I have...a situation," she admitted morosely. "Um. My door lock is not working."

To his credit, he immediately stood back and gestured her inside. "Not working how?"

"I might have fried it," she grudgingly stated. Instead of looking at him, she looked in every other direction. For some reason, she had assumed that Cameron's apartment would look like hers—half unpacked. That was not the case. It looked pristine, actually. There was an overplush chair in the corner, a leather couch along the wall with the usual holoshade headsets and speakers for television watching. A picture above the couch featured what she assumed to be his parents. There were others, too, of friends and presumably family, all branching out from that main picture. There were bookshelves, knick-knacks, everything exactly in its place. "You're unpacked already?"

"Yeah, Amy did it. She's borderline OCD, so she took one look at my place and went haywire. Works for me, I didn't have to kill myself unpacking." Cameron took the groceries out of her hands and set them on the table. "Now, you fried the door? Seriously?"

Who was Amy? No, a question for another day. Noriko heaved a resigned breath. "I might as well warn you now. I'm bad with electronics. When I'm tired, my energy levels go a little haywire, just enough to mesh badly with anything electrical. I touch them, they go poof."

"So door and..." his eyes trailed down to the phone still strapped to her wrist.

"And phone, yeah," she growled, vexed with herself.

"Got it." In an unexpectedly gentle gesture, he took her by the shoulders and led her to the couch. "Sit. I'll handle the door."

While that sounded wonderful, letting him fix her problems, Noriko didn't begin to see how he'd manage it. "How? By breaking it in?"

"First, I call the expert." Cameron tapped his phone, brought up the holoscreen, and scrolled through a short contact list before double tapping the person he wanted. She could see it, of course, but from this angle it was nearly impossible to read. K-something. It rang twice before Cameron's face lit up in a smile. "Hey, man. Yeah, something's up. Tell me how to break into an apartment. No, dead serious, and it ain't criminal. Well, if I have the consent of the owner, it can't be criminal, right?" To her, he mouthed, *He doesn't believe me.*

Well, with that kind of explanation, she wouldn't believe him either.

Cameron took the Bluetooth out of his ear and set it on his palm between them, switching to speakerphone so they could both hear and talk.

"*—next thing you're going to say is that you're playing white knight for some cute damsel in distress,*" a male voice was saying, tone rich with laughter. "*Come on, man, don't josh me.*"

Taking that as her cue, Noriko tried to perk

her tone up a little so she didn't sound like death warmed over. "Hi. I'm Noriko, Cameron's partner."

The phone went silent for a long second. *"You really have to catch me up on things, Cam. Hey, Noriko. My name is Kirk. Are you the damsel in distress this evening?"*

"Unfortunately, yes. I, um, have bad luck with electronics when I'm tired. I tend to accidentally melt them."

"...Well that's dandy. So Cam, as I see that you really do have permission from the lady in question to do a little B&E, I shall tell you forthwith how to storm thy yonder castle gate."

"I am ready, my general. Give me your orders."

Did they regularly go into mock-archaic language like this? The ease with which they did so made her think it was normal.

"First, Sir Knight, find thee a stout card. Something you don't mind destroying."

Cameron leaned over onto one hip, taking out a wallet from his back pocket, and started rifling through them. "Old library card?"

"That'll work. Now, march thee to the castle gate in question."

He immediately stood and headed for the door. Noriko started to follow, belatedly remembered her groceries still sitting on the table, and doubled back to fetch them. Cameron paused in the doorway to wait for her, talking to Kirk as he did. "I gotta ask, General, how does an old library card help in this situation? I mean, don't I need a screwdriver, or a hammer, or something?"

"No, actually, you don't need any of that. See, the security and the locks for these doors

have improved by leaps and bounds over the years, right? I mean, we've even gotten to the level of palm prints and dual passcodes in one system. But the actual lock itself is still mechanical. Nothing electronic to it."

Only as she listened did the question occur to her: who was Kirk? A criminal? Cameron was completely the type of personality to have friends from all walks of life and not question what their occupation was.

"I see. So?"

"Before I continue, as an officer of the law, I must make you swear an oath. Harmony Cameron Powers, do you so solemnly swear to use what I am about to teach you only for mischief and not evil?"

"I so swear, officer," Cameron intoned with a grand, rolling tone.

Wait, officer of the law? Was this perhaps the same friend that was a highway patrolman? The same one that had also reported the surging ley line to them?

"Excellent. Alright, are you at her door?"

"I am."

"Take the card and slide it between the lock and the door frame. What you're aiming to do is jiggle the tumbler in the door just enough to give it the pressure it needs to open. Slide from top to bottom, angle it as you go."

Sensing this was not the moment to ask questions, Noriko set them aside. She watched with her breath in her throat as her partner bent to the task. Cameron followed the instructions precisely, but it didn't work on the first try. He did it again, jamming the card in a little further, jiggling it back and forth as he did so. There was a mechanical click, but the door stayed shut.

"No luck so far?"

"Not yet, but I think I almost had it."

"Oh, I forgot to ask. Hey, Noriko? Did you deadbolt the door on your way out this morning?"

"Ah, no, I only deadbolt it at night."

"Sweet, okay, we're still good, then. If it was dead bolted, I would have suggested that Cameron pick up the bill for the inevitable brick through the window that you would have had to do instead."

Considering how many times in the future that Noriko would likely fry her lock, she carefully filed away the instructions to herself: never dead bolt the door unless she was inside, always carry around a card that she could destroy if she needed to. Taking a half step to the side, she carefully watched Cameron as he worked on her stubborn door. This was going to be something she would need to know in the future.

The door quietly clicked open. Cameron let out a crow of victory.

"You're in," Kirk stated knowingly.

"I'm in. Thanks, man."

"No prob. The next time you want to do something only semi-legal, I will have changed my number and not tell you about it." The way Kirk laughed as he said this, he wasn't at all serious.

"Right, I'll remember to call you first," Cameron replied, for all the world as if he were agreeing.

"Some friend you are. Toodles. And goodbye,

fair maiden Noriko. We gotta meet soon, maybe dinner or something? I'll tell you everything there is to know about our man Cam, here."

Now that was a dinner she definitely wanted to have. "I look forward to it."

Most people in that situation would be a little alarmed, but of course Cameron wasn't, and he grinned down at his phone. "Only if I'm invited. Dinner's on you."

"After I've turned you into a harden criminal and given out the best advice of your life for free? No way, hombre', dinner's on YOU."

"Dinner's on me," Noriko stated firmly. "After all, it was my door."

"Groovy. Then our fair lady of perpetual beauty will pay. Hey I gotta bounce now, I gotta go kick the neighbor's cat again." The call abruptly ended.

Noriko was a little startled by this abruptness. And she still wasn't sure what to make of him. "Your friend is really a police officer?"

"A CHP." At her blank stare, he rephrased, "California Highway Patrolman. I never speed in LA. If he ever catches me, he'll have waaaaay too much fun with it. Now, your phone is fried. You probably don't have an old phone lying around that you can use?"

She shook her head sadly even as she made a beeline for the kitchen. Getting the ice cream into the freezer was a priority. "No such luck. This phone is actually GF issued."

"Oh man, bad luck all around, then. I'll email Cap for you and explain the situation. If we do get an emergency call, I'll come down for you, okay?"

That worry had yet to occur to her until he'd said it. Then she winced. Oh, that would have been bad. "No, I'll get a new phone after we get this sorted out."

He gave her a pat on the head, like she was a five year old that needed comfort. "Put your groceries away. I got this."

Was he trying to be supportive of her or trying to tease her? Noriko couldn't figure out which. Or maybe she was just too tired to analyze him at the moment. Giving up, she obediently put her groceries away. Except the ice cream. That she pulled back out as it had just become breakfast.

It had just been one of those days. Seeing Cameron turn and look her direction, she demanded, "What?"

"Nothing. I know better than to ask a woman who's eating ice cream straight from the carton how she's doing."

Well. Maybe he was smarter than he looked after all.

10TH MERLIN

BECAUSE they had pulled some overtime the day before, their team had been given the next day off. Noriko was beyond thankful, as she was bone tired. More than that, her heart still hurt from what she had seen and lived through. Part of her was still a little rattled at how close she'd come to being buried alive, too. If not for Cameron's quick reflexes, they'd both have been severely hurt.

She took advantage of having the day to herself and slept far later than she normally would have. She woke up to a chain of text messages from Tye and Sam. The two of them were planning a get together for Friday night, although neither of them were thinking of doing anything elaborate. Impulsively, she sent back a message to both of them that they needed to have a pedicure party at her place that evening instead. She got back enthusiastic responses.

It was just as well that she had a day off, as she really hadn't finished unpacking yet. Having guests over would give her the needed motivation to get everything out of boxes and properly cleaned up.

Shower first, though. Even after washing twice, she still felt like she was covered in grime.

Once under the spray, with shampoo in her hair, Noriko started thinking of other things than preparing for tonight. How was the investigation going? Before going to sleep, she'd gotten no updates from either Jack or Banderas, which made her wonder. Were they really having that hard of a time deciding on where to set up shop? Had something else been discovered after they'd left?

Worried, she stepped out of the shower long enough to send a quick email to them both. By the time she'd scrubbed up, dried off, and had most of her clothes back on, she'd gotten this response:

Noriko,

Everything is progressing well. We have offered Mr. Goudie a conference room here in the station, which he has already taken over. We've also been contacted by one of the engineers you helped to save, Mr. Mike Yockey. He wishes to help us with the investigation, but has not been medically cleared to work yet by his company. We are currently waiting for his medical checkup and reports to come back before we can move forward.

You still have today off, so don't worry

about it until tomorrow.

Do not worry about the possible backlash either. I have already notified the other stations, and they are all on alert and patrolling the ley lines.

Jack

She read through the email quickly, then again more slowly. Mike Yockey...Mike? The one that had helped her with the injured woman? Must be. True, having an engineer would be extremely helpful to them. He could give them a firsthand accounting of what the setup was, what had happened, and how the test cell was configured before it blew. Just having all of that knowledge would surely help Goudie sort out the important facts from the unimportant.

It was brave of the man to volunteer to help them, so soon after living through such a horrible experience. Noriko appreciated his pride and mettle.

She sent back a quick reply, thanking Jack for the update, and felt better for asking. It cleared her mind so that she was able to relax and not have thoughts of work hanging over her head.

Humming a song to herself, she finished getting dressed and tackled her disorganized apartment.

It was just as well that the pedicure party was set for six that night, as it took almost until five for Noriko to finish unpacking and get the apartment cleaned up. It wasn't that large, a one bedroom with kitchen/dining and living room, but she had basically ignored her boxes after arriving in Tehachapi in favor of studying. Really, she'd been living out of a suitcase more than anything else. Now it looked like someone actually lived there. Pictures were up on the wall, the furniture wasn't drowned in a sea of boxes, and she had a few decorative touches around that made it feel more like home.

There was a quick rap at the door before Tye waltzed inside, brandishing a tote as she did so. "I got us everything we need. I think. My dears, we got munchies?"

"We have munchies," Noriko confirmed. It may have been very impromptu, but now that she had people arriving, Noriko felt like it had been a good thing to do. She, Tye, and Sam had been in the same schools since basically elementary. Well, Sam she'd met in Junior High, but regardless, they'd known each other for years. It felt wonderful to have people to talk to that she knew how to react to.

"You know, I would have thought that after being transferred to the same town, we'd have met up more often than this," Tye observed as she started unloading the tote onto the table. There were quite a few bottles of polish, most of them in shades that Noriko would never, ever wear. "But it's been, what, a week since I last saw you?"

"About that," Noriko agreed, bringing two plates of nachos and salsa to her coffee table. "Tye, don't take up the whole table. Where am I supposed to put these?"

"Oh, sorry." Tye obligingly scooted the bottles closer together to give her room.

There was a knock on the door, but with her hands full, Noriko wasn't able to answer it herself. Knowing who it probably was, she called out, "Come in!"

Sam entered, two pizza boxes balanced on her hip, dark curly hair flying all around her face. She looked ready to go to work as she had makeup on, or as much makeup as Sam ever wore. It was a good thing her fair skin was naturally clear and didn't need much in the way of foundation, because Sam hardly used the stuff. "Can you believe my hairband broke just as I got to your door? And this wind up here is something else." Spitting out strands of hair, she handed the boxes over to Tye. "Nor, got a rubber band I can steal?"

"Sure do, hang on." Noriko went for the blue dish next to the door, where all of the odds and ends seemed to end up, and fished out a rubber band before handing it over. "So? How is life in Tehachapi?"

"You know, it's a good little town." Sam plopped down on the couch, the only place to sit in Noriko's apartment aside from some thick cushions stacked in the corner. "It's growing on me. People are nice here, I get a tan while working, and the weather's nearly perfect all of the time."

"I can't comment on the tan," Tye drawled, which made the other two laugh. After all, Tye was African American and her dark skin could get slightly darker but 'tanning' wasn't a possibility. "But I am liking this weather. My new partner isn't bad to work with, either."

Noriko had heard a little about him, but not much. "You said his name was Gage?"

"Right, Gage Halden. About ten years older than me. He lost his first partner to cancer, poor guy, and he's still a little rough over that. Apparently the two were real close. But he's treating me good, and he's patient while we're feeling each other out." Tye shrugged as if saying she didn't have anything to complain about. "But girl, I saw *your* new partner, and that's what I want to hear about. He is lickable."

Knowing that these two would appreciate the story, Noriko plopped down on the floor so that she formed a rough triangle between them. "Harmony Cameron Powers."

"Repeat that again?" Tye's eyes flew wide, mouth opening in a ready laugh. "His mother did *not* name him Harmony."

"She really, truly did," Noriko assured them, laughing as they laughed. "His mother is apparently a hippie out of time or something. He goes by Cam most of the time."

"I sure would," Sam responded, shaking her head. "That poor guy. So what's he look like? I haven't gotten a glimpse of him, as we're on totally different shifts."

"Surfer bum?" Noriko offered, then nodded at her own choice of words. "Don't know how else to describe him."

"Yummy surfer bum," Tye corrected, a laugh still lingering on her face. "Tall, rather good looking, blond hair, perfect tan. He looks like he's our age."

"About that," Noriko agreed. She'd heard his age but had promptly forgotten it. Her retention on things told to her orally was abysmal. It took seeing it in written form before it stuck. "He's got an interesting personality. Definitely a 'my pace' kind of guy."

"But he's treating you right." Sam's tone said *'if he isn't, I'll do something about him.'* Which she would.

"Oh, he's fine to work with," Noriko assured her. "In fact, he's well-grounded, ability-wise. He's just quirky." Realizing they were letting the pizza get cold, she popped to her feet and headed for the kitchen, gathering up plates. "I think I'll get used to his strange sense of humor eventually," she added over her shoulder. "Did anyone think to bring drinks? I only have water, apple juice, and milk right now."

Tye reached for a pizza box. "Water should work for—" she paused at a knock on the door. "I thought we were all here?"

"We are." Noriko frowned and headed for the door.

Tye, being Tye, answered it instead.

There in the doorway stood Cameron, a six pack of soda in the crook of his elbow and a hopeful look on his face. "It sounds like you're having a party down here."

Noriko blinked at him. "Can you really hear everything through the ceiling that clearly?"

"What can I say, walls are thin," he responded with an illustrative gesture toward the ceiling. "You doing nails?"

"We're having a pedicure party," Sam warned him, tone gentle and amused. "That's generally a girl thing?"

"Cool. Count me in."

Tye bust out laughing, slapping her leg. "Sweets, if you want one, you can have one. Come on in. Be one of the girls."

"Okay." Brightening instantly, he stepped inside, offering the sodas with both hands like an offering to a pagan god. "I bring beverages."

"And we needed them," Tye accepted cheerfully, snapping them out of the plastic handles and passing them around. "I'm Tye Lewis, by the way."

"Cameron Powers," he introduced himself, offering a hand and taking Tye's in a firm grip. "Oh, nice, I like how you feel. You've got nice control. Can you do that climbing-beam trick too?"

It took Tye a moment to realize what he meant. "Ah, you saw Noriko doing that? Yup, sure can. Sam can too. Oh, this is Sam, Sam Stoliker."

Cameron extended a hand, brows climbing as Sam shook it. "Nice to meet you. D-4?"

"Same as you, feels like," Sam confirmed.

"You from the same school as Spidey?"

Both Tye and Sam gave him blank looks and repeated in unison, "Spidey?"

"She climbs buildings with her bare hands," Cam explained, pointing to his partner. "So she's Spidey."

Sam snorted, amused, but Tye set off laughing all over again. "I have a feeling I'm going to like you, Cam. Can I have a nickname too?"

"Sure," Cam responded, going along with the flow. "Which superhero do you want to be?"

"Let me think on that." Tye actually sobered, as if giving this serious thought. But then of course she would, as her personality was almost a perfect match for Cameron's in some ways.

Noriko shook her head, resigned to the whole situation of her male work partner crashing her girl's night. That was just Cameron all over. "To answer your question, Cam, yes we all went to the same schools together. Sit, get yourself some pizza."

Without an ounce of hesitation, Cameron sat next to Sam, pulling a pizza box around. "Oooh, meat lovers. So why didn't you match up with Spidey or Tye?" he asked Sam.

"Because Teddy would have had something to say about it." Sam handed him a plate, studying him openly. "Why?"

"Spidey's one of the best Mægancræft I've ever seen," Cameron responded frankly. "I can't figure out why she hadn't already been snapped up."

Noriko flushed at this unexpected praise.

Without changing a whit of his expression, he continued, "She's also cute and really fun to tease. So you can see why I'm confused."

It was instinct on her part, mostly habit from growing up with younger siblings, that had Noriko reaching out and lightly smacking him on the back of the head. Then she froze, realizing belatedly that she wasn't close enough to him to react like that.

The room froze with her, all except Cameron, who twisted to give her an open grin of pure delight. "I was wondering how far I'd have to push before you'd smack me."

What? He'd been *aiming* for that? "Are you a masochist?" she spluttered.

"Nope. Just believe that people can't be friends until they tease each other." Happy, he bit into his pizza.

Sam gave him a once over with her eyes before giving Noriko a look that said, *Yup, I see what you mean, definitely a 'my pace' kind of guy.*

Strangely, though, his reaction made her realize that what Cameron really wanted wasn't just a work partner, but a true friend. He'd been teasing her, pushing her, and trying to get past her line of 'professional relationships.' Even crashing the party with the girls tonight was likely because of that desire. It felt rather strange to treat someone that she'd only known for a short time like she would a long-term friend. But she had to admit, they'd both be more comfortable as friends than otherwise. So if that was what he truly wanted, maybe she could treat him like one of her brothers?

Alright, if he wanted teasing, she'd do her best to oblige. "So if I pick out a color for your pedicure, you'll go along with it, right?"

Cameron's head jerked up sharply, reading her expression, and a slow smile won over his face. "You're going to choose something outrageous, aren't you?"

"You bet I am."

"If you do the honors, Spidey, I won't refuse."

Idiot. She grinned as she thought it and plopped back down to the ground, angling herself so she had access to his feet as she moved. Then she reached for the colors and picked out two of the more glaringly bright bottles, shades that she herself wouldn't wear. "Passionfruit or Yowza Yellow?"

Good to his word, Cameron didn't back down or even flinch. "I'm in a passionfruit kind of mood. Paint me up, Spidey."

11ᵀᴴ MERLIN

WEDNESDAY morning rolled around bright and early. Noriko went for her daily run early, trying to beat the heat, then spent the rest of the morning doing necessary errands and chores. She walked into work thirty minutes before her shift was actually due to start because curiosity was driving her mad. She'd been waiting to hear if they had discovered an answer to the cause of the explosion, and she hadn't heard a peep. She really, truly didn't want it to be because a ley line had abruptly gone unstable and made the engine explode, but she wasn't able to put the question out of her head.

Curiosity might have killed the cat, but satisfaction brought it back. It did her no harm to walk in and ask, right?

As it turned out, Goudie had been given the very back conference room. Jack's description of Goudie having 'taken over the room' was dead-on. It looked like a constructive cyclone had hit the place. There were papers taped up on the projection board, the walls, and one even hung from the ceiling. Another table had been shoved in to the far corner and it was buried in charred remains from the blast site. The conference table itself had more charred remains on it, although these were more spaced out and sat on white sheets of paper clearly labeled. Trying to preserve a chain of evidence?

The only clear space to be found was at the very head of the table, where Frank Goudie and Mike Yockey sat. Three plates rested in front of them, all covered in aluminum foil, and delightful scents wafted in the air, mixing with the smell of burned metal in a very interesting aromatic clash. At her entrance, both men looked up and smiled in greeting.

"Mr. Goudie," she acknowledged, "Mike, how are you?"

"I'm well, thank you. Michelle asked me to tell you many, many thanks for wrapping her ribs. The doctor said she had a bruised lung and if we'd lifted her into the ambulance without it being wrapped, it would have done even worse damage."

That thought made her a little queasy. "Very glad I wrapped them, then."

Mike gestured her into the free chair at his elbow. "Come, join us. My wife, when she heard that I was coming here today, insisted that I bring something to thank all of you. She's very glad that I was able to come home in one piece."

"As to that, sir, we had little to do with it,"

she observed, although she readily dug into the offerings. There were brownies, chocolate chip cookies, and lemon bars, which happened to be three of her favorite deserts. It was really hard to choose just one. "All we did was dig you free."

Shaking his head, Mike denied, "I heard the doorway to the block house collapsed after we left. You got us out just in time."

Noriko thought about explaining that the reason for the collapse was Cameron. Naw, probably best to not say that. It felt like a betrayal to her partner. "Either way, these are welcome. Mmm, and good! Thank your wife for me."

"I will," he promised. "I understand that this is only your first month of work?"

She had to chew and swallow before she could respond, "Yes, it is."

"Your partner, Cameron's, too? I never would have guessed that. You both were so calm while helping us."

"Cameron's always calm," she responded with a slight shrug. "I'm actually a little afraid to know how bad a situation has to get before he panics. Mike, I'm happy you came in. I have a lot of questions about that site."

Mike gave her a sad nod. "Yes, I thought you all would. I want to know the answer too. I'm willing to help any way I can. I had some of the plans to the test cell in my car, and with base's permission, I'm cleared to give them to you. These are more up-to-date than the copies on file."

Goudie handed her a stack of papers, most of them rather large in nature, big enough to be poster size. Noriko shoved the remains of the lemon bar in her mouth to free up her hands so she could hold them up and get a look. At a glance, she understood what Mike meant, as these plans had been red-lined with changes.

"I've already found these helpful," Goudie informed her, "as it details pipes and wiring that I didn't know existed from the original plans. Mike has helped me sort through the debris we bagged. Everything on the table is what was at the blasting point."

Oh, hence the separation?

"I smell cookies." Cameron waltzed into the room and zeroed in on the plates like a hound dog. "Oh, hey, Mike."

"Hello, Cameron," the engineer returned, standing and offering a hand. "The cookies are a thank you from my wife for getting me back home in one piece."

"All in a day's work," Cameron returned with a grin, and took the hand with a firm grip. "It looks like you've been at the problem for a while. You turn up an answer yet?"

Mike silently encouraged him to take a cookie, which Cameron promptly did. "We know which fragments were on top of the blast site and which weren't."

"That's a good start," Cameron agreed easily even as he bent to look over Noriko's shoulders at the plans. "Send my compliments to the cook, Mike."

The man seemed pleased his gesture of thanks was so well received. "I will. Noriko, you had questions?"

"I did. First, with a blast of that size, was there

anything on the Richter scale?"

Goudie leaned back in his swivel chair to point to the chart taped at the very top of the white board. "There was. Very local, in fact it didn't spread much past the Lab area."

"Was there any other sign of an earthquake?"

"I've found no evidence of such and no one's reported anything," Goudie denied. "If it was an earthquake, it was very localized, and it happened just at the time of the explosion."

Cameron sank into the chair next to her, catching her eye as he did so. The odds of that happening were very, very slim.

The explosives analyst caught their reaction. "Neither of you believe it was an earthquake."

"We don't," Noriko admitted, folding the papers back up with a snap of the wrist. "There just wasn't enough power in the area to set off a quake, not even a minor one. It takes weeks to build up enough to cause an earthquake. Six days wouldn't be sufficient enough time." Unless it was an abnormal de-stabilization of a ley line. But that wouldn't be something Goudie could figure out. That was on her own team's head to solve.

"I'm also disinclined to think that it was an earthquake," Mike concurred. "As I told you, Frank, we had our Dwolcræft and Mægencræft come in an hour before the test. Wesson and Landers confirmed that the area was stable enough for a test. I think Landers did stay for about thirty minutes, draining off some of the power to feed into the Base generator. He said something in passing about doing it because the coast was a little low on power at the moment."

"If he did, then there really couldn't have been enough power." Cameron eyed the plates as if he really wanted another cookie but was trying to restrain himself.

Noriko sat up a little straighter at this information. She had not known that the team had gone in that close to the test. She'd assumed, for whatever reason, that they had either looked at the area the day before or maybe that morning. Why the pairing had gone in a mere hour before the test was an interesting question, as they could usually do it a day in advance, but in this case she was relieved to hear it. The odds of an unstable ley line being the cause for the explosion just became practically nonexistent.

"So if not an earthquake," Goudie's tone suggested this was more a rhetorical question than anything, "then it was the explosion registering as a seismic event?"

Cameron gave a one shouldered shrug. "That's the most likely explanation."

"For a minor quake, say a 2.0 on the Richter scale, it would only take 800 KMs," Noriko confirmed for him. "The printout above your head is about twice that size. It would take an explosion like this to register on that level."

"I'm switching the question. I know that unstable ley lines lead to earthquakes. Something of this size, this intensity," Frank gestured to the two of them. "Power-wise, is it something that the two of you can handle?"

"We're Level 4, sir," Cameron denied. "It would take a Level 3 to do that."

"Not necessarily," Noriko objected, turning to

her partner. "It's not like you have to drain *all* of the power out of that area in order to make it stable again. You could do half of that and get the same outcome."

Cameron gave a slow, thoughtful nod. "She's got a point. In that case, yes, someone on our level could handle it. Assuming we have time to bleed it off slowly. Jerking all of that power out at once would set off an earthquake for sure."

"Mike, I believe that your Dwol/Mægen team are Level 5?"

"Yes, that's right."

"Would they still have the necessary power to diffuse an earthquake of this level?" Goudie asked the pair.

"Still would," Noriko assured them. "They can handle up to 69 KMs at a time, after all. Even if they took half of that, it would still prevent an earthquake."

"So even if Landers drained just 300 KMs from the area, feeding it to the Base generator, it should have been sufficient to prevent an earthquake," Mike summarized. "Do we have a report from him yet on how much power he pulled?"

"Not yet, no, although I understand he's writing one for me now. He did give me a preliminary report over the phone, but he didn't tell me exactly what he pulled, just that he had." Goudie puffed his cheeks out in a frustrated breath. "So the earthquake was caused by the explosion and what the Dwol/Mægen pairing did would have mitigated any chance for it to be an earthquake. I was hoping for a more clear-cut finding but I'm not getting it."

Confused, Noriko asked him, "Why were you hoping for that?"

"Because I can't find any evidence of an IED. There's no trace of an incendiary device to be found. Mike recognized every piece on this table as belonging to either the engine or the test cell itself. Nothing is out of place here."

"It's still very possible that it was the engine itself that blew," Mike assured Goudie.

Cameron leaned forward to brace his forearms against the table, making his chair squeak slightly. "How often does that happen?"

"In the thirty years that I've been doing this, I've only seen an engine fail on its own about six times." Mike paused, seemingly gathering his thoughts, before continuing his answer. "Sometimes it's a design fail, something that wasn't made right before the engine was even put together. I had one experience about four years ago where an engine would just go into meltdown for no explainable reason. It would run for five minutes and then it would tear itself apart. Never did figure that one out."

Goudie was especially interested in this. "But don't you test rocket engines in these test cells? I thought part of the standard testing included putting in airborne debris. Like the chicken gun."

The...what now?

Seeing their confusion, Mike explained, "One of our tests for engines and windows is to fire chickens at it, to make sure it can withstand the force. Not live ones, of course. We have a specially designed gun to fire them for us."

There was a five-year-old's type of smile on

Cameron's face. "And what are the odds, Mike, that we can fire that gun?"

"Dismal. We haven't used it in about two years." Mike had a small grin on his face even as he said this. "Sorry to burst your bubble."

Deflated, Cameron sank back into his chair.

"To answer your question, Frank," Mike stated in a more serious vain, "while we do test for that kind of thing, it's not done in 2A. To begin with, we only test rocket engines in that test cell. Also, we are actually very careful to make sure there's nothing in the test cell when we fire the engine. We don't want even a loose screw out there. These engines are still in the preliminary stages of testing. We don't want outside forces factoring in when something goes wrong. Makes it harder to hunt for the problem. There's also the factor that we keep very little fuel in the engine itself. We have a run line hooked up from the engine and to a storage tank nearby. Actually, there are two of them, one larger than the other. We do it that way to prevent explosions like this. There are four different fail-safes on that line, and at the least sign of something going wrong, they cut off all fuel supply instantly."

Goudie's mouth screwed up to the side, peeved at this answer, but he didn't argue the point. "So really, I'm down to one of two choices: either something went seriously wrong with the engine, or this is sabotage and I just haven't found the evidence to show how they've done it yet."

12TH MERLIN

ANY HOPE that Noriko had of getting an answer before her shift started was axed by her meeting with the men. She had to report to Banderas that she was on duty, and by the time that she got back, Mike had left. Understandable; it was already past four. He probably had dinner waiting for him.

Goudie was still there, and when he saw Banderas in her wake, he gestured for the man to come in. "Have a cookie. Mike's wife baked them, they're quite good."

"It's always nice when we get a thank you from people." A wide smile on his face, Banderas grabbed up a brownie and bit into it. "Woman's got good skills. Well, Mr. Goudie, any findings for us?"

"Too early at this stage for that, I'm afraid. What I need now is more information. Nothing I have on hand is giving me answers. Captain, I wonder, if there was a quake, then would the area around the Lab show signs of it?"

Banderas gave him a slow blink. "There should be. But I thought you had this confirmed for you already?"

"The reports I'm getting from the Lab Dwol/ Mægen pairing, plus Mike's account, isn't adding up. I believe they're telling me the truth, but if they are, then why was there a localized quake? You see my confusion."

"I do, and share it." Banderas licked his lips free of any crumbs, thinking. "Tell you what, Mr. Goudie, let me pass along a request to the other teams in the area. We'll all investigate and see what traces of the quake we can see."

Noriko had had no idea that earthquakes left traces behind, aside from the obvious physical ones. This should prove to be interesting to learn.

"If you'll do that, Captain, I'll go back to the site tomorrow and comb through it again. It was very dark out there. Maybe I missed something."

"Should we go with you, sir?"

"I might need your help, yes, but the higher priority for you is to examine the area and figure out if there was a quake there. And if there was one, what caused it. I truly need that confirmed one way or another before I can get much further."

Banderas gave a grunt of understanding. "Then that's what we'll do. Noriko, pass word to the rest of the team that we leave for the Lab in an hour. I want to call people and get them searching as well before we go."

"Yes, Cap." She gave Goudie a quick duck of the head as a goodbye before leaving the room and retreating toward their team office. When she entered, she found that all except Jack were there. "Captain says that we'll leave for the Lab in about an hour," she announced to the room in general. "Mr. Goudie has requested that we search for any signs of the earthquake around the Lab and confirm how extensive it was and what caused it."

"An hour? Why the wait?" Charlotte asked.

"He's calling the other teams to examine their own areas before we leave," Noriko explained.

"Ah, gotcha. Pass that along to Jack. He'll want to know."

Noriko had every intention of doing just that. She lifted her radio band to her mouth and relayed the message to their coordinator. As she did, most of the team chose to leave the room on some quick errand, leaving just her and Cameron behind.

Their desks were right next to each other and she had to scoot a little around him in order to reach her chair. She perched on the edge of it, trying to claim her gear out from underneath the desk and talk to Cameron at the same time. "Did you know that you can see the traces of an earthquake even if it's very minor?"

"Only in theory. Never had a chance to do it in person." Cameron had a perkiness to him that suggested he looked forward to learning something new. "All of this going back and forth makes me wonder, though. I know they said we can study here at the station if nothing's going on, but can we do that while we're traveling too?"

It was a good question. Noriko had wondered the same. She had not been able to study much since Cameron's arrival. At the rate they were going, it would take them ten years to get a Bachelor's. "Let's ask Cap or Jack when they get back. I would think it would be fine?"

"I hope so. A degree is going to take forever otherwise."

"Yeah. I know they said we don't have to finish in four years, but—"

An emergency siren blared from the main screen on the wall. All around the screen scrolled the words *"Protocol Delta — Mojave."* Swearing, Noriko dove over her desk and slapped her hand against the screen, letting it scan her palm print. She still didn't have a voice activation code yet and had to do things the physical way. "This is Noriko Arashi, Team Pathmaker. What is the emergency?"

The woman that blipped onto the screen had honey colored hair twisted into a wild knot on the top of her head, skin unnaturally pale, dark eyes wide with terror. *"We've got a ley line here that's dangerously unstable. My team is off shift and not answering, I can't get through to them. You're the closest station. I'm just past the mountains, near the weigh station."*

"Send me coordinates, my team is moving," Noriko promised her. "Our radio channel is 3."

"I'll switch to the radio band then."

Whirling, Noriko found that Cameron was already on the team's radio band and relaying everything they were saying. Assured the alert had been spread, Noriko snatched up both of their bags and raced for the side door. By the time she made it out to the parking lot, half the team was there, pouring in from different angles, and Jack was disappearing into the van.

She hopped in, scooting over to make room for Cameron, and listened as Jack took over coordinating where they needed to go and how much help he should be bringing. Listening to him calmly asking questions and relaying orders soothed her fraying nerves. If he wasn't panicking, then she had no call to be.

Banderas was the last person in and he slammed the door behind him. "Go, go, go!"

Jack slapped the van's engage button and it tore out of the parking lot. How had they programmed the AI to respond like this, anyway? Noriko knew that most police cars were still driven manually because they couldn't be pre-programmed for most of the situations policemen encountered, but how did they get an AI to break the speed limits like this?

As they tore down the main boulevard, heading for the freeway onramp, Noriko bent her attention back to the woman that was reporting the situation to them.

"—*don't know how this happened,*" she was saying, tone distraught. "*We were just here three days ago, and I passed by the place this morning and didn't notice anything unusual. I was actually on my way home when I felt the air go weird and stopped to double check things. I'm without my partner out here, I can't do anything about this, and for whatever reason no one at the Mojave station is responding.*"

That sounded very weird. Even if there was no one at the station to answer, the call should have been automatically routed to police dispatch, who had ways of contacting people.

Jack must have had the same thought as he asked, "Not even dispatch is responding?"

"No, no one. It's like the lines are all dead."

Now that smacked of sabotage. No way a police station just lost all communications.

All of a sudden the woman let out an audible gasp and a keening noise that sounded almost animalistic in pain.

Banderas, if he had possessed the ability, would have transported himself through the radio channel in that moment. "Jack, get this thing to go faster."

Jack immediately spun, hit the manual override, and floored the gas pedal. The van jerked forward, throwing them all off balance and rocking into each other.

This demand didn't make sense to Noriko. She looked to Charlotte, who was the only one not confused by Banderas's reaction. "Charlie?"

"Only one time Javier and I have ever heard a person make a sound like that," she explained. A shaking hand reached up to push a stray lock of hair away from her face. "It was a Mægen that had gotten too close to an open ley line. She nearly fried herself. Took her two months to recuperate enough to return to work."

Oh. Oh no. That woman was still standing out there, near an open line? A Mægen couldn't do much of anything in a situation like this, not by herself. What was she thinking, staying in an obviously dangerous area?

Lizzie slapped open her phone's app, called

up the station, and demanded through the phone, "Dispatch, this is Team Pathfinder, I need an ambulance headed this direction. Make sure that one of our medics is on board, too."

Banderas waved a hand to get her attention. "Get Khanh and John over here as well. Someone has to figure out why the Mojave Station isn't responding; it might be technical trouble."

Waving a hand to him to show she'd heard him, Lizzie repeated, "Send Khanh and John Vo to Mojave Station. They're not responding and we think there's a communication problem. Tell them not to use the 58. I repeat, NO ONE is to use the 58. Take the back highway there."

Fortunately for Noriko's strained nerves, the drive was a very short one. The only thing separating Tehachapi from Mojave was the Tehachapi Mountains, and once through that mountain pass, they were almost in Mojave's jurisdiction. The weigh station sat just at the front of the pass, a leftover from earlier days when weigh stations still had to be manned. Now there was a completely automated one near the Mojave Bypass that did the job. The old one had been closed for a good three decades, but the gates were open as the van barreled across the four lane freeway, skirting around the concrete barriers, and inside the shell remains of the station.

A small red coupe sat just inside the gates, a woman collapsed on the ground and vomiting into the sand. From her red jacket and the insignia of the tree on her left arm, it was clearly the person who had put the call into them.

Banderas pointed to her. "Lars, get a shield

around her now before she burns herself out. Stay with her until the medics arrive, then come help us. Cameron, you go left, I'll take right. Stabilize this thing before it blows us all to kingdom come."

If Cameron responded, it was lost on Noriko. The ley line before, the one on the old highway, had been bad, and of course the one at the Lab had spewed power like a miniature gusher, but this was a hundred times worse. This one ran completely exposed to the open air for a good half a mile, visible even to the naked eye, as it looked like lightning shooting out of the ground. The air was so electrified that when they opened the door, she felt statically charged and actually shocked herself on the door as she stepped out.

Grabbing her hand, Cameron hauled her directly to the left. She felt his hand trembling a little and knew that he was reacting like her. The earth shook under the force of the power, and because ley lines always ran in between fault lines, there grew a very real chance that they stood on top of a budding earthquake. Groans rumbled in the air as the land slowly wrenched apart, ground crumbling in on top of the active ley line so that it looked as if it were melting over an open flame.

As they moved, two different holes appeared at random, like sink holes, power glowing out of them. Noriko felt like she was navigating a mine field, one that would explode even without her tripping over it.

This was frankly terrifying and if there had been any way to do it, she would have run in the opposite direction. But there wasn't. No one could outrun something like this, it would be like trying to outrun a tsunami. This thing had minutes before it blew apart, taking everything with it. Her only chance was to fix the situation before it could detonate in her face.

Somehow, miraculously, Cameron turned to her and gave her that patented devil-may-care smile of his. "Time to test our limits, Spidey."

She gasped around the nauseous pit in her stomach, actively fighting the urge to throw up. "You got a place to put it?"

"Yup." He jerked a chin to indicate an area just behind them.

Turning, Noriko saw that what she had walked over without a second glance was a nearly drained ley line. It was large enough to house half of the energy she saw dancing in front of her eyes. Is this where all of that excessive power had come from? Must be.

Noriko tried to draw upon some inner strength, some well of courage, but even then she felt inadequate to the job facing them. It was the steadiness of Cameron's eyes on her, his patience as he waited for her to give him power to work with, that focused her. There was trust in his expression, a trust that she could not bring herself to betray. So she took in a breath and informed him, "I'm sitting down for this."

"Go for it."

It was either sit or collapse. She chose the dignity of sitting. Dropping into a seiza position, like a martial artist before a bout, she found some internal balance. Then she grabbed at the power sparking right in front of her.

Yooooowwwwouch! It felt like grabbing hold of

a lightning bolt. If power started shooting out of her eyes or fingertips, Noriko wouldn't have been the least bit astonished. Still, she had expected it to be at least this bad, and after the last time, she wasn't surprised. Hurting, but not surprised, and she knew how to handle insane power now. Experience was a wonderful teacher.

Channeling it, she shot it toward Cameron, who was open and waiting to receive it. He flinched at the first touch, jumping back a half step. "Wow."

"Sorry," she apologized through gritted teeth. "I'm modulating it as much as I can."

"Don't apologize, Spidey, this is just jacked up. Give me more, I can handle it. The sooner we get this back where it's supposed to be, the better."

Now that she could agree with one hundred percent. Remembering what he had told her, that his max was seventy-eight kilomerlins, she fed him seventy-five. It felt insane to her, to tackle this much power all at once. It was equivalent to seventy-five thousand watts, after all, and barely .2 amps was all it took to kill a normal human being. Not even Mægencræftas and Dwolcræftas, who had the special talent and training it took to handle raw power, were immune to electrocution. A wrong step and they could kill themselves.

Of course, it was her job to make sure that neither of them did that. Usually that was easy. Right now, not so much.

She could not spare the attention to see how anyone else was doing. It took every ounce of skill and focus she had to not endanger either of them. But she could feel the power being steadily drained, she could hear the wail of the sirens as the ambulance arrived, and the way that people shouted information back and forth.

Someone—likely Jack—had had the sense to call in for backup, and they arrived on scene and immediately pitched in. Noriko recognized at least one voice in the crowd—Sam. Jack had to have pulled another Tehachapi team in.

There was no knowing how much time had passed—her senses were completely skewed by the situation, feeling like she had been here at least a decade. But the taut, dangerous energy abruptly lessened as more people applied themselves to it. Someone else shifted the bedrock that had been upheaved back into place, cutting the exposed air off, which helped significantly. Noriko went from feeling very exposed to just tenderized, as if she had been baking in the sun too long.

"Team Pathmaker!" Banderas boomed out. "Retreat to the van, take a break!"

Could they do that already? Noriko lifted her head to take a good look around her. Indeed, the ley line was still unstable, but not nearly as bad as it had been. They now had three new partners on the job and they were working steadily all up and down the line. She caught Sam's eye, who was standing next to Teddy, and they both waved and gave her a thumbs up in reassurance.

Feeling better about letting go, she glanced up at Cameron. He was nearly bent over, hands on his thighs, breathing hard enough to make a person think he had just run a marathon. On a magical level, he had. He caught her eyes and somehow managed a smile. "Ready to quit?"

"Beyond ready," she responded, voice creaking. She sounded like an eighty-year-old woman. Felt like it, too.

"On three, then. One, two, three."

Noriko cut off all power flow and watched as Cameron put the last of it into the ley line behind them. Now it looked almost as it should be, flowing with energy and not lifeless.

Cameron sank to a knee, hand planted against the pavement to keep himself from completely falling over.

Recognizing the signs of power burnout, she struggled with her pack and dragged out a water bottle. "Drink something."

"Gimme a second," he panted out.

"No, now," she insisted, nearly forcing the bottle into his mouth. "A swallow at least. You're about ready to pass out."

"Trust exercises," he responded. "Your turn to catch me."

"Harmony Cameron Powers, *drink something right now*," she insisted, feeling a lump of fear climb into her throat.

"Ouch, full name, huh?" Finally, he stopped joking long enough to raise the bottle properly to his mouth. He started with a swallow, but soon tipped it back and drained half of the contents in one long pull.

There, that was better. He didn't look as shaky or drained. Partially satisfied, she grabbed a power bar and stuck that in his hands too before finally seeing to herself. When he'd told her that 78 kilomerlins was his max, and that he could only sustain it for three hours before being "tapped out," what he'd actually meant was before he passed out.

Clearly they needed to have a talk about unduly pushing his limits.

Jack hurried over to them, actually running, which was a very rare sight. Dropping to one knee, he looked them both over. "Neither of you faint on me."

"Is that an order or a request?" Cameron managed around a mouthful of the power bar.

"Both." He glanced at their hands and seemed relieved to find them refueling. "Glad to see you have some common sense, at least. Can you make it back to the van?"

Good question. Could she? Noriko pushed herself up to her feet and wobbled like an ungainly foal trying to find its legs for the first time.

"I'll take that as a no." Jack caught her around the waist. Her independent nature squawked at having a superior physically support her like this, but the sad truth of the matter was she could not be trusted on her own two feet. Just trying to stand had taken a lot out of her. Grabbing her arm, he put it around his shoulders, then reached for Cameron. "Up you go, Powers."

"I can make it under my own power," Cameron assured him.

"Don't listen to him," Noriko informed Jack. There were dark spots dancing in front of her eyes, a sure sign she had pushed herself too hard. She promptly drank more water and fought the urge to pass out.

Jack fortunately didn't, just manhandled

Cameron into leaning on his other side. If Cameron had been as fine as he was pretending, he would have been able to fight the man off, but of course he wasn't, so Jack succeeded without much effort. Supporting both of them, he more or less frog marched them back towards the van.

To no one in particular, Cameron said fuzzily, "I now totally understand why this job comes with hazard pay."

13TH MERLIN

IT TOOK a while for her body to recover enough that her mind could think. Noriko lay flat on the floor of the van, Cameron stretched out right next to her, close enough that their arms nearly overlapped. They were not the only ones, as Charlotte was on the bench above her, a cold cloth over her eyes. Their captain was sitting up in the doorway and exchanging words with Jack and anyone else that came by with a question. Noriko was 100% positive that it was sheer willpower keeping the man upright, and if he'd had the luxury, he'd be on the opposite bench from Charlotte.

They had to be wrong. All of their assumptions about the ley lines, the reasons why the ley lines had gone spastic recently, the time it took for that to happen, all of that had to be wrong. Because the first ley line that had gone out of control had been out of sight for nearly five days, they'd assumed it'd taken time for a power buildup. But this one had been well within sight of hundreds of people, as it was just off a main highway, and experts had seen it not eight hours before and all had been well. That suggested to her that time had nothing to do with it.

It also meant that this couldn't possibly be natural, or a backlash from some minor quake, or anything else they'd thought of. Since their near escape with the other one, every team in the surrounding area had been almost anal about patrolling their ley lines. If they had been cautious before, every GF officer was downright paranoid now. If anything even remotely strange had happened, it would have been reported—Noriko had no doubt of that. They'd had two red herrings already and the explosion at the base had sent people into overdrive making sure they didn't have a backlash from it.

So for this to happen? Without anyone being aware that it could? It simply wasn't possible. Not naturally possible. "Someone's doing this on purpose," she concluded aloud.

Cameron let out a pained groan, sounding like a mountain with a bellyache. "She's right."

"I know she is." Charlotte lifted up a corner of her cloth to peer over at Noriko. "We have a very short list of people who possess the ability to do this, and they'd have to be certifiable to even want to try. I certainly wouldn't do it, even if I was crazy, as I risked blowing myself up in the process."

That was very true. "We're looking for someone with a suicide bomber mentality."

"That's exactly what we're looking for."

Charlotte slumped back with a weary sigh. "You know what scares me most? My kids both had an away game today. Sometimes they play with Rosamond, which means they would have taken the highway this direction. It's only chance they were going towards Bakersfield instead."

Now that was worrying. "Ah, Charlie? Are your kids...?"

"Both Dwols."

Noriko pictured two juvenile Dwolcræftas passing by a scene like this and winced. They would have become extremely sick being in the vicinity of this.

Banderas turned toward them. "This event is unfortunately a game changer. We're going on high alert until we catch the SOB that is doing this."

That didn't surprise Noriko one little bit.

Cameron lifted his head a little. "Cap, I know that the Lab has more security and everything, but this doesn't look like coincidence. I mean, if someone could screw up this ley line so easily, stands to reason they could have done it at the Lab too."

"Unfortunately it's a very real possibility. We're going to have to do some calculations and experiments to see how fast a ley line can be turned this volatile. I've already sent a message to Goudie about it."

Of course he had. No matter what Jack's complaints were about the captain's inability to communicate properly, he never failed to give people the information they really needed to know.

"The other team has a handle on this now. We're out of danger and into cleanup mode." Banderas slapped a hand against the side of the van, the sound echoing and tired. "Pathmaker, load up. We're off shift as of now and if I catch any of you at work tomorrow, I'll fire the lot of you. Rest."

He didn't have to threaten her twice. She fully intended to.

How could she have possibly been so stupid? Noriko couldn't believe she had done this to herself AGAIN.

Really, any fool would have been able to predict what would happen. She could have prevented this whole thing if she had taken even a split second to think about it. But seeing the situation at the weigh station had panicked her, and so she hadn't thought at all. She'd reacted.

Which ended up with her having a fried phone, radio band, and Bluetooth. At least this time she could still get into her apartment, she hadn't accidentally killed her door lock again.

Because of what she had put herself through for nearly three hours, Noriko's usually excellent control was...not. In fact, one could describe it as nonexistent. Her inner bastion of power arced and sputtered so much that she knew that doing anything power-related for the next twenty-four hours was an extremely bad idea. It's likely why the captain had banned them from coming into work the next day.

Taking extreme care, she touched the flat panel of her security system, letting it read her palm, and then waited with baited breath for it to key open. It did so with a quiet chime. Phew. She *had* to remember to set a verbal password for this thing later. That was a far safer option for her to use.

Stepping inside her apartment, she shed the useless electronics on the little table next to the door and headed directly for the kitchen. Anything in the fridge was deemed edible and she consumed all of it so quickly that she barely took the time to breathe.

The food helped. Food always did. Something about using her ability for long periods of time drained the blood sugar in the body, which was why eating had such a rejuvenating effect. No longer feeling like she would pass out, she headed for the shower, taking ten minutes under cold spray to gather herself again. The coolness of the water on her overheated skin felt like bliss. She just stood there and let it pummel her until she was afraid that she would fall asleep standing on her feet.

As tempting as collapsing in her bed was, she couldn't do it, however. She had to replace a phone first.

Struggling out of the shower, she threw on the only clean uniform she had left—Noriko simply had to do laundry tomorrow—and shoved her feet back into her shoes. She did take two minutes to program the door with a verbal password, as putting it off any longer was dangerous, and then she was out of the apartment and in the stairwell.

Seriously, this day felt like it had been a decade long already. And to think she'd woken up with plans to study during their 'lunch' break and catch up on some assignments. Maybe she could do that tomorrow.

She turned the corner and nearly plowed right into Cameron, who was coming up. In his hands rested a pizza box and a 2 liter of soda. "Take-out?"

"Yeah, want some? I had no food, so I had to order for delivery, but it's a little big for just me."

Even though she had eaten her fill, the smell was wonderfully enticing. Regretfully, she shook her head. "Can't. I need to head into the station."

Cameron's eyebrows twitched together. "Cap said we're to stay home and recoup."

"I know, but I fried my phone and radio band earlier," she explained. "I have to go in and requisition another one." And boy that wouldn't go over well considering they'd now given her two phones in a single month.

His mouth formed a silent 'ah' of understanding. "Ouch. I guess with what happened earlier, it's understandable that happened. Next time we'll have to make sure to leave them in the car. At least the phones."

Truly, she would make sure to do that in the future. "Remind me if I forget."

"Will do, partner. But save the forms for tomorrow, yeah? You're beat, go sleep."

Before he could even get the sentence out, she was shaking her head. "I need to replace them today."

Cameron gentled his voice, ducking his head a little to the side in a charming lilt. "No, Spidey, you reaaaaaally don't. It can wait for tomorrow. You're swaying, okay? Swaying people should not be on stairs. Go to bed."

Stubbornly, she shook her head again. "I need to replace them today. If something happens, they won't be able to reach me."

Growling, he ran a hand over his face, clearly exasperated. "Listen, you little rule-maniac, they are NOT going to call for us before tomorrow. We are literally at the end of our ropes, everyone knows that, they'll call for other teams before ours. Go. To. Bed."

"I made a promise that no matter what, I would always have a way to be contacted, on or off duty!" she snapped back. "So I need to get a new phone. Move."

He didn't. Cameron did the exact opposite and planted himself firmly in her way. "Screw the rules. You're in no shape to do anything, alright?"

"It doesn't matter if I am, and it doesn't matter if nothing actually happens, that is not the point!" Heavens, why was she yelling?

"Then what is the freaking point?!" he yelled back. "Because I don't get it!"

"No, of course you don't," she growled to herself as much as to him. Frustrating, frustrating man. Why couldn't he just let her go in, fill in a simple requisition form, get a new phone, and come back to bed? He was taking up more of her time arguing about it than it would take to actually do it.

Cameron's eyes took on a glow, power

sparking a little in the air around him. "And what does that mean?" he snarled between clenched teeth.

"Regulation Four, ring a bell? 'All members of the Gældorcræft Forces shall have a means of communication on them at all times, regardless if they are either on or off duty—"

"Yeah?" he cut her off, taking another step up so that he could glare at her eye-to-eye. "How about this one for size? 'When in the field, the captain's orders to his team take precedence over regular protocol, especially in the cases of injury. The captain's commands to his teammates are to be followed to the best of his team's abilities unless it would endanger the team or the surrounding area.'"

Noriko's temper sparked and burned. How dare he suggest that it was she, and not him, that was breaking the rules! "What is wrong with you? I did obey that order!"

"You're not obeying it right now!" he shot back, volume climbing.

"All I'm trying to do is obey regulations and replace a phone!"

"Injured personnel—and news flash, we count right now!—are not supposed to be available as a response team in any emergency! Hang the stupid phone, Noriko, and go rest like you're supposed to!"

"I will *after I replace the phone!*" she yelled back at him. Seriously, what was *wrong* with him?! She wasn't in the best of shape right now, even she could admit that, but it was just a short walk. The station was at the end of the block, it wouldn't take her twenty minutes to walk there, fill out the right form, get a replacement, and walk back. "Why am I even arguing with you?"

"Good question," he sniped, pushing past her. "If you want to blackout on the stairs and break your neck all for a phone, go right ahead."

She turned to watch him blaze up the staircase and yelled after him, "An injured person wouldn't be able to spring up the stairs!"

What he yelled back wasn't exactly repeatable.

It had been years since she had been so mad at someone that she had ended up yelling like this. To make matters worse, she wasn't entirely sure what had made their argument escalate so abruptly into an actual fight. There was nothing wrong with obeying the rules, and yet he had made it sound like she was committing treason. Upset and shaky, she continued down the stairs and slammed her way out of the building.

If he thought she was going to meekly retreat to her apartment just because he told her to, he had another thing coming.

14ᵀᴴ MERLIN

SAM found her hunched over the requisition forms crying and muttering curses to herself. She'd been sitting there for who knew how long, not a single word written on the form, and with everyone actively skirting around her. Which was funny, really, because she was sitting in the narrow hallway just outside the IT office, and there wasn't any space to be had, but they were almost gluing themselves to the wall in order to avoid her.

Sinking into the chair next to hers, Sam slid an arm around her shoulders. "Okay, honey, put this down."

Stubbornly, she clung to it. "I need a new phone."

That made her friend really look at her. "You fry yours earlier?"

"Yeah."

"Okay. Give it to me, then, I'll fill it out for you."

See? Sam understood that when her phone was broken, the right thing to do would be to replace it. She surrendered the clipboard without a fight and watched as Sam easily filled in the form. It took her less than two minutes. Two minutes, and she'd spent at least fifteen arguing with Cameron.

John popped his head cautiously out of the office. She'd met him before because of the last phone she'd fried. He'd been sympathetic (after laughing) and helpful as he set up a new phone for her and copied over all of her data. He was Vietnamese, although born in the States, rather like she was. "Ah, everything okay out here?"

"John, if you could replace a phone?" Sam smiled and handed him the form. "She fried hers while fixing the exposed ley line earlier."

He was a smart man and didn't ask any questions. "Sure thing. Noriko, want it set up like I did last time?"

She gathered herself enough to respond to him. "Please."

"Okay. Just hang tight for a few minutes." He took the form and disappeared back into his office.

"Now." Sam focused back on her once more. "I doubt that frying a phone, which you've done dozens of times, has made you cry like this. So what happened, honey?"

Noriko tried to formulate the words to explain only to pause and frown. Even in her head, the explanation seemed inane. "I don't know."

"You don't know," Sam repeated doubtfully.

"I was on my way here to the station and

bumped into Cameron on the stairs," she started, with no idea how to end the story. "And he told me to go back to my apartment, the phone could wait for tomorrow."

"He was likely right?" Sam offered, gauging her reaction as she spoke. "I heard your team was given temporary medical leave until Friday."

"We're supposed to be accessible 24/7," Noriko maintained obstinately.

"Ah, well, I suppose. Anyway, go on."

"He didn't want me to come here. He had all sorts of reasons." Some of them dead on, although she could only now admit that. "We argued about it. I ended up yelling at him."

Sam rubbed at her lips, with something that might have been laughter glinting in her eyes. "Haven't seen you argue or yell in a while. How did he take it?"

"He yelled back."

"I see."

Morosely, Noriko slumped further in on herself. "It was a stupid fight."

"With you, they always are. You never seem to argue about the things you should argue about. Want me to play mediator for you?"

Noriko shook her head and took a swipe at the drying tears on her cheeks. "Captain Banderas told me the first day that if Cameron and I couldn't get along, he would find me a new partner, that it was alright to do so."

Sam's eyebrows climbed into her dark, curly hair. "You really think you should break off the partnership with him? Just because of a fight that you yourself admitted was stupid?"

"It's not that we don't get along," she sought to explain. "But Cameron's the type that can get along with anyone. It's just that, at the end of the day, we're polar opposites in personality. We approach almost everything differently."

"On a power level, you told me that your work together seamlessly."

That was true.

"You also told me that he has a great work ethic, it just doesn't look like he's working on the surface, sometimes. And I know how important a work ethic is with you."

That was also true.

"Nor, I know from painful and personal experience that decisions made when you're strung out and tired are never good ones. You are so exhausted that you're trembling, your magical core is twitching, and you can't even sit up straight. This is clearly not the time to make decisions that will affect you long term."

While emotionally, Noriko didn't want to agree to any of that, her mind could acknowledge that Sam's argument was a valid one. "So you think I should sleep on it."

"Sleep is a very good first start. Then sit down and think about the argument again, and figure out why Cameron was arguing with you in the first place. He's a fun-loving guy, your Cameron, and a jokester, so if he's serious enough to get in a screaming match with you, then maybe you should think about why. Also consider that he's also extremely exhausted, strung out, and not thinking clearly. He might be overreacting like you are right now."

While all of that might be true, she wasn't in the mood to think about any of it.

"Sleep first," Sam advised. "Now, I'm going to fetch your phone from John, and then I'll take you home."

"I can get myself home."

"Honey, if you can get out of this chair without passing out, I'll be very surprised. Just sit tight, I'll get your new phone." Sam was out of the chair and in the office before she could get a full protest out.

She tested her balance a little by half-rising out of her chair. Her vision went a little grey around the corners. Maybe Sam had a point about her physical wellbeing right now. She sank back into the hard plastic and brooded.

It might not matter what she thought about their argument or whether she wanted Cameron to be her partner or not. He, too, had the right to choose to stay with her or switch to someone else. And after tonight, his choice might not be her.

A police blue uniform stopped in front of her and a man knelt, asking tentatively, "Everything alright, Noriko?"

She slowly brought her head up to stare fuzzily ahead. Conrad. He was a cop she had met on her first day. He was one of those men with the all-American boy next door look to him and a nice personality, so she'd had a good first impression of him, although they hadn't seen much of each other since the world had gone upside and sideways. "Conrad."

"She's dead on her feet," Sam informed him

bluntly as she came back out the door.

"Then I'll drive her home, yeah?" He gave them both a charming smile.

Noriko thought about arguing. It was only a block to her apartment, she could make it just fine. But the truth of the matter was just sitting there was draining her energy. And if she tried to walk home, she was sure Sam would put a stop to it, and she didn't want to argue a second time tonight over something pointless. So she said, "Sure."

It was amazing how much clearer the mind could function after properly sleeping. Noriko floundered awake with the sense that she had been lying in the same spot for a very long time. Flopping over, she picked up her phone and blearily read the glowing numbers on the band. 12:45. Seriously? She'd slept straight into the afternoon? That meant, what, that she'd slept for nearly sixteen hours?

Alright—maybe she had been more done in than she had realized.

Rolling out of the bed, she staggered into the shower. Somehow—no one had ever explained to her how—showers had a magical effect on her. Maybe it was the massaging motion of shampooing her head, maybe it was something about the spray itself, but showering always woke her up and gave her insights.

Sam had been dead-on last night. Breaking

off her partnership because of a stupid argument was a very bad decision. Was she convinced that they should remain partners for decades and decades? Of course not—she'd only known him a short time. There was no way she could make that judgment call now. But it was precisely because she was still learning about him that she shouldn't make any rash decisions.

This did beg the question, though, of what to do next.

Noriko just didn't know Cameron well enough to predict what he would do next. She'd only seen his jokester side, really, on a day-to-day basis. It really had to hit the fan before he got serious. As soon as the emergency was over, though, he went back to his usual cheerful self. Did he even argue with people? Noriko was inclined to agree with Sam's analysis, that their fight was more because of strung-out nerves and exhaustion than anything. Did it take pushing Cameron to his absolute limit before he got in a fight with someone? If that was the case, it likely didn't happen often, so he might not know how to forgive and forget.

She herself had only limited experience with it outside of her family. With siblings, she of course got in squabbles with them, but it was different arguing with family than with friends.

Her phone beeped. Twisting her arm about, she punched the little messenger icon. It was from Sam: *You up yet?*

She sent back the reply: *I'm up. How are things with the ley line?*

Back to normal, no worries. Still trying to find the cause.

No leads on who's pulling this insane crap?

I wish, she texted back. That was the most worrying point, actually, that they still didn't know what the cause was. Or more accurately, who was behind it.

The messenger binged again: *Head's up.*

Head's up? What was that supposed to mean?

There was a knock at the door, sounding like the beginning steps to a tap dance.

Noriko frowned at the door. Who would knock out a particular rhythm that way?

A voice, one she was growing to know well, spoke something in a low rumble and the door clicked open. Cameron had somehow learned her door password to be able to open it like that. Noriko wasn't quite sure how to feel about him having such easy access to her apartment, but that wasn't the immediate concern. She got half to her feet, not sure what to brace herself for. A continuation of the fight? Some awkward reconcile? An announcement that Cameron had thought things through and didn't want to be partners with her anymore?

But Cameron didn't enter. The door opened perhaps a foot, and a plastic 'silver' tray was pushed inside. Then it promptly shut again, although not entirely, as she didn't hear the lock re-engage.

Noriko stared in astonishment at the tray. How in the world had he discovered that her one weakness in life was icing shots in chocolate vases? There were six of them in a rainbow of hues, and just looking at them made her mouth water.

Eyeing the door cautiously, she sidled up and picked up the tray, then retreated just as cautiously back toward the table. Sitting next to it, she picked up one and bit it in half. Ahhh, bliss. Sugar was exactly what she needed this morning. Afternoon. Whatever. But what was he playing at, shoving her favorite treat into her apartment and not showing his face? Was he that scared of her right now?

A few minutes passed, and the door opened again. This time, it had a new radio band on it, in GF red. It was the thing she hadn't thought to requisition last night, as her main goal had been a phone. And how did he know that? It was clearly hers, she could see her initials inscribed on it even five feet away.

She waited for him to appear, but he didn't. Having a sneaking suspicion what he was waiting for, she crawled the short distance over and picked up the band before retreating to her spot.

He promptly opened the door again, pushing in a present that was actually wrapped this time in silver paper with a pretty white ribbon around it.

Apparently Cameron had the hearing of a bat, as he didn't budge until he heard her move.

Not sure what this one was, but getting more into the spirit of the game he was playing, she more promptly scooted over and picked up the present. Not bothering to retreat the whole way, she did scoot back about two feet before tearing off the paper.

She'd had no idea what to expect, but even still, this was outside her expectations. It was a hard case protector, designed to protect electronics from EMP, merlins, or any other electronic-like energy bursts. They weren't exactly expensive, but they were not by any means cheap or easily come by. In fact, she'd bookmarked one as a potential birthday present her siblings could get her but had been too cheap to buy herself.

The thought it took to think of this gift, practical but luxurious at the same time, touched her. How long had it taken for him to come up with this idea?

The door cracked open again and a white handkerchief was waved. "Safe to come in yet?"

Noriko had to swallow to re-find her voice. "Come in."

Opening the door, Cameron slid inside like a hunter entering a known predator's lair. He watched her face and body language for any and every nuance, and his expression screamed caution.

To put him at ease, she smiled at him and raised the gift. "However did you think of this?"

His tension fled at her smile and he grinned back. "You're welcome. I admit I was a bit stumped at first, we don't know each other well enough to guess at likes and dislikes, but I knew you'd need one of these in the future. To avoid, you know, what happened."

Yes, they couldn't avoid that topic. Noriko's eyes fell to the present in her lap and she chewed on her bottom lip. What to say? How to say it? She wasn't mad anymore, but....

"Hey." Cameron sank onto his haunches and tilted his head sideways, trying to meet her eyes. "Hey, don't look like that, Spidey. Look, we were both tired, right? Exhausted. Past exhausted. And we're stressed out because weird crap keeps happening, and it's dangerous, and we're not sure how to handle it. All of that on top of being in a new place, with a new job. It's crazy. We were bound to hit a limit at some point."

While all of that was true, it sounded like an excuse. Noriko hated excuses. "So when it all hits the fan, you yell at people?"

"Not usually, I admit." His tone became very gentle. "I just got mad. You were nearly grey, you know? And there was a fine tremor in your body and I was afraid that you'd collapse right in front of me. It didn't make any sense that you were so set on replacing your phone right then and there."

This sounded like he was going to re-start the argument again, if in a more reasonable tone. Her back automatically went up. "You still want to argue that?"

"Nope, don't need to. In hindsight, I realize my mistake. I was arguing with a tired woman and that is never, ever a good idea."

Well, yes, that was true, but.... "Cameron, even if I wasn't that tired, I would have gone immediately to replace my phone, y'know?"

"Yeah, Spidey, I get that." There was no anger on his face, no judgment, no readiness to leap back into the fray. Just calm acceptance. "I get that it's important to you to follow the rules. Do you get that if you weren't that exhausted and shaky, I wouldn't have been arguing the point to begin with?"

Noriko looked at the present in her hands, the icing shots, the radio band he had replaced that was now on her wrist, and back up at him. It had to have taken him at least two hours to gather up all of this. Two hours of his time when most would have tried a simple apology first. How much did she mean to this man? There had been times when she wasn't sure what he really thought of her. He liked working with her, he liked teasing her, but she had never seen much past the surface. That smile of his was like a mask to what he was thinking.

The saying went that actions speak louder than words. He had not once said 'I'm sorry,' but the presents all around her were nearly thunderous with their intent. "Honestly, I no longer remember the argument well enough to figure out what we were even arguing about," she admitted.

He choked, then laughed outright. "Seriously?"

A little shame-faced, she nodded, and went back to chewing on her bottom lip.

"What do you remember?" he asked, still laughing.

"That you were mad, that I was surprised to hear myself yelling at you, and it was all about me not going to get a new phone." Reviewing it in her head, she offered, "I think you were in the stairs because of a pizza delivery?"

"Oh boy. Seriously? That's all you remember?"

The way he asked that worried her. "What more did I say?"

Cameron raised both hands in surrender. "No way am I re-hashing it all. If you don't remember, that's for the better. It was a stupid argument to begin with and if we'd been less punch-drunk, I doubt it would have happened at all."

Now that much she did remember. Noriko felt like she owed something to him. He'd had the courage to come to her first and try to smooth things over, and he was being perfectly honest about everything without trying to hide. The least she could do would be to meet him halfway. "Cameron. I like working with you."

That stopped him dead, and he stared at her with growing delight. "Yeah?"

"You're the best partner I've ever worked with," she continued, "and I don't think I'll ever find a person that matches me better when it comes to syncing power. I like how hard you work. I just worry, sometimes, because our personalities are so different from each other. We're like oil and water."

"Sometimes, yeah," he admitted freely. "But you know, I don't think it'll always be that way. We really haven't known each other long. A month? Less than that, actually. We're still figuring out where the lines are with each other, and when not to cross them, and that just takes time. We didn't get the calm, quiet time we needed to figure each other out before insanity ensued."

Noriko felt a sort of maniacal hysteria rise in her throat. "That's such an understatement."

"Right? So I think we shouldn't leap to any conclusions yet. Yeah, we're different from each other, but no one's exactly the same. You're right—we work really well together, and I'd hate to lose that because we're not sure if we're going to drive each other crazy. So let's give this a proper go, okay? Don't give up. At least, not yet."

What was it about him that made her think

that everything would work out wonderfully? This enthusiasm of his was catching, and she felt herself being swept up in it. What he was asking for was simple: time. Time for them to really know each other better. How could she possibly say no to that? With a firm nod, she agreed, "Not yet. You're right, three weeks isn't enough time to make any sort of judgments."

His smile went bright and wide. "Exactly."

"I do have two questions for you."

The smile dimmed a little. "Questions? Okay, shoot."

"First, how did you know my password?" she inclined her head toward the door.

Without batting an eye, he admitted, "Sam."

She huffed out an amused breath. Of course. Of course it was Sam. Sam had learned it by taking her home last night. "And how did you know about the icing and the radio band? Sam?"

"Tye."

Her eyes went wide. "Both of them?"

"I might have tracked Sam's apartment down through a little illegal hacking and knocked on her door this morning," he offered with a completely straight face. "If a man looks pitiful and spins the story right, you wouldn't believe what information he can get out of a girl's best friends."

T-t-that...ooooh....there wasn't a word to describe him! "I seriously don't know whether to laugh or hit you."

"The women of my acquaintance generally do both." Even as he admitted this, he raised both hands in a half-defensive posture, as if braced for her to take a swing at him.

She held firm for all of three seconds before laughter won out.

"That's the smile I was working for. You know, when you laugh like that, your eyes disappear into this half-moon shape. It's really cute."

For that, she did hit him.

"Oww! Jeez, it was a compliment. Now, I have a question for you." He dropped his arms and asked seriously, "Your password. Asphalt? Why asphalt?"

Noriko stared at him. "Is that really my password?"

"You don't remember?" he demanded in astonishment. "Ooookay. Spidey? My lovely Spidey, from now on, you are not to make any decisions when sleep deprived."

Considering the events of the past twenty-four hours, she really didn't have a leg to stand on.

15ᵀᴴ MERLIN

AFTER a full day of rest and relaxation (actually, she had spent part of that time doing school assignments), Noriko returned to work. She walked into the office and frowned when she realized that no one else was there yet. Granted, she was early, but not *that* early. It was only fifteen minutes 'til. Had something else happened?

"Rare to see the room empty," Cameron observed as he walked in. Slinging his bag under the desk, he sank into his chair. "I wonder if everyone is just running late."

Maybe that was it. Noriko admitted that she was now a little paranoid. Emergencies were constantly cropping up, and being in this room, not knowing where everybody else was, felt unnerving.

She sat at her desk and opened her message app, as her phone had dinged on the way into the station. The message was from Sam and read:

Things better with him today?

Yeah, we made up, she sent back. But to her it still felt awkward. Even though she didn't remember most of the fight, she remembered being stupid and it left a strange aftertaste in her mouth.

To cover up the silence, she asked, "What do you think we'll do today?"

"Probably some investigation. I mean, we still have the test cell explosion to figure out, and those ley lines, so either way we're going to be outside doing some poking around."

That was very likely. "Since we're tasked with helping Frank Goudie, I bet it'll be at the Lab."

"Probably." He gave her a once over. "You packed sunscreen, right? Cause you got a little sunburned when we were at the weigh station."

She hadn't thought to protect herself from the sun, and after three hours of exposure, she had been a little pink. "I've got a tube in my bag. Do you really not—" she cut herself off as her phone rang. Noriko frowned down at it. She recognized the number, all too well, from a survey company. That she didn't have anything to do with. This would make the sixth call in the past month, and for the life of her she couldn't figure out how to make them leave her alone.

"Problem?" Cameron asked, peeking over her shoulder to see the number scrawled out along the band.

"Telemarketer," she explained, still frowning. "From a company that I don't have any connection to. I can't get them to stop calling."

With a 'give it here' gesture, Cameron took it

from her and answered, "Hello?"

"Hello, I'm looking for Noriko Arashi."

Cameron deepened his voice. "This is she."

There was an audible mental hiccup over the line.

At that moment Noriko decided the safest thing to do would be to sit properly in a chair, because otherwise she was sure to hit the ground laughing. Cameron had that glint in his eye that suggested that this was going to be good.

Now clearly uncertain how to address him, the telemarketer continued, *"I'm calling on behalf of the Geographical Survey for—"*

"Geographical survey?" he repeated with sweet, innocent confusion.

"That's right, sir, ah, ma'am, specifically dealing with underground rights—"

"Underground? Oh, you mean where the lizards are."

This time the mental hiccup was more pronounced—dead air for two full seconds. *"I'm sorry?"*

"The lizards. The giant lizards that live in cities under the ground. You do know about them, right? Wait, maybe you don't. Not a lot of people do. Listen, okay, this is very important. There are giant lizards that live under the crust of the earth and they survive by feeding off of us. They control us with specific energy that's way, way advanced for us, we can't understand how it works, we just know that it does. It controls us, makes us angry, and depressed, and every negative emotion you can name. They feed off our negative emotions. The reason why we have all of these wars in history? It's the lizards, man, the lizards feed best when whole nations are fighting against each other. Can you imagine? The fighting, and the injuries, and the rage, all of that is like a banquet to them, man. A freakin' feast."

"O-oh. I see. I mean, is that right. Ah, well, and what do we do about that?"

"Only one thing to do. Weed, man. You got to stay high. If you're high, you don't feel all of that negative energy, it's hard for them to connect with us, so we feel good. And if we all feel good, then no one gets into war or any of that, and we achieve world peace. Can you imagine? It'll be sweet. If we can all get high, it'll starve the lizards, and they won't be able to survive. We'll have a peaceful world at last. You feeling me on this?"

"I'm feeling you, absolutely. Stay high, okay?"

"You too, stay high. Don't let them lizards win and stay high."

"You have a good day now." Click.

Cameron looked down to find his partner on the floor, holding her stomach with both hands, tears leaking out of the corners of her eyes. "Whatcha doin' down there, Spidey?"

"Safest place to be," she gasped, struggling to breathe through her silent laughing fit. She hadn't dared let herself be heard for fear of missing what Cameron was saying. "Cam, please, please tell me that you will handle all of my telemarketer calls from now on?"

"It'll be a pleasure," he assured her genially, offering a hand up.

It was at that moment that their captain

walked in. He took one look at the situation and rolled his eyes. "Powers, what did you do this time?"

A thought struck and Noriko hopped to her feet. "Sir. This room has audio and visual recording, correct?"

"Correct. Why?"

She threw a fist pump into the air. "YES! Be back in five." That said, she raced out of the room. If she was very charming, she might get the security guys to cut a sound clip of the conversation. Cameron's story was too priceless, she simply *had* to share.

By the time she made it back to the room, the whole team had assembled except Banderas. Noriko stopped in the dead center of the room and cleared her throat loudly. "Attention. Your attention please. I have something that I must share with you."

Cameron grinned at her, his feet kicked up on his desk. "You got it?"

"I got it." Everyone else was confused, of course, but they closed in on the laptop in her hands. "Please listen and enjoy."

Noriko laughed just as hard as she watched the fresh reactions of her co-workers who had unfortunately missed the original rendition. Even Lizzie was hanging off the chair and begging for mercy.

The only person not laughing was their coordinator, Jack. Noriko still wasn't sure how his sense of humor worked. He didn't react much at all except a brief twitch of the eyebrows. As the recording ended, he turned to Cameron. "Powers.

They're reacting as if this hasn't already been validated."

The room went dead silent, so still that a dropped pin would have sounded like a war drum.

Cameron went still as well and his demeanor become very serious. "You've read the file, sir?"

"I have, Powers, I have. It's a matter of national security after all."

"Ah," Lars lifted a finger in the air, "what are you two talking about? This was just a joke, right?"

"That's above your pay grade, Torvald."

Lars jabbed a finger in Cameron's direction. "He's in the same pay grade!"

"That's classified." With a knowing look at Cameron, he gave a slight nod before quietly exiting the room.

They stared uneasily after him. Lizzie cleared her throat slightly. "Ah...he wasn't serious. Was he?"

Cameron's mouth twitched, as if he were fighting a sneeze, then he abruptly doubled over in a laughing fit.

At that point it clicked and Noriko rolled her eyes. "He was playing along with you."

Lars drawled, "Did you two work that out beforehand, Cam?"

"Completely improv," Cameron denied, wheezing as he got his breath back.

Banderas chose that moment to enter the room, although he didn't do more than just pop his head around the doorframe. "Get ready to roll, people. We're moving out. Frank Goudie has requested we go to the Lab today. Our goals are cleanup but also we're looking for any further evidence of what happened. So look sharp."

Still chuckling to themselves, sometimes quoting their favorite line, they all grabbed their gear and shuffled out. As they moved, Noriko heard Lars join Cameron behind her.

"Cam, I do have a serious question for you."

"Shoot," Cameron encouraged.

"I've been wondering this for a while, but… Why are your toenails purple?"

Noriko's eyes flared wide in realization. He *still* hadn't taken the toenail polish off?! She whipped around to stare at him, spluttering. Why would he show up to work with the polish still on and wearing flip flops?

Cameron caught her reaction and cast her a wink before he drawled, "Classified."

16ᵀᴴ MERLIN

BEING out in the Mojave Desert in the later part of the afternoon was very different than doing it at night. Even at five o'clock, it remained hot enough to bake an egg on the pavement, the air sucking every bit of moisture out of a person. Noriko wasn't used to this kind of dry heat. She drank water bottle after water bottle, trying to stay hydrated, and felt like she was in a losing battle.

The only consolation she had was that everyone else was doing the same thing. Cameron would sometimes be drinking with one hand even as he worked with the other. Even California natives took the heat and possible dehydration seriously.

Like Goudie had that first night, they started at the Lab and worked their way out, using their knowledge of the blast source to their advantage. Noriko fully understood why Goudie wanted them out here. While being mostly sure that it was sabotage, he didn't have any proof of it—just a gut feeling and some circumstantial evidence. None of that could stand up in court and it didn't tell them who the culprit(s) might be. Their job today was to first look for the incendiary device (if there was one) that might be scattered all over the desert floor. Their second, equally important task, was to figure out if the ley line had gone berserk and if so, how it might have played into the explosion.

Since they had never done anything like this before, their captain stayed with them after he deployed everyone else out. This was one of those rare moments where the Mægencræftas could work separately from the Dwolcræftas. They could see the ley lines just as clearly as their partners, after all, and it took no magic on anyone's part to be able to do so. It worked out nicely this way as they could split up and cover ground much more quickly.

Hands gesturing as he talked, Banderas started them off at the base of the Lab hill. Even here there were traces of scorch marks, black against the red and tan rocks. "Now. You two know how most geologists measure an earthquake's effects?"

Having just studied this, Noriko could give the answer off the top of her head. "Tilting of horizontal surfaces, fault displacements, general ground motion and architectural damage."

Cameron gave her an approving look. "You're on chapter sixteen, aren't you?"

Now how did he...? "You too?"

"Yup, got to it this morning."

Sidetracked, Banderas gestured between the two of them. "You're both finding time to study? I'd meant to ask that earlier but it keeps slipping my mind."

"Yes, well, at least I am," Noriko confirmed. She watched her partner as she answered the question, somehow surprised that Cameron was diligent enough to study even with everything else going on. "Not at the rate I was going before, of course."

"That's understandable," Banderas assured her. "As long as you're still progressing, the Force won't complain. Do let me know when you're approaching midterms or finals, though. I'm required to give you at least two days off in advance so you can study. We want good grades from all of our members."

That was a fact Noriko had not known. "We'll take advantage of that, sir."

"Keep it in mind. Now, back to this. Are either of you aware that if there is a surge along a ley line, that it will widen the stream?"

Cameron gave a slow blink. "News to me, boss."

Actually it was news to Noriko as well. Why, she wasn't sure, as it was perfectly obvious when she thought about it. The ley lines were like underground rivers. They had their own paths carved out in the bedrock, and they moved along that set course instead of going about willy-nilly. If something came along that was more powerful than the usual power stream, of course it would widen the pathway. "By how much?"

"Depends on how much power went through it. Now, we keep a measurement of the ley lines in our areas as a matter of course. We also keep an updated sketch of the ley line's stream so that we know what it looked like."

Noriko nodded understanding. Modern science had still not caught up enough to where it could register magical power as an energy source. There was no tool, no piece of equipment that could really discern merlins of power as anything except random electrical surges. It certainly couldn't quantify or measure it. They had to rely on a Mægencræftas or Dwolcræftas readings, illustrations, and experience to measure anything. "How updated is it, Captain?"

"Documented, about two weeks old. Experience? Ten days." He gave the two of them a pointed look. "The last people who took a look around the hill before the explosion were you two. Normally that wouldn't be the case, because Main Base's people come out here regularly to take a look, but, because of that flu, they're badly behind schedule. I think that's part of the reason why we got this gig."

Noriko didn't quite follow that. "Jack told us during our tour that the Lab team would cover for the Base and vice versa, though, if something happened? I thought we got this job because there's only four people on station at the Lab." It was a huge stretch of desert out here and thinking that just four people could patrol it all was ludicrous.

Banderas pointed to the area directly behind her head. "The Boron Mines are back there, as well as Boron City, if you can call it that. There are quite a few things that the team up here has to cover that's just around the Lab area. Which is why, because we're in between Lab and Main Base, its Main Base's teams that have to take care of this area."

"Makes sense to me. So you want me and Spidey to take an extra careful look, see if anything matches up with our memory."

"Because of the explosion and the power that rocked through it, there's going to be changes. But there are too many conflicting reports about the ley lines. We need to take measurements and drawings of our own, see where things actually stand now. Anything short of a large discrepancy won't be something we'll be able to see with the naked eye. We might have to take the numbers and illustrations we get today and match them up with what's on file to see the differences." Banderas handed Cameron a tape measure. "Do this in increments of every three feet."

Noriko took up the other end of the tape measure Cameron handed her and helped him bridge the underground ley line.

"Sixteen feet, nine inches," he said.

Banderas gave a command to his holoshades and jotted the number down. "Power level?"

"16 KMs," Cameron reported. "Didn't we get a report that one line was almost drained?"

"Right after the explosion," Banderas confirmed. "But of course we fixed that immediately. Even with power levels that low, unstable ley lines right next to each other are not wise to leave be. 16...16 is good. It was just at 15 when we left. It means the line is growing to healthier levels again."

The other ley lines, the ones that had gone berserk, were also reported to be slowly regaining their usual power levels. Noriko was relieved to see that these lines were following the same trend without needing a team to babysit them.

As they walked and measured, the captain drew out what he was seeing. His strokes were quick and sure. Because they were all linked to the same page via their holoshades, she was able to follow what he was doing. It turned out that her captain was a capable artist. He'd never be able to make a living off of it, but it was clearly detailed and in proportion.

It was a time consuming task, a little on the side of drudgery, and they were at it for nearly a half hour before Cameron got bored enough to start chatting. "Spidey, you get calls from telemarketers very often?"

"No." She now felt highly disappointed about that, too.

"Shame. Fourteen feet, three and a half inches, Cap."

"I've been wondering," she eyed him sideways as they stood again and moved three feet, "did you come up with that on the spot?"

"No, didn't have to," he responded, a wicked gleam in his eye. "It's a legitimate theory."

"Get out."

"Really, it is. It's old now, like I think it was first published in the late 80's, but it was written up by a guy named David Icke. My uncle had some of his books on the shelf. I used to read them as a kid just for laughs. There were some really crazy elements to it." Cameron shrugged. "My uncle's a great guy, but he's super paranoid and loves conspiracies. Like, any conspiracy will get his attention. So when a telemarketer calls me up, I have a ton of conspiracies I can throw at them. Gets them off the phone every time."

"And here we thought you were able to come up with that on the spot," Banderas drawled.

"Not quite that creative, Cap," Cameron denied with a grin.

"Huh. And that very bright color of purple nail polish on your toes? That isn't some outcry of your creative spirit?"

Far from being uneasy at this direct question from his boss, Cameron's grin grew wider. "Nope. I crashed Spidey's girl party. In revenge, she painted my toenails."

Banderas's expression gave the impression that getting a pedicure was the same as being tortured. So when he gave Noriko a questioning look, she assured the man forthrightly, "He's odd, but we can work together, and at least he's never boring."

Cameron preened. "She called me odd. I love you too, Spidey."

Flicking her sunglasses down an inch on her nose, she stared at him. "Let me guess. You're one of those people that thinks 'normal' is an insult."

"It totally is. Normal is boring."

"Uh-huh. I figured that was the case. Ten feet, eleven inches."

Their captain seemed not so secretly relieved at their bantering. Clearing his throat, Banderas gestured for them to move on to the next spot. "So Lars mentioned that you know how to climb metal, Noriko?"

"That's right, sir. It's an old exercise from my Jr. High coach. He had all of us do it."

Banderas stopped drawing long enough to study her for a silent moment. "Why are you so good at feeding multiple people power at once?"

"That was the point of the exercise," she informed him with a slight smile.

Cameron added nonchalantly, "That and she can pretend to be Spiderman at Halloween."

Ignoring this sideline, Banderas asked, "How difficult is this to learn?"

"Difficult for a Mægen, not much at all for a Dwol. Why?"

"I think it would be beneficial to teach the others how to do this. Yours is one of the most seamless transitions I've seen for multiple partners. I think, out of the Tehachapi area, only two other people can rival you, and both of them have at least a decade of experience in the field. It's a practical exercise that increases skills, and I'm always looking for those. What's the timeline for learning this? For a Mægen?"

Noriko found this praise to be highly flattering, and she had to fight to keep a blush down. "I learned the basics in about a week, sir. Of course, I was very new at it, only thirteen when I started. I think a trained adult could learn it faster. After that, it takes months of practice before you can actually go up any distance. Just going up the steel beam in the training gym takes concentration on my part."

"That's what, a twenty-foot climb?"

"Somewhere in there, sir."

"Hmm." Banderas went back to sketching and pondering at the same time. "We might not be able to start this immediately, we do have a case to solve after all, but I would like to do this soon."

Cameron knelt, Noriko following his lead, and they measured. "Three feet, ten inches. Cap, this is a heck of a lot smaller than near the Lab."

"Yes, it is." Banderas stopped sketching and really looked at the area. "We're about a mile out now, I think. This should be enough information to be able to answer the question. But at first glance, what do you two think?"

Pointing down at the ley line, Cameron immediately answered, "This was the width of most of the ley lines. I don't remember it being much wider than this. The Lab's lines were a little wider, but I don't remember them being as large as we were measuring."

When Banderas looked to her, Noriko confirmed, "I don't remember it being that big either, Captain. And if memory serves, the change in width was much more gradual. This...this is more abrupt. It went from ten feet to four within two measurements. It reminds me of a shock wave, like the one up at the test cell. Or it could be the point of a power entry."

"Your instincts and memory are good," Banderas approved. "I think you're right. Let's get back to the van and verify this information. Frank Goudie will prefer hard numbers to prove his theory, I think." Lifting his radio band to his mouth, he pushed the team frequency. "Everyone gone out about a mile? If you have, meet back at the van."

There were various affirmations from different members of the team as they walked back. Banderas took them a slightly different route, crossing over the other ley line in a circuitous route. As he did, he peered down hard toward the ground. "Huh."

Noriko hadn't been paying any attention to him until he uttered that sound. The inflection struck her as slightly wrong. She, too, immediately studied the ley line under their feet. "It's not as wide as the other one. Can there be a natural reason for that?"

"Not one I can think of off-hand," Banderas said, tone still odd as if he were responding to her on auto-pilot while his brain whirled in a different direction entirely. "Perhaps the explosion messed with the ley lines, but I wouldn't think so. The one experience I have with a situation like this, both ley lines were overloaded with nearly identical levels of power."

That made perfect sense. All ley lines were kept at more or less the same level of power. It was the easiest way to keep them all stable while siphoning off power to feed the coastline generators. An explosion wouldn't prefer one ley line over another, not when they were within the same proximity of the blast. In theory, they should have overloaded with the same power levels.

The overloaded lines on the old Mojave Highway and the other line near the weigh station just off the main highway had looked just like this—one line much wider after its surge and the other narrowed in comparison.

Her blood ran cold for a moment and she shivered despite the intense desert heat.

Jack had stayed in the cool interior of the van as they went out and worked. He had not been idle, as he was on the phone when they arrived. To whom, Noriko wasn't sure, but he had a strange look on his face.

Banderas caught it too as he stopped halfway inside and asked, "What?"

"Mr. Goudie apparently mentioned the possibility of sabotage to the higher-ups today. They're now insisting that we stop using any personnel from either the Lab or Main Base until we can prove that it was not sabotage."

While Noriko understood that, she couldn't help but ask, "What about Mike Yockey? Or any of the others that were in the control bunker?"

Shaking his head, Jack assured her, "They're more or less above suspicion. Only the truly insane would stick around for the test after sabotaging it to blow, after all. But they did ask us to be cautious, to only get information from them, not to give it."

That seemed a little wrong, somehow, but Noriko couldn't very well say so as the newest person on the team.

Perhaps some of that showed on her face, as Banderas assured her, "None of us think they're responsible. Don't worry about it. We just need to focus on finding out what actually happened and who was responsible for it."

That was true. Only partially satisfied, she climbed into what was becoming her seat in the van and sat down. Taking another water bottle out of the van cooler, she started guzzling it down.

"Alright, people," Banderas held out his hands. "Give me your sketches. I want to see what you found."

Lizzie popped the retractable table out of the floorboard and pulled it up and into position. She flicked on the holoprojector, which gave the GF symbol on a field of red for two seconds before coming online. Everyone synced their holoshades with it, so that it was easy to compare everything. Five different sketches popped up, side by side, aligning into an overall grid of the immediate area. Banderas put his down with everyone else's. Almost instantly he frowned. "Powers, Noriko, give me yours too."

They hadn't taken any sketches or measurements on their own, though...? Puzzled, she handed hers over promptly.

Banderas took over controlling the system and pulled the file from two weeks ago to compare with the others. Cameron's was used for the second ley line.

Novice she might be, but the difference was obvious even to Noriko's eyes. The line near the Lab looked ragged, as if someone had taken a ton of water and tried to force it through a firehose. The other looked almost pristine and neat in comparison. "Captain, I've got a bad feeling that this is what the lines near the weigh station would look like now."

"You would be absolutely correct," he answered quietly. "It's extremely rare lines look like this. I've been in this career for nearly twenty years and I've only seen it one other time."

Charlotte glanced up at him. "White Sands."

"White Sands," he agreed grimly. "Charlie and I have seen this before. A great deal of power was shoved into the ley lines, setting off an earthquake, and it looked just like this."

They all went taut in their chairs. Jack leaned forward, tone brisk and professional. "For what purpose?"

"We never figured out if it was intentional or accidental, to be honest. But the result was massive damage to the White Sands Base. I still think some fool kid, who was new to handling power, drew too much from the ley line all at once and then panicked when he couldn't manage it. It was shoved back into the ley line in one go, causing something that looked a lot like this."

"Javier, I need an answer: was this sabotage?" Jack demanded, nearly sitting on the edge of his chair.

"I can't give you an answer, not yet. I need numbers. We need comparative data of sabotage attempts like this, and we need to completely eliminate the possibility that what happened at these ley lines was linked to natural events. Only then can I say for certain. What did Goudie figure it up to be?"

"He wasn't sure either. He said it depended on what you found out today."

The captain was not happy about this. He kept rubbing at his chin and grimacing. "He's gone home for the day by now, surely."

Considering it was almost seven o'clock in the evening? That was very likely.

"First thing tomorrow, we'll ask him," Banderas promised Jack. "In the meantime, back to station. I want us all to go over every inch of data from the past three months. Let's make sure we're not jumping to conclusions."

17TH MERLIN

"NORIKO, Cameron, this is Elizabeth, our archivist," Lizzie introduced.

"Nice to meet you," Elizabeth greeted pleasantly, holding out a hand.

As Noriko returned the greeting, she gave the woman a quick once-over. Elizabeth was one of those people who may not have been stunningly beautiful, but instead had a particular charm that made her instantly likeable. Her curly brown hair swung at chin length, skin on the paler side from lack of sunlight, and she was dressed in the simple blue police uniform jazzed up by her stylish glasses. When she smiled, Noriko smiled back without realizing it.

"You're Cameron?" Elizabeth asked in a searching tone. "The same one that spouted off the conspiracy theory involving lizards?"

"That's me," he admitted, not at all shy or defensive about it. "Easiest way to get rid of telemarketers, y'know, are conspiracy theories."

Elizabeth's eyes crinkled into a silent laugh. "I didn't, actually. You will have to share some more of these theories with me so I can unleash them on the unsuspecting at will."

"Absolutely."

Noriko glanced between the two of them. Was she the only one wondering? "Ah, how do you know about that?"

"The security footage was mysteriously 'leaked' on the Net," Elizabeth explained innocently. "We've all been laughing over it."

Taking a moment to process, Noriko offered, "I take it that there are no secrets in this station?"

"None whatsoever," Lizzie confirmed. "Elizabeth, you pulled the files for us?"

"I did," Elizabeth confirmed and waved them to follow her. "I set everything up for you in the research room so you can work undisturbed."

Noriko took a good look around her as they moved through the archive. It was laid out like a warehouse, but it had an archaic air and more warmth to it than she'd expected. There were hundreds of volumes of books, some large enough to be terrain maps and stored horizontally, some slim like monthly ledgers, others hidden in protective boxes and ostensibly too old to be exposed to the fluorescent lighting. Most of those that were visible were bound in stiff leather hardback, a few worn and frayed around the edges with age and use, others looking relatively new in comparison. Interspersed through the shelving were desks with computer consoles, flat wooden library tables, and holo screens set up here and there. The place was a little on the dimmer side, quiet, and had that musty smell of old paper. Noriko inhaled a deep breath and felt right at home.

"I'm surprised by all the books," Cameron noted.

"Everyone says that," Elizabeth grinned over her shoulder. "We're surrounded by relics, but the truth is, books and paper can outlast the lifetimes of our children's children, far longer than any type of digital file we've created so far. But in order to survive, we need the information from books and papers to be machine readable and right at our fingertips." She wiggled her fingers for emphasis. "There are archivists all over the world scanning books and documents and digitizing audio and video recordings that date as far back as 1970, as well as those managing the databases that contain the constant influx of born-digital content. It can take some serious engineering to extract data from filmstrips, photo negatives, old music records, or ancient floppy disks. And don't get me started on how every new technology makes our current methods obsolete."

She opened the door to windowless private research room and gestured them inside. "Here you are!"

In the center was a wide rectangular table that could seat twelve people comfortably, with one side smooth, solid wood and the other side equipped with a state-of-the-art holo screen. From this a 3D projection lit up the room, and Noriko stepped forward and took a better look. It was a rendering of the ley lines in the immediate area. "How recent is this map?"

"A complete 3-D graph of the planet is completed every six months," Elizabeth explained. "As different teams map out the ley lines in the field, they send the data to me and I update the graph piece by piece until a full rendition is complete. Then I save the data with a series of secure back-ups, and it becomes the master file until the next rendition is done. It's a constant process. For your sakes, since I understand this is urgent, I merged the newest data I have with the master file. This is by far the most current graph I can offer."

What the woman had done was a mountain of work. Noriko turned to her and said with a grateful inclination of the head, "We appreciate your hard work."

"To itashimashite," Elizabeth returned with a wink and a slight bow.

Noriko blinked, doing a double take. She had not expected Japanese from an obviously American woman. *"You speak Japanese?"* she asked in her parents' native tongue.

"Yes, but I'm poor at it." Elizabeth laughed, as if admitting that she was bad at the language was nothing to be ashamed about. And indeed it was not; as a non-Japanese, being able to speak it all was remarkable. "Have you met Katie from Legal, yet?"

Katie? "No, I have not."

"She also speaks Japanese, but far better than I do. Actually she and I became friends because we both have a great love for Japan's unique culture. You definitely need to meet her and come see us again, as we're both always looking for someone to talk to and practice our Japanese. It would be great to have lunch sometime!"

Noriko made a note to do that. Making friends in the workplace was always important and knowing that she had common ground would ease things along. "I'll go meet her."

"Excellent!"

Elizabeth switched back to working mode and pointed to a stack of thin books on the table beside the holo screen projection, each with several paper bookmarks. "I did find a few documented cases of the ley lines in this area surging. Not quite in the way that Lizzie described to me, and the investigations all resulted in concrete causes, but I thought they might still prove useful. I pulled them just in case you wanted to take a look."

"I certainly do." Lizzie made a beeline for the stack. "If nothing else, maybe it will prove a negative. Right now we're thinking it's deliberate, but we need to make absolutely sure that nothing else can explain all of this."

"Can I help with anything else?" Elizabeth checked with all three of them but got shakes of the head in response. "Then I'll go back to work. I'll be around here somewhere if you need me— just holler."

"Thank you," Lizzie called after her. "Well, she saved us quite a bit of time by setting all of this up," she noted as she dropped into a chair.

"Yeah, she really did." Cameron touched the holograph display and rotated it, tilting it at a different angle before peering intently. "It's completely 3-D. It really shows where the ley lines go and how they connect, even if they go deeper into the ground rather than running along the surface."

That was excellent. "How do we want to divvy this up? Lizzie, do you want to take the books on?"

"I do," Lizzie confirmed, waving Noriko and Cameron on. "Why don't the two of you mark the paths that connect. We know that our surging ley lines connect to others, but I couldn't begin to tell at what points or how many lines. Trace them out so that I can see if any of these incident reports correlate."

In a recessed pocket near the holo screen, there were fat stylus pens available. Noriko picked up one and twirled it idly in between her fingers as she tried to find her bearings on the map. "Let's see. The line near the old Mojave Highway was here, I think."

"It is. Correct." Cameron had a stylus of his own in hand and stabbed the line, making that area glow a brighter blue. "I'll trace it backwards if you want to go forwards."

"Okay." Carefully, she followed the line, making it glow as she traced it. For a while that was easily done as the line was a straight shot. But then other lines started to intersect it, or feed into it, and she had to mark those as well. Her progress slowed as she traced those other lines and she became completely absorbed in the task.

There was the sound of a book closing, being set aside, and then Lizzie asked, "Didn't see anything in there, but this one mentions shenanigans at the southern Bakersfield outskirts. Any of our lines connect to those?"

"Not directly," Cameron responded. "This one gets to the base of the mountain, not really near Bakersfield, and then veers off west. So I guess sort of in the area?"

Lizzie leaned forward enough to compare what she was reading to what Cameron was pointing at. "Nope, not close enough."

Noriko kept tracing, but her mind wondered if this was really possible. In theory, yes, power surges in one spot could certainly affect the rest of the line. But it usually had an immediate effect. It was like any other electrical surge that way—it would be strongest near the impact point, and then grow gradually weaker as it dispersed different directions. To think that power could travel a long distance before suddenly causing havoc did not make any sense to her.

Testing the waters, she asked, "How far out should we go?"

Lizzie glanced up, saw where she had stopped, and shrugged. "I'd say that was plenty far. Maybe too far. We're trying to find anything within a fifty-mile radius as anything further out than that is impossible."

They agreed on that at least. Seeing that she had gone too far on this one, she switched over to the area near the weigh station and started in again. This time she marked it out straight to the fifty-mile mark and then back tracked, tracing any branching or intersecting ley lines.

The area went quiet again as they worked, and it got to the point that the rustling of a page or their own breathing became loud.

"How's it going over here?"

Noriko nearly jumped out of her skin as Elizabeth appeared right behind her. Was the woman a ninja?! She hadn't even heard footsteps.

"Sorry, sorry," Elizabeth apologized, laughing. "I didn't mean to spook you all."

Cameron lightly thumped a hand to his heart. "Just let me get my heart back in my chest. It's all good."

"You get used to the quiet in here," Elizabeth continued. Coming up to stand in between Noriko and Cameron, she took a close look at their work. "Not being a Mægen myself, I only partially followed the explanation Lizzie gave me earlier. Is this what you needed?"

"I think it is," Lizzie assured her, "We're just not finding the answer we wanted to find."

Noriko—for that matter, the whole team—had known what they would find before they were even assigned to go look. She didn't need to trace out the last ley line, the one at the Lab, to know what the answer would be.

The truth of the matter was this: there was no possible way that three ley lines could go out of control all within the same month and in the same area without them being related. And, as the saying went, once was happenstance, twice was coincidence, three times was enemy action. The whole team had known, when that last ley line had gone berserk, that the odds of this being a natural event was extremely low.

They were all hoping beyond hope that they would be able to find a reason, a natural reason, for these instances. It was why Banderas had assigned the three of them to the research room while the rest of them either helped Goudie or went to the station holo room to construct a crime scene model. But no amount of research would tell give them a different answer, not to this question. There were only two reasons why a ley line surged like these three had. Either a natural disaster happened, physically impacting the lines....

Or someone deliberately sabotaged them. It always circled back to this but no one talked about it.

"Criminal," Cameron stated, for once not a trace of the jokester on his face.

Noriko was jarred back into the present as someone said what she was thinking. Lizzie dropped her book a few inches to stare up at him as well.

"It can't be a natural disaster," Lizzie agreed grimly. Shutting the book with a soft finality, she laid it back on top of the stack. "There's no cause for it. And with something that powerful, we'd darn well be able to detect a cause. We'd feel it."

Truly. A Mægen or Dwol was just as sensitive to merlins as a dog would be to scents, or a bird to changes in air currents. It was an occupational hazard of sorts. If there was any kind of change in their surroundings, anything that would influence the ley lines, they would feel it. Even in a dead sleep they would feel it.

"Who?" Noriko wondered aloud, not really expecting an answer, but having to voice it regardless. "I mean, who would be crazy enough? The people that have the ability to do this aren't insane enough to want to. We go through a crap-ton of psych evals to make sure of that. So who in their right minds would be doing it here?"

"I really wish I had an answer to give you, but it's probably not our department to figure this out," Lizzie responded wearily. "Our job is to figure out if someone else should be investigating this properly, and I think we have the answer to that." Lizzie lifted the radio band to her mouth and stated clearly, "Captain."

"Here. What did you find?"

"Nothing even remotely natural to explain this. All three of them had to have been the work of someone."

There was a long, weary sigh. *"I was hoping…. Alright, good work. Clean up and return to the office. You're still on duty for the next…ah, forty-five minutes and then you can call it quits and go home."*

"Roger that, Cap."

18TH MERLIN

"SPIIIIIIDEY." Scratch, scratch, scratch. "Spiiiiidey, you home?"

Noriko, still with her hair wet from a late shower, stomped to her own door and yanked it open. There in the doorway was her partner, looking as lackadaisical as usual, an e-reader in his hands and a bakery box of some kind tucked in his arm. "Cameron Powers, why are you scratching at my door like some cat that wants to be let in?"

"Because I tried knocking and you didn't answer?" he responded, as if that was the most natural and obvious reason in the world.

"I was in the *shower*," she riposted, beyond exasperated. She did appreciate that he hadn't used her password to just barge in, though, even though he knew it. "Now, what do you want?"

"We got midterms soon, but I can't study. I need someone to quiz me."

Understandable and reasonable. Noriko

actually needed a study session herself with someone else as the material was getting stale and hard to retain. "And that box?"

"It's cake. I thought this was a Japanese thing, to eat sweet things when you're tired."

It was also true that she was tired. Of course, she had every right to be. In the past three weeks, she had moved across the country, started a new job, and then got thrown into a very intense investigation. "We've only got two hours until we need to report for our shift."

"Two hours a day is better than trying to cram everything in last minute."

"You do make a point." She waved him inside. "Want spring rolls? I was going to make some for a late lunch."

"Sounds good," he agreed. "These Japanese?"

"Vietnamese. I had a friend teach me how." Noriko waved him to the couch, which he largely ignored. He set his e-reader and box down on the table and instead followed her to the kitchen.

Since he seemed intent to stick with her, she put the ingredients for the sauce out on the counter and squirted a large amount of Hoisin sauce into a small pan. "Stir this slowly. When it gets hot enough, add a heaping spoonful of peanut butter."

He took up the whisk she handed him readily and started stirring. "You make your own sauce too?"

"Half the fun of eating spring rolls is the sauce." Noriko didn't have to make the rest of the ingredients—they were already in the fridge. She just pulled out the containers, the rice paper, and filled a large bowl with water. Dipping the rice paper in it, she then laid it flat on a plate and loaded it full of goodies before rolling it up tightly. "How many do you want? I should warn you, they're rather filling."

"Three? If I want more than that, I'll wrap my own. I think I know how after watching you do it."

It's true that this wasn't rocket science. Their simplicity was one of the reasons why Noriko made them so often. "Is the sauce hot?"

"Adding in the peanut butter."

"Pour some of the coconut soda in there too. Not much, say two tablespoons worth."

He did as she directed, and Noriko felt rather impressed that he knew how to follow those directions. Her brothers were notorious for messing even simple instructions up. "Don't let it boil. Once it's hot and mixed, it's done."

"Okay."

She reached for two sauce bowls, handed them over, then carried their plates over to her small coffee table. To make up for lack of chairs, she pulled out two thick cushions from the stack in the corner and placed them near the table.

Cameron plopped down on one like he had sat this way his entire life, legs crossed and off to the side. A grin on his face, he dipped a roll liberally into the sauce and ate with obvious pleasure. "You're a good cook, Spidey."

"Cameron, if you consider this cooking, we're in trouble."

He grinned at her, mouth full, and didn't try to deny it.

Noriko only ate two rolls, as she was saving

room for the cake. With them done, she popped up and fetched plates and forks from the kitchen before returning. When she flipped open the box lid, she sat and stared at it for a panic-stricken moment. "Is today your birthday?"

"Nope. Mine's in September."

Phew. Wait. "It's not your birthday. But you bought birthday cake."

"The cake won't know."

Rolling her eyes, she translated, "In other words, all they had available was birthday cake."

"It's like your psychic." He grinned at her.

At least she didn't have to worry about somehow celebrating his birthday on such short notice. She cut herself a slice and bit into it. Ahh, ambrosia. It was good cake, true, but the sugary sweetness was a boon to her tired body. Halfway through her piece, she felt mentally aware enough to tackle the books. "Alright, you said you wanted me to quiz you?"

"Yup. Go through the end of chapter questions, that'll work."

She obliged, starting at the first chapter and working her way through them, often doing them in a semi-random order in case he had tried to memorize the answers in a specific way. This degree wasn't a case of 'let's just graduate.' Even the basic information of geology would be vital in their field. She wanted to make sure that he knew it and knew it well.

He did. In the hour of them going back and forth, Cameron missed two questions, and on one of them he half-knew the answer. It was the same chapter Noriko had struggled with, as the author's definition of terms had been somewhat confusing. "I think it's just chapter fifteen you really need to review."

"Were you confused by it? At one point, I swear he had a logical fallacy in the definitions."

Noriko grimaced agreement. "It sure read that way. Lars has a geology degree, right? Maybe he can explain it to us better."

"Now there's a thought." Cameron cleaned off the last bite of cake with a soft sigh of approval. "We should bring the rest of this into work."

"Scrape off the rest of the 'Happy Birthday' first."

Cameron blinked at her, innocently confused. "Why would I do that?"

She gave him the same Look she reserved for her brothers when they were up to mischief. "You like causing confusion and panic, don't you?"

"Who doesn't?"

At that point, Noriko started to worry for herself. "Fine, I don't care." Pushing herself up, she headed for the bathroom. She was dressed and ready to go except for her hair and putting on a touch of makeup. In the bathroom doorway, she paused and bent half-backwards to look at him. "Are you an only child?"

"Nope. Why?"

Huh, really? "Just curious." He'd come off as the only child. Or maybe there was a large enough age gap between the siblings that he'd been raised like one. It wasn't in her nature to pry, so she let the question lie there and finished getting ready.

By the time she came back to the living room,

Cameron had washed all of the dishes and put them away, the cake was properly back in the box, and he was listening to something on his e-reader. Noriko blinked in shock. She normally had to bribe or threaten the men in her family to clean up. "Thank you."

"What for?" He pulled out an earbud, expression genuinely confused instead of playful for once.

It was her turn to respond as if the answer were perfectly obvious. "For cleaning up."

"You cooked. Of course I clean."

"Music to my ears." She grinned at him. "Alright, let's go to work. Maybe today we can find some answers."

"The perk to this job," Cameron said, eyes on the twisted metal debris that he was lifting, "is that we get great tans."

"Shut up," Noriko growled in aggravation.

He twisted his head to look over his shoulder, blinking at her innocently. "Maybe with enough exposure, you'll adapt and start to tan?"

"You say one more word and I will kick you off the cliff," she warned direly. Noriko had put on three coats of sunscreen already on her exposed skin but she still felt like she was burning.

A grin on his face, he turned around and focused on the work he was doing. Of course, he didn't leave it alone. "Should I buy you a parasol? You can be like those old-fashioned ladies, shielding yourself from the sun."

"Powers," she growled.

That got him chuckling. "I do love teasing you. You have the best reactions."

She eyed his unprotected backside, thinking dark things to herself. If she took one giant step forward, she would have the reach she needed to plant a boot in his backside. He'd never see it coming.

"Don't kill me off, Spidey."

Was the man a telepath? How did he know he had just made the endangered species list? "Who says I will?"

"The paperwork for killing off your partner, even if it looks like an accident, is horrendous. Trust me."

Sidetracked by this, she demanded, "How would you know?"

"Classified."

Really, it would just take one giant step forward. Paperwork or not, she was fairly certain it was worth it.

Perhaps Cameron's survival skills were better than she gave him credit for. He stopped working for a moment, the piece he was carrying hovering in mid-air, and half-turned toward her. "I'll buy you birthday cake."

Pursing her lips, she glared at him suspiciously. "Chocolate birthday cake."

"Deal." Eyes sparkling with laughter, he turned around again as if his life hadn't been in jeopardy a moment before and continued on.

The man had a talent for getting on her last nerve. Their previous times, he had been focused enough on the job that he didn't think to tease her much. But today was different, as he was obviously bored and taking that boredom out on her. Four hours of cleanup work was likely to blame for that.

When something the size of a test cell blew up, taking part of the neighboring test cell with it, it created quite a bit of debris. Most of it was black and twisted past recognition. Some of it had been blown into the side of the hill, some of it went onto the desert floor, and unfortunately for them, the rest was strewn up and down the hillside. The very steep, turned-into-a-cliff hillside.

Rather than use a work crew with cranes to lift it all out, the GF team had chosen to focus on the hillside first. They had divided the area into zones and lifted things out one at a time, moving it to a designated area behind them so that Goudie could take a good look at things and decide if he wanted to keep them or not. If not, then another pair that stood at his elbow lifted everything into hazardous waste disposal dumpsters sitting nearby.

This would not be a single day's work. Perhaps a full week would see the worst of the mess cleaned up. It would've gone faster if everyone could put things directly into the dumpsters, but it would also be counter-productive. Goudie had to make sure that there wasn't an incendiary device somewhere in this chaos of charred metal. If he could do that, then half of their mystery was solved, and they could move past the 'how it happened' stage and onto 'why and who.'

"See another piece," Cameron announced,

edging sideways to get a better look. "Man, it looks almost wedged in there. How'd that happen?"

Everything else they'd found so far was loose, which was understandable. "Maybe it was hot enough to melt stone and dug itself into the hillside?"

"Maybe?" he said doubtfully. "Spidey, give me a little more juice. It's not budging."

She obligingly fed him more power even as her heart started to climb into her throat. He was edging far too close to the cliff for her piece of mind. "Cameron…" she said warningly.

"I'm stopping here," he promised. "Ground's unstable any further out." He gave a grunt of effort, for once looking frustrated instead of bored. "I might need to dig this thing out. Or tag team it." Still maintaining his grip on it, he called to the neighboring pair, "Lars? Can you gimme a ha—"

In that split second of inattention, the hunk of metal that had been so stubborn broke free. The weight of it was much heavier than Cameron, and because of his grip on it, it jerked him off his feet. Noriko felt it happen all at once and saw from the startled look on Cameron's face that he hadn't been expecting this development at all. His balance was completely thrown off and he was heading head-first for the cliff.

A scream lodged in her throat, she threw herself at him, catching hold of his shirt, then flung out her left hand toward the base of the test cell. There wasn't much left of it, perhaps a foot sticking above the ground, but enough for her purposes. Years of training kicked in and she magnetized her hand toward the steel pillar, locking herself in place.

Cameron's shirt made an ominous ripping sound under her hand, but her grip on him was strong enough to jerk him to an almost stop. He twisted enough to lock his hand around her wrist, keeping himself from falling.

His blue eyes were wide in his face, breath coming out in pants, like hers was. Noriko was sure that her heart beat fast enough to go right out of her chest.

Lars and Lizzie were there in seconds, grabbing hold of both of them and dragging them well clear of the cliff. Noriko did not let go of Cameron until she was absolutely sure that he would not go over.

A cold sweat trickled down her spine, and it felt like she had aged about five years from the terror of that moment. "I thought we agreed," she panted out, voice squeaking, "that we wouldn't be doing any more trust exercises?"

Cameron had to be just as scared as she was, just as rattled, but he actually had the audacity to laugh. Grabbing her up in a hug, he just held on to her, almost rocking. "Last one. Promise, Spidey."

"You break that promise, you will owe me a *year's worth* of birthday cakes. We clear on this, Powers?"

"Crystal, partner." His voice sounded calm enough, but she had her ear next to his heart, and it was thumping hard enough to be a drum in a metal band.

There was the crunch of gravel as someone sprinted their direction. Their captain skidded to a halt on his knees and grabbed them both by the shoulders, nearly shaking them. "What happened? Who's hurt?"

"We're good, Cap," Cameron promised, still not letting go of her.

"Speak for yourself," Lars muttered, looking a little white around the eyes. "I aged about ten years."

It was Lizzie, practical as always, that explained, "Cameron had a grip on something in the hillside that was giving him trouble. He called to Lars for help, but just as he did, it finally came free. It was so sudden that it jerked him right off his feet. If not for Noriko, he would have gone head first over the cliff."

Banderas didn't like the sound of this one bit. "How close were you to the edge?"

"I stayed within the two feet minimum, Cap. But it was a lot heavier than me." Cameron's shrug implied that physics was the evil one here, not him. "But we're good. Only loss is my shirt."

Rubbing at his face, hard, Banderas muttered to himself, "When I was younger, my mother cursed me that I would have children just like me. I didn't realize that curse carried over to subordinates."

Noriko actually found that amusing. "Were you that bad as a child?"

"Worse. At least you two have come out both times unscathed." He unbent enough to give her a fleeting smile before taking off his jacket and handing it to Cameron. "Wear this until we can get back. And take a break in the van, get something to eat. Tired, hungry people make mistakes."

She, for one, would not argue.

They retreated to the van and pulled out ready-made sandwiches and drinks from the cooler. Noriko's system still ran high on adrenaline, so she wasn't sure if she could really eat just yet. She focused on hydrating first.

Her phone rang. At a glance, she could tell it was her favorite pest: Haru. For once, she was relieved to have him call, as she needed a dose of normal right now. "Hello, Haru-kun. What are you looking for this time?"

"Your Advanced Channeling textbook. It's not on your bookshelf."

"That's because I have it with me," she drawled. She kept re-reading the chapters on channeling to machines, hoping she'd eventually get the knack for it and stop frying them.

"Nee-chan!" he whined in that particular pitch that only young teenage boys could manage. *"How am I supposed to read ahead if you have it?"*

"I'll pray for you."

Cameron slid over on the bench and grabbed her Bluetooth, switching it to speaker. "Hey, Haru. Your sister was pretty cool just now."

"Cameron? What'd she do?"

"She saved my life."

There was a startled beat of silence on the other side. Noriko struggled, in vain, to retrieve her Bluetooth. She knew from that smirk on Cameron's face that he was enjoying her blush, and wasn't it just like the man to use her one good deed to tease her?

"No way."

"Way, man. I was heading head-first over a cliff, and she caught me and held me steady until help could pull me back up. It was freakin' cool."

Alright, fine, two could play this game. "What he's forgetting to mention is that he saved me last time. I was returning the favor."

"Half-saved," Cameron denied, eyes crinkling up in the corners.

"*What happened last time?*" Haru demanded, attention completely diverted.

Cameron plucked the phone out of her hand and shooed her toward her sandwich. He had a grand time re-telling the tale of how broken slabs of concrete had nearly crushed them. Noriko dutifully ate and watched him. Just when had these two people, who had never met in real life, gotten to the point where they enjoyed conversing with each other so much? Haru tended to be a little on the shy side with complete strangers. Was this some magic of Cameron's, that he could charm anyone into talking to him?

Eventually she managed to wrest the phone back so that Cameron could eat, and answered some of the questions Haru had so that he no longer lamented about her taking her own textbook. By that time, their break was likely long over, and after re-applying sunscreen, they went back to work.

It might have been slow progress but it was still progress. Most of the hillside was cleaned up, except one section near the 1A test stand. Everything near the Block House was cleaned up so that they could actually see what was left of the building. There were pathways carved through some of the debris strewn about.

Before the team loaded up for the ride home, Noriko jogged over to Frank Goudie and asked, "No luck, sir?"

"No, and I don't think there will be." Goudie had a contemplative look in his eyes that suggested he was thinking more than he was willing to say out loud. "I have a hunch that this really was sabotage, Noriko, but not in the usual way. Now that I've gone over this area twice, I see the overall pattern. After thirty years on the job, I can read it well enough. But I don't think it was done in the usual way." Locking eyes with her, he said softly, "I already told your captain this, but tomorrow, half of you should stay and do that legwork I asked for earlier. I think our answers are going to come from there, not here."

After what happened today, Noriko had a feeling on who would be assigned desk work for the near future. "We'll comb through it carefully."

"Good, thank you. Good night."

"Good night, sir."

Walking home that night, she got a call from Teddy, something of a rare moment. Teddy was one of those minimalists that spoke when necessary. He was completely charming when he wanted to be, but normally didn't feel the need to exert himself. Sam always joked that Teddy was in stealth mode most of the time. As his twin, she would know.

Beyond curious, maybe even a little alarmed, Noriko punched accept. "Hello?"

"Hey." Teddy's tenor was calm and unhurried so whatever reason he called for it was not emergency related. *"What was that text about you sent us?"*

After Noriko had wrestled her phone back from Cameron, she had sent a brief text to people that she had earned her hazard pay today. She hadn't elaborated, as it wasn't the sort of story that one could tell through a text message. "Well, my partner nearly took a nosedive over the side of a cliff today."

"Wait, wait, let me put you on speaker. Sam and Tye're with me, they'll want to hear this."

As it saved her from having to repeat it later, Noriko waited three seconds and after getting a reassurance that everyone could hear her, told the story. There was a part of her that felt she didn't do the event justice, but how could she describe the terror of watching someone nearly get fatally injured in front of her eyes?

Tye made a keening noise as if her heart was trying to come out her throat. "Nuh-uh. Nope, nope, nope tell me you're joking."

"Wish I was. It was terrifying," Noriko responded, and for a moment her heart skipped a beat as she relived that moment. "I'm so glad my reflexes kicked in as fast as they did, otherwise I'd be short a partner right about now."

"I bet he's even more glad than you are," Teddy opined.

"Obviously," Sam agreed, a touch sarcastically. *"But you're both okay?"*

"Both of us are fine. Only casualty was Cameron's shirt."

"*I think she sounds a little shaken,*" Tye declared. "*Noriko, why don't you come over to my apartment? Dinner's almost ready, you'll be able to eat and chill, and I think you need to chill.*"

"Dinner sounds great," she responded honestly. "I'll be there in five."

Not having to cook was always a bonus, but Noriko hoped that maybe the other three could unravel the questions swirling in her head as well. Her terror today, was it just because a person nearly died in front of her eyes?

Or had she in fact become more attached to her partner than she realized?

19TH MERLIN

NORIKO plopped into her desk at the station with a certain sense of inevitability. "I knew he'd give it to us."

Cameron thumped into his own chair with a half-formed pout on his face. "I feel like I've been grounded."

That was because they had been. The grown up version of it, at least. "I think it's more a precaution," she responded. Only secretly was she relieved to work inside instead of outside. Yesterday she had still mildly burned despite all of her precautions. A second day of full exposure would not have helped her. "I mean, we *did* almost get hurt twice."

"And we saved ourselves twice. That should count for something."

In a tone she normally used on her brothers, she levelled a Look at him and said, "Want some cheese with that whine?"

Grumpily, he subsided and pulled the files over so that they straddled both of their desks. They sat so closely together that this wasn't much of a stretch. He was still grumbling to himself about not being cut out for deskwork even as he picked up the one off the top.

Noriko steadily ignored him as she grabbed the second one. It was true that Cameron wasn't the type suited to being indoors most of the day. That dark tan of his did not come from a tanning bed. If it was possible to do something outdoors, that's where he would be.

He plugged in earphones into his computer, pulled up some e-folder, and started listening to it. If music helped him concentrate, then she certainly wasn't going to argue with him about it.

Noriko settled more comfortably into her chair, grabbed a highlighter, and started reading. She was perhaps a third of the way through the file when she stretched her neck out, giving it a break from that slanted downward angle. As she looked up, she realized that Cameron's file was still open on the first page. His eyes were closed, elbows on the table, head propped onto his hands. Had he fallen asleep sitting there?

Put out that he would dump the workload on her, she grabbed an earbud and yanked it out of his ear.

His eyes snapped open. "Hey!"

"Somewhere out there, a tree is working very hard to replace the oxygen you consume," she griped, brows snapped together. "Now go apologize to it."

Cameron blinked at her, confused why she

was angry, then his eyes darted to the folder on his desk and back up. The light flickered on. "Ah. I'm not reading the file, Spidey."

She rolled her eyes. "Obviously."

"I'm listening to it."

Her head cocked in confusion. "Come again? Listening?"

"Right. You know how in an emergency like this, they have all personnel involved with the site give a verbal report first? I'm listening to those."

It had escaped her mind completely that those had existed. "But aren't those files typed up and in here?"

"No, anyone that gave a report will make a more formal version of it themselves later. Sure, they're supposed to basically type up what they said in their verbal report, but Jack warned me that they don't always match up like they're supposed to. You're a speed reader, aren't you?"

"Yeah, so?"

"So, you read. I'm better with listening."

The way that he had most of the textbooks on audio, and their out-loud study sessions, and his approach to their work today all clicked into an overall picture. "You're an oral learner."

"Yup," he agreed easily. "And you're visual."

Now, finally, his behavior made more sense. In fact, every time that she had come into this room and found him with headphones on and eyes closed, he'd likely been studying. She'd thought he was just chilling to music. Really, did the man have to throw out confusing signals so much? "Alright. I'll do the visual search, then."

"Let me listen through this whole folder," he

suggested, "and then we can use the board to write out the highlights. See if anything doesn't jive."

It was the only sensible way to approach it. "Okay."

Neither of them had any prior experience in investigating something. Not in real life. At boot camp, they'd had a course on investigation that had two different case studies. One of them had been a lab, where they'd had a "natural disaster" play out, and then they had to gather their own evidence, write reports, compare notes, and whatnot until they figured out what had happened. Since Noriko had limited experience in this, she decided to question everything. So she highlighted every number, every time and date, and what area. If nothing else, maybe a timeline of what people were doing when would help.

Three files in, her thighs started cramping on her, her neck was screaming with tension, and she literally couldn't stand sitting in that position anymore. Gathering up all three files, she went to the large holoboard on the other side of the room. Taking up a stylus pen, she clicked it over to black and drew out a long line, marking out time in half hour increments for a full twelve hours before the explosion. Then she chose a red for the GF pair, writing out what they'd done and when. Clicking over to a blue to represent the Air Force engineers, she started filling in their information.

A pair of hands landed on her shoulders and with strong strokes, kneaded into the taut muscles. Noriko almost dropped her folder. "Ahhh," she moaned in bliss.

"This is why I hate reading for a long stretch of time," Cameron observed rhetorically. "Puts my shoulders into knots. So, if I see something on the board that doesn't match with what I've heard, what color should I use to mark it?"

That did not sound like a casual question. Noriko was loath to lose those magic hands, though, so she didn't try to see his face. "Why? Is there something that conflicts?"

"Yup, sure is. The GF pair reported that they sent 36 KMs to the Main Base generators."

"Yes, and?"

"They also reported that doing it left the ley lines both equally running at roughly 48 KMs."

Noriko's eyes flew to the numbers she had just written on the board. "That doesn't quite match with the report I read..."

"Right. The numbers changed a little. Also doesn't agree with our own findings." Cameron's hands dropped as he came around her, picking up another stylus to encircle the numbers of the ley line and what was fed to the generator with a bright orange. "Something's wonky here."

"Maybe in their shock of what happened, they didn't quite remember it right?" she voiced, doubting her own words. "And when they wrote the report, they'd double-checked, and that's the more accurate account?"

"It's possible," Cameron allowed. "They're only human, it's natural to make mistakes when rattled like that. Also possible they goofed and they're trying to cover for it. No matter what they say, it doesn't make sense with what we found."

That point was very true. "Maybe we should

double check with Main Base and make sure that everything agrees."

Cameron gave her a sloppy salute. "I like your thinking, Spidey. Let's double check the facts. Something smells here and it isn't fried chicken."

"Do not mention food," she groaned, her stomach giving a petulant rumble. "It's way past lunch."

"Make the call to Main Base so they have time to get the report here today," he suggested. "Then we'll get lunch."

"And cake," she added firmly, tone brooking no disagreement. "I need sugar in order to face the rest of those files."

"I do still owe you a chocolate birthday cake?" he suggested innocently.

Yum, that's right, he did. "Motion carried."

They finished their timeline right about quitting time. Everyone else was due to go straight home when they were done at the Lab, so there was no one to report their findings to. Noriko gave the board one last, lingering look before shutting off the lights and heading for home. Tomorrow's shift was soon enough to report what they'd discovered.

Noriko did take the remainder of her chocolate cake home with her. There were certain things in life that a woman was not willing to share. Chocolate was one of them. She had another slice for desert after dinner and didn't feel the slightest bit guilty about having two slices in the same day.

As she lingered over the desert, she reflected back to what she and Cameron had found. The truth of the matter was, the GF pairing had lied. They must have. Their reports conflicted, for one thing. The written reports stated that they sent 36 KMs to the base, leaving 52 KMs behind in each line. But if their verbal reports were to be believed, they'd sent 36 KMs to the base generators, which left 48 KMs in the ley lines. Both ley lines were at more or less equal strength, with the number so close they hadn't bothered to note the difference. Main Base reported that they had received 36 KMs from them and all of the power was immediately stored in the generators. That much, at least, was confirmed.

And yet...and yet when her team had gone in that night of the explosion, they'd found 28 kilomerlins in one line, barely 2 kilomerlins in the other. Such a disparity was not possible. If Goudie's math was correct, then what the ley lines should have been was equally 20 kilomerlins a piece. There were approximately 10 kilomerlins missing that should have been there. Even with the uncertainty of the explosion, they should have been there.

Eating chocolate usually helped unwind her, made whatever stressed her out more manageable, but in this case a whole cake wouldn't do the trick. Noriko was very much afraid that the answer to their initial question was this: in the case of the test cell explosion, Wesson and Landers had played a hand in creating the disaster. Either through idiocy, laziness, or criminal intent, their actions had made the explosion much more intense than it should have.

At this moment, the only questions she had were these: Were their actions intentional? If so, what had been their goal? Had they intended to blow up the test cell or were they after a different outcome?

When she made it back to work the next morning, she found both Banderas and Jack in front of the board. She stopped dead in the doorway, not quite sure how to interpret their expressions. Both men were taut, as if ready to spring into action, mouths slightly agape with surprise or suspicion, she wasn't sure which. It felt as if she had just walked in after an argument had exploded, the silence was that deadly.

Not sure if she wanted to walk into a room where angels feared to tread, she nervously cleared her throat and offered, "Good morning?"

Banderas's head snapped around. "Arashi. Are these numbers accurate?"

Alright, if he had already read the full timeline, she now understood his reaction. "Cameron and I double checked them, sir. I admit it doesn't paint a good picture, so if you want to triple check them, I won't be offended."

"I want to quadruple check them," Jack stated in a toneless way that nevertheless made the fine hairs on her arms stand up. "Noriko, show me where you found these numbers."

Now very glad that she had highlighted everything the day before, she readily went to her desk, pulled the reports, and showed both men the numbers. They grew progressively more quiet, a deadlier sort of quiet that made her glad they weren't armed at the moment.

Cameron came in mid-way through this briefing and perched on the edge of his desk. When Noriko finished, Jack turned to him and asked quietly, "The orange letters that conflict with the others on the timeline. Where did those come from?"

"Verbal reports," Cameron answered succinctly. "I marked time and file, if you want to listen to them yourself."

"Pull them up, Powers," Banderas demanded.

Double tapping his desktop to wake up the computer, Cameron obligingly pulled up the files and turned his speakers up high enough so everyone could hear them.

Noriko didn't pay a lot of attention to what was being played. After all, she had listened to it twice yesterday. Instead she watched the reactions of Banderas and Jack. They became increasingly agitated as they listened. Banderas clutching his fist tighter and tighter until his knuckles were white. She didn't know the man well enough to gauge how he would react next. Was his temper such that he would strike something? Should she be ready to duck?

"That was the last file I listened to," Cameron announced, hitting pause to stop the recording. "We didn't get through all of it yesterday. Partially because we went back to double check things."

"There were many reports to wade through, we didn't expect you to get through all of them," Jack assured him. Even though the words were reassuring, the tone spoke of graveyards.

Not sure if she wanted to know the answer, but still unable to stop herself from asking, Noriko put voice to the doubt that had plagued her all night. "Sirs. Did the GF pairing in the Lab cause the explosion?"

"It certainly looks that way." Jack stared hard at the timeline as he said this.

Banderas made a sound like a volcano ready to explode. "I'll be in the gym." With that announcement, he whirled and stomped off.

Noriko let out a breath she wasn't aware she'd been holding. Phew, so he wasn't the type to punch people or things. Well, no doubt the punching bags in the gym were likely to take some abuse, but he didn't indiscriminately hit things.

Jack watched him go and commented rhetorically, "I thought for a moment he'd punch a hole in the wall again."

Again?

Cameron's face split into a slow grin. "And when was the last time he did that?"

"About five or so years ago. When he missed the birth of his last daughter because of a bad train wreck that was caused by an engineer's carelessness." Shaking his head, Jack moved past the memory. "We just came in to check on you two, to make sure that you knew what to look for, but it seems that you found more information than we did yesterday. I'll confirm with Banderas, but we might have the team stay here today and plow through the rest of the reports. I have a feeling the answer is going to be here rather than at the Lab."

She, for one, was relieved to hear it. "Sir, having never done this outside of a simulation, I have to ask: did we miss anything?"

"I won't know that until I review the reports." Jack unbent enough to assure her, "But I think you're on the right track with this approach. If nothing else, you certainly gave us the right questions to ask. That is half the battle in mysteries like these."

20TH MERLIN

"CAMERON. Is there any particular reason why you're lying on the floor and nuzzling the tiles?"

"The floor is cold."

It took a second for her to translate. "Your brain is overheated and the floor is cold, so it feels good?"

"It's a good floor," he purred, still nuzzling the tiles.

Noriko had learned how to file things under the mental heading of: Powers, Cameron, General Strangeness Of. It was safer for her sanity that way.

Granted, after three straight days of crunching data and reading reports, she rather understood why his brain had overheated. The reports were all starting to sound the same, her brain wanted to confuse numbers because some of them overlapped while others disagreed entirely, and they still had to double check what the others had read yesterday. Because of the direness of the situation, Jack had split them into two groups: Lars and Lizzie on one, she and Cameron on another. They read the same files the other person did, double checking each other's findings, and then double checked again with the sources to make sure the information was correct. Part of this was to make sure that they had all of their legal ducks in a row.

Part of it, too, was because no one wanted to believe that a GF pair had caused such horrible destruction.

Even on the best of days, Cameron was not a studier. He openly admitted that. He was a man of action, so reading (or in his case listening) day in, day out, for three days was hard on him mentally.

"Someone should have warned me," he whimpered against the tiles.

"What?" Lars asked him, shoving back from his desk with a tired sigh. "That this job occasionally calls for you to play investigator? And doing that requires a boatload of paperwork?"

"Yes. That."

"Hate to tell you this, man, but going to the civilian side instead of the GF would not have saved you from the paperwork. You'd be stuck doing it either way."

"Lars would know," Lizzie inputted absently, still bent over the file on her desk. "He started out as a civilian contractor."

"Worst mistake of my life." Lars apparently had enough of reading and stood up. "Alright, walk me through the timeline one more time."

"You hoping we missed something?" Cameron asked him, turning his head to find a different spot on the floor.

"Yeah, I am." With a stylus, Lars air-tapped the holoboard under each point as he read them off. "Seven o'clock, the full team of engineers and techs arrive and prep for the test. Seven-fifteen, the GF pair arrives to clear the ley lines of power. Should we write their names down?"

"I don't want to confuse them with the other pairing that work at the Lab, so I think we better." Lizzie popped out of her chair and scribbled their names in: Wesson and Landers. "Alright, so they arrive and transfer power from ley line to Base generator. According to their report, they were only there for about an hour."

"Check in with the other test cell, which they went to next, confirms that." Noriko frowned at the board. That seemed like a very short amount of time to do that much power transfer. Maybe it really was a case of carelessness on their part? Not wanting to say something stupid out loud, she kept the thought to herself.

"At eight-thirty they report to the lead engineer, Bill Collins, that they were clear to test. Collins stated that they finished off prep, did a final check of the system, and then actually started testing at about nine o'clock."

"And the test cell blows not even a minute after they hit the switch," Cameron said, still flat on his back. His eyes weren't even open, but he was clearly paying attention.

"Our assumption is that Wesson and Landers did something, and that's why the ley lines went unbalanced and blew. But then why would it take another half hour to explode?"

That was a good point. Noriko frowned at the board. "Good question."

Lars gave her a bleak grimace. "We need an answer to that question before we can do anything to these douchebags. When we find a pairing that's careless like this, we don't let them off the hook. We don't want them recklessly going around pulling stunts like this. Even if it had been accidental, they might do serious damage later."

A very valid point and one that Noriko was not inclined to argue. She stared at the numbers, the way the timeline laid everything out, and fervently hoped that she would never become like these two. Maybe she was still new to her job, and this strange place called the work-world, but she took pride in what she was doing. She enjoyed it, even though it had proven to be more stressful than she anticipated. Doing something like *that*, where people's lives were in danger, seemed anathema to her.

"Hey, I think we need a break," Lars suggested. "We're supposed to be practicing Noriko's climbing trick anyway, right? Let's go do that for an hour."

Cameron got to his feet so fast air vacuumed in his wake. "Great idea."

Noriko came into work the next evening to find the office empty. Noriko was beginning to wonder about this. Did anyone actually use their desks? Sit in them for more than an hour? Or were they constantly running about doing other things instead? Since no one was there, she stuck her head in the library next, then the conference room, but those were both empty as well. They had been working in the holo room the day before, maybe they hadn't finished?

With that thought, she went to the end of the hallway and out the door, into the one outside building that was not directly connected to the rest of the station. She left stark bright sunlight for a very dim interior. She did not enter the room proper but instead came into a small entry foyer that separated her from the rest of the room by a glass- paneled wall and door. There was a keyless security pad next to the door and a sign above it that read: *Please do not enter without booties over your shoes.*

Booties? Casting about, she spotted two bins to her left, one with plastic booties in sealed pouches, the other for disposing the used booties. Just how sensitive was this holo room, that even the floor could be damaged with regular shoes?

She ripped open a package, snapped the plastic on over her workboots, and then very timidly put her hand against the door lock. It scanned her print, made a happy beep, and the door clicked open. Phew, okay, didn't fry that one. Poking her head inside, she found that a holo program was already in motion. It looked like 2A, still intact and pristine, and the remake was so realistic that she could actually feel the heat from an artificial sun beating down on her. Noriko had seen state of the art holo programs before, but never quite to this extent.

"Ah, Noriko, come in," Goudie invited with a wave of his hand.

With her wonder at the program, she'd missed that Goudie and another man were inside. Shutting the door, she crossed to them, taking in this new person. He looked very international, thick dark hair cut close, dark eyes, a light skin tone, and relatively short stature. He probably could look her right in the eyes, they were so similar in height. From his looks, he could be Cuban, Spanish, Italian, or something else entirely. His looks were so versatile any spy would envy them. "Hello, I don't think we've met yet?"

"I don't know you," he confirmed with a smile that said he didn't mind that. Holding out a hand, he introduced himself, "Anthony Pacheco. I'm the lord and master of SHRR."

The way he said it, it sounded like 'sure'. "Noriko Arashi, Team Pathmaker in the GF."

"Oh, one of the newbies? Nice t'meetcha."

"Nice to meet you too." Not sure if she should ask, but wanting to clarify, she repeated, "Sure?"

"Simulation Holographic Reconstruction Room," he elaborated. "SHRR. I don't normally see anyone from the GF, like maybe three times a year, as you guys don't deal actively with investigations like this. How did you get pulled into it, if you don't mind me asking?"

"Severe ley line fluctuations have been happening recently," she explained without a qualm. After all, he was a fellow officer, she could discuss things with him. "One of them occurred just as the explosion happened at the test cell."

Anthony gave Goudie a strange look. "I thought the ley line burst was an effect of the explosion, not a cause."

"I'm not sure which it is," Goudie denied.

Oh? He must not have heard from Banderas yet. "Ah, sir, we're 95% sure that it was done deliberately. We have not been able to find any natural disaster or anything like it that would cause the line to go berserk like that."

Goudie let out a low breath, more like a condensed stream of air, and rocked back on his heels. "That would coincide with my findings. I have to tell you, I don't like what I've discovered."

Noriko hadn't liked it either, when she'd made the logical conclusion yesterday. "If you don't mind, sir, can I watch the re-enactment you've programmed here?"

"Not at all, not at all. Anthony, if you'd do the honors?"

"SHRR," Anthony stated calmly to the room in general, "restart program. Play 2x speed."

The test cell was peaceful, calm, the sunset sinking slowly into late evening. Noriko watched as men went about in a fast forward mode, doing the various tasks they needed to prepare the test cell for testing. Then night did fall. There were two elements that jarred her out of the virtual reality she was standing in. On the floor near their feet were numbers: one was the time, the other was a large zero that made no sense to her.

She saw Wesson and Landers come in, do their transferring of power from the ley lines as they said they had, then leave again. The lights near the gates flashed red to show the test cell was in testing mode, the engineers and techs all went inside the block house, and the engine fired.

What happened next was so fast that she couldn't follow it with the naked eye. It seemed as if the engine just blew up on its own, and a wave of light and fire swept over her. There was no wind or physical force, which caused her body some disorientation, as it felt as if there should have been because of all the other stimulation. In its wake, there was the destructive scene that she knew well.

Taking in a breath, she glanced down at the floor again and found that the time now read 9:02 p.m. and there was another, much larger number beneath it. "Sir. Am I reading that right?"

"250 gigajoules," Goudie read for her with a sad smile. "That's the force of the explosion in total."

Her breath came out in shaking gasps. That sort of force was unimaginable to her mind. In fact, her brain refused to compute it for a moment and kept trying to shut down on her. "250 gigajoules." She found herself incapable of saying anything else.

"This was the number that the simulation came to, and one I've confirmed myself." Goudie huffed out a breath and shook his head sadly. "I think I've found the answers I need here. Thank you, Anthony, your assistance was invaluable."

"Anytime, sir."

"Well, Noriko, shall we go?" Goudie extended a hand toward the door as he ushered her out. "I think it's time we all got together and shared what we've learned."

21ST MERLIN

"250 GIGAJOULES?!" Charlotte repeated in complete astonishment. "That's—that's—"

Cameron let out a whistle. "That's an insane amount of energy."

"It is that. Hence the complete destruction of the 2A Test Cell." Goudie gave the team a shrug, although he seemed to enjoy their flabbergasted surprise.

They'd come into the conference room to report their own findings and hear what Frank Goudie and Anthony had figured out. But no one had suspected this bombshell to be dropped on them. No one aside from Noriko, at least.

"Captain Banderas," Goudie's chair creaked a little as he swiveled to look at the man more dead-on, "I understand that a merlin of your power is basically equivalent to a joule of energy?"

"That's correct. Which is why we're all so surprised. It would take a Level 1 to be able to manage a megamerlin of power, which is rare enough, and now you're saying that this explosion was in the giga range." Banderas tapped the report he had nicely printed and stacked in front of him with a blunt fingertip. "And it doesn't match our findings at all."

"It won't." Goudie gave a shrug, one hand splayed. "Most of the blast energy wouldn't go into the ground. It's like water, or air, it will take the path of least resistance. So most of this energy went out and up. What I couldn't easily figure out was how much went down into the ground, and the ley lines, which was why I asked you to go look for me."

Now their expedition made more sense.

Banderas spun his report around and pushed it toward the other two men. "This was our finding. The Richter scale showed the earthquake to be just under a 3, mostly a localized earthquake, which the outer area supports. We showed that level of energy through the ley lines. The immediate area is another thing. It was more like a 4 or 5 on the Richter scale. I believe anyone on the hill would have felt it and it probably knocked more than one picture off the wall."

"It did that," Mike Yockey agreed somberly. "Is that why our equipment in the Block House was knocked loose and thrown around?"

"That and the shock waves," Goudie confirmed, flipping through the report. "You make sketches of the ley lines like this?"

Banderas nodded. "On at least a weekly basis. Until some scientist can find a way to actually measure ley lines and merlins, we have to keep our own records. As you see, there was an abrupt shove of power into the ley lines right around the test cell area, which splintered off in every direction before burning itself up and settling into the known ley line paths. Even the ones further out were broadened slightly."

Mike especially seemed fascinated by this, as he was leaning sideways in his chair in order to read over Goudie's shoulder. "How much energy went through there?"

"We can't give you an exact number, but from our own readings and charts, we think it was between 28 to 30 megajoules/kilomerlins. Outside this immediate area at the base of the hill, it tapered off to about half that."

"So, roughly the size of about a half ton of dynamite going off," Goudie translated to himself.

"There is a mystery still lingering." Banderas flipped several pages, switching to a map of the general area. "We've had two other instances in the past month where ley lines went berserk, much like what happened at 2A."

Goudie's attention sharpened. "What's the reason?"

"I was hoping you'd have one for me. The only explanation I know of is not a good one."

With a slow shake of his head, Goudie denied, "I don't know. This might be a fluke, but I'd like an answer to that question. Unknowns are rarely a good thing in circumstances like these." He pondered that page for several seconds before flipping back to the previous one.

Noriko had been trying to follow all of these numbers flying about, taking notes as fast as her hand could write them, but at this she stopped and looked up. Goudie's expression made her think that something was not quite right. "Something wrong?"

"Hmm?" His eyes had been trained on the ceiling, staring off into space as he thought, but when he realized he was being asked a question, he glanced down at her. "I have a curiosity of my own pestering me. I would have expected less power to go into the ley lines. After all, it's not like the test cell is in the ground. It was exposed completely to open air. Very, very little of the energy should have traveled into the ground at all."

"Especially since the tanks are propped up above the ground?" Mike asked him, the wheels clearly turning in his head too.

Charlotte lifted a hand. "Sorry, some of us aren't following this. What tanks?"

"The run tanks," Mike explained to her. "You've been up to the test cell before, right? I thought so. Remember those large, white tanks that were sitting off to one side of the test cell? There was one that was very large, one that was about a third of its size sitting close by. Those are—were—the run tanks. See, we never put a lot of fuel in the engine itself when we're testing it. Too dangerous. These things are in the experimental stages, anything could happen, and if the engine goes we don't want it to turn into a bomb. So we have a run line connected from it to the tanks, which supply the fuel. That way, if something goes wrong, we can shut down the run tanks from the Block House and prevent anything from seriously blowing up."

Noriko silently applauded this thought process. The Air Force had obviously thought this through. Under normal circumstances, it would have prevented a disaster from happening. Although that begged the question, what had happened this time that was abnormal?

"The tanks are actually what caused the massive explosion this time," Mike continued when he realized he had the whole table's riveted attention. "Well, I shouldn't say "caused," but they're what magnified the explosion. You see, between the two of them, they contained about twenty thousand gallons of fuel. Since we only test rocket engines in that test cell, that means there were twenty thousand gallons of liquid hydrogen in the tanks."

Cameron let out a low whistle. "Liquid hydrogen would make a pretty big bomb."

"The equivalent of sixty-three tons of dynamite," Goudie agreed in dark humor. "I had not known until Mike explained the standard operation procedures to me that the engine itself wouldn't have the fuel to create an explosion of this nature. Now, at least, I understand why there was a chain reaction in the evidence I was finding. I thought that something had used the engine as camouflage to ignite the tanks and make them explode. Now I realize that's not necessarily the case."

"It could be the reverse," Mike suggested. "It could be that there was an ignition source near the tanks, and because of the run lines, the engine was blown up along with it."

Goudie gave him a frustrated glare. "I do not

want more possibilities to explore, thank you very much."

Only slightly abashed, Mike gave him a small grin. "Sorry?"

"It's a theory I have to investigate, though, as it's very possible." Goudie rubbed at both eyes with the pads of his fingers for a long second. "Anyone else have something they want to tell me?"

"In the case of the ley line, we are almost completely convinced that it was deliberate sabotage," Banderas announced grimly. "Like I said, we've already had two similar cases pop up recently. So unless you tell me that the explosion caused this one, then I'm inclined to think we have someone running around doing it on purpose."

That made the room grow very still, almost funeral quiet. Goudie slowly shook his head and said quietly, "I have no explanation to offer."

"Then we'll have to work under the assumption that this was sabotage until proven otherwise."

Goudie growled out a curse. "Now that leaves me with a whole new set of questions. Was the off-set of the ley line done deliberately with this timing? Was it intended to help blow up the test cell? Or did it happen without our saboteur realizing the consequences? I believe, Captain Banderas, that you told me before that if someone is too careless, they can set off an explosion without intending to."

"That's correct. I'm not sure in this case if it was intentional or not. It could well be that the ley line wasn't unstable enough to blow yet, that it was priming itself to do so, when the test cell explosion happened. I can't imagine that the GF pairing on the rock wouldn't have noticed such elevated ley lines and done nothing about them."

Goudie rocked back and forth in his chair, eyes returning to the ceiling. "So either the GF pairing is in cahoots with the saboteur or the power surge had not arrived in the ley line by the time they left."

"Those are our two options," Jack admitted. "The GF does not experiment with how much time or energy it takes to make a ley line unstable. We're actively trying to keep them from doing so, after all. Would it help if we ran simulations with SHRR to come up with possible answers?"

"That would help tremendously, Jack. I don't know enough about your abilities or merlins to be able to come up with the right questions, much less the right answers."

"Then we'll do that for you, try to give you some models and numbers to look at," Banderas assured him.

"I did have a thought," Jack offered. "Mr. Goudie, as I understand it, all base personnel are basically under suspicion except for those caught in the blast. Is that correct?"

"That is correct, sir."

"In that case, do you want us to double check the reports coming in to make sure that people actually did what they said they did? Especially on the GF side of things, this team would be able to tell if someone is lying or not. Or at least, if we compare reports, we'd be able to see the inconsistencies."

Goudie brightened slightly. "That would

certainly help me. I don't have the time to run down every lead and then research the answers. Captain Banderas, can you do that?"

"Of course, Mr. Goudie, we're at your disposal."

"Excellent. I have a stack of reports here that I need double checked." Goudie shoved his chair back, spun to grab a stack of folders from the edge of the table behind him, then propelled his way back to hand them over. "I'm currently waiting on lab results, so aside from shifting through what I have on hand, there's not much any of you can do. I don't know what questions to really ask right now until I get more information."

Noriko had followed most of that explanation except that first line. "Lab results?"

At her question, Goudie seemed to remember this was her first investigation. Snapping his fingers, he said, "Of course, I'd forgotten. In cases like arson or explosion, Noriko, we always take an undamaged sample from the area nearby as a 'standard reference' if you will. We do so in order to make sure that there was nothing in the area that was inherently flammable. We also do it in order to set a baseline for what should be in our destroyed remnant. Anything outside of the standard reference is considered to be evidence."

So that was why he kept scooping up dirt into those little jars. "I see. So the samples you sent to the lab aren't back yet. How soon do you get results?"

"Entirely depends on how backlogged the labs are. Right now, we have a higher priority than usual because it was a government facility that blew, and we need to know if this was terrorism or not. I had an email from the lab this morning and they promised results by the end of the week, or the beginning of next. Apparently they have a machine down and they're not sure how long it will take to fix it."

Since she really wanted to know what happened, Noriko hoped for the results back this week.

"This is getting more and more complicated," Lars said to no one in particular, tone almost rhetorical. "What are we looking at, here? Saboteurs, idiots that are accidental saboteurs, what? Do we have a group that is actively trying to re-arrange the Mojave landscape? Do we have two individual saboteurs that aren't aware of the other person's movements, and so they're crossing paths without realizing it? Or do we have one saboteur that was messing with ley lines and happened to take out the test cell with it?"

It was an excellent question and no one at the table had an answer for it. It could be any mix of those possibilities, really. Noriko was inclined toward the second option, of two different saboteurs that were accidentally stepping into each other's plans and making a mess of things. Her eyes happened to catch a strange look on Mike's face. Something about it suggested to her that he had an answer, or at least part of the answer, but for whatever reason he chose not to say it aloud.

She must have been the only one to notice as Goudie said, "Captain, I've been informed that we're reaching our time limit in collecting evidence." Goudie gestured to the team as a whole with the sweep of his hand. "Even though we don't have an answer yet, I need to go through the area one more time. If you don't mind, I'd like to start in on the cleanup of the area tomorrow. If we stumble across anything as we go, I can bag and tag it."

"Understood, we'll do so. I assume you want us out there bright and early?"

"If possible, yes."

Banderas turned to his team. "In that case, short shift today, people. Go home at nine and sleep. Be here at 8 a.m."

Everyone gave him an analyst's salute and said more or less in unison: "Yes, sir!"

22ND MERLIN

FOR SOME reason, she and Cameron were left with strict instructions to stay by Goudie's side and help him sort evidence as everyone else finished cleaning up the test site. They were also warned (threatened, really) that they were not to go within ten feet of the cliff side.

She couldn't imagine why.

There wasn't much left for them to do. After all, half of the team had been out here with other base GF personnel for the past two weeks helping to clean up, and with that many people working it was bound to clean up quickly. They were barely there two hours when the last of the large debris was settled into a dumpster.

"Well," Goudie stated with a satisfied nod, "I found nothing else to indicate an incendiary device was used."

Noriko knew that he intended to sit down with Mike next, going over every facet of the engine design, and visiting SHRR again to make up another model. He'd stated that intention on the way here, at least. She was just glad that they were going to retreat back to the station sooner rather than later. Two hours was the magical window for sunscreen protection after all. If she escaped into shade now, she wouldn't need to reapply it.

For a moment, she took the time to really look at the area. It wasn't the clean place with towering structures she had seen the first time, nor the disastrous rubbish heap she'd seen the second, but had turned into a clean desert space that didn't have a building standing. Even the block building that housed the control center had been completely removed so that it could be re-built from the ground up. From what Noriko had heard, this decision from the higher ups was met with much rejoicing, as some of the equipment in the control center had been at least thirty years old. This was a beautiful chance for an upgrade, and no one was passing it by.

They loaded back into their red van and returned to Tehachapi. As they rode along, she tuned out most of the conversations going on around her, thoughts spinning. The reason why all of this had happened still puzzled her. Why were the other two ley lines also tampered with? Was it an attempt to make the lab look like an accident? Look, this one happened over here, this one happened over there, so what happened at the test cell must be a natural disaster too—that sort of thing? It might have worked, if the person doing it had coincided them with some sort of natural phenomenon. Or even with the explosions that the Boron mine nearby did. But with literally nothing to tie them to, of course the default reason for them would be human involvement. Power surges didn't just happen.

That assumed that all three incidents were tied together which, granted, she had no real proof of, but it made no sense that they were isolated. Unless the first one did have a cause, just something they couldn't detect, and a person had used that instance to blow up the test cell? Then, afraid that it wouldn't look random enough, did it again at the weigh station?

The simulations and experiments in SHRR had proved that unbalancing a ley line didn't necessarily take an explosive insertion of power. In fact, give it just 40 or so kilomerlins of power more than the line was able to handle, and it would unbalance itself. It was almost like a domino effect that way. One slight push, and everything would topple, making the situation more complex and destructive with every power ricochet. The more energy that was poured into a line, the faster this happened, but it was that slow start that worried all of them. A small dose of power wouldn't be as noticeable until far too late. Which was likely why a certain pair at the Lab had been able to go in, mess with the line, and walk out again without suspicion. With this technique, it would indeed take thirty minutes or more before the pressure would rise enough to cause problems.

This whole situation made her head hurt.

Smoothly, the van pulled into the precinct parking lot. "Everyone out," Banderas ordered calmly, moving as they did. "Someone needs to start the legal paperwork to get a warrant."

As Noriko had been intending to get over to the legal department and meet the infamous Katie, she responded, "I'll go, sir."

'It's true you need to learn the process. Lizzie, go with her."

Lizzie paused outside the van doorway and explained, "We have to give her the files and flag them for reference first. She's not going to want to sit there and untangle the web to figure out what the warrant should be for."

Made sense. Noriko thought of the report she had prepared for Goudie and asked, "Something like the timeline we gave Goudie?"

"Much like that, yes. Did you link all of the written reports to it?"

"Yes, but not the oral ones. I'm not as familiar with them, Cameron's handled that side," she explained.

"In that case, Cameron, link those up for us. We need to copy all of these files into a central folder for Katie so she has access to any and all of it whenever needed. It's not just for the warrant; it's also to hand over to the prosecuting attorneys when it's time."

So they built that foundation from the very beginning? Granted, it would be easier to do it that way than to frantically try to pull all of the information together in a cohesive pile the day before. Noriko's understanding of due process was very basic, but she did understand the core of it, at least.

Because she had laid some groundwork

already, it didn't take long to pull the rest together, and bundle it all neatly into the legal department's intranet folder. With it there, Lizzie nodded satisfaction and then waved Noriko to come along. She trailed obediently in the woman's wake.

Legal was basically the central office in the station. The building spidered out several different directions, each hallway being its own division, but the core four rooms were claimed by the legal department. Lizzie gave a cursory rap against an open door before waltzing inside as if that was the most natural thing in the world to do.

Sitting just inside, desk buried in a stack of files that threatened to interfere with the holographic ability of the computer, was a petite woman with pale skin and dark auburn hair. She was swathed in an oversized grey sweater, hair pulled up in a messy bun, and it looked as if she were doing two things at once as her hands flew even as she spoke, "—no, no that is not probable cause. That isn't even close to being probable cause. Have you forgotten the definition of probable cause since leaving the academy? I keep saying probable cause in hopes you'll remember what probable cause is and come up with some. Larry. Larry, please. I cannot write 'cop's instincts' as the reason for an arrest. Otherwise tomorrow's headlines will read: 'Cop Instincts Used In Arrest, Taste In Donuts Not A Factor.' And then I'll have to start sneaking in Bear Claws and jelly filled for you and I'm far too lazy for that level of espionage. But I would do it, Larry. I would do it until you're so buried in powdered sugar, they'd ban you from working coke busts out of fear of cross-contamination. Then go find evidence, watch the guy, but I can't give you any warrants until you give me some evidence to back it up with." She rolled her eyes and tapped the Bluetooth to end the call. "Every time. Every freakin' time he calls, he tries to sweet talk me into a warrant with no ground to stand on."

"Maybe it's his way of flirting with you," Lizzie suggested as she dropped into a plastic chair nearby.

"If so, his sweet talk is coming from a galaxy far, far away, but that's a whole new level of horrifying, thanks for that. It already feels like he's the date that just would not end no matter what you did to sabotage it. The word 'Larry' is *this close* to becoming a swear word around here." Spinning sideways in her chair, she zoomed in on Noriko. "Hello, new face."

The name plate hanging on the wall above her head was in Japanese, so Noriko was absolutely sure this was the same Katie that Elizabeth had mentioned. To her, she said in Japanese with a smile, "*Hello, I'm Arashi Noriko. I look forward to your guidance.*"

Katie's face lit up in a brilliant smile. "*And I as well.* How lovely, someone else to talk to! Sit, Arashi-san. You're on Lizzie's team?"

"I am," Noriko confirmed while sitting down in the adjoining plastic chair. "Elizabeth informed me you were here and I was to absolutely introduce myself to you."

"Good girl. She did mention we had a fun person in house, but I didn't have time to strangle details out of her cryptic little neck."

Lizzie cleared her throat meaningfully. "Let's get business out of the way, and then I can leave while you two get to know each other."

Katie made a face at her. "Fine. Be that way. What do you need?"

"A warrant for the arrest of James Wesson and Henry Landers."

Katie swung back around and started typing things out at blazing speed. Interestingly enough, there was a very mechanical sound accompanying her typing, as if she were using an old fashioned keyboard. Noriko had only heard the like in old movies and television shows, as with holographic keyboards there wasn't any sound at all. Was this a preference of Katie's?

"Crime?" Katie prompted.

"Right now we only have enough evidence to prove criminal negligence that led to the destruction of the 2A test cell on the Research Lab."

Katie's mad typing abruptly stilled. "Wesson and Landers are pulling up on my screen as being GF. You're telling me a Mægen and Dwol were responsible for that mess?"

"At least partially," Lizzie clarified. "We're still trying to untangle the rest. We also suspect them of having purposefully unbalanced the other two ley lines in the area."

The paralegal stared at her for a long moment, a disturbed expression on her face. "I don't normally ask this, usually it's pretty obvious, but what was their motive?"

"Motive's unclear. The only reason why we

suspect them of messing with the other ley lines is because it had to have been done by humans. Natural disasters certainly had nothing to do with it, and believe me, we looked for a cause."

Hoping to clarify a little, Noriko added, "We're not sure about the first one, but the third ley line that went out of control? They were no longer working at the base at that point, and we believe they might have attempted to camouflage what they did at the Lab by making one more go haywire."

"A red herring," Katie stated softly. "But there's no evidence to suggest they were involved in the first?"

"No, just the second," Lizzie confirmed. "We have a timeline, complete with links to the original reports, and a summary of our conclusions in your folder. It's labeled Base Explosion Investigation."

Katie abruptly swiveled and pulled it up. Her eyes flicked from top to bottom as she read through several files. "Half of your evidence is circumstantial, but you've got evidence of means and opportunity. You should get the warrant just fine."

Fascinated by this statement, Noriko edged a little closer in her chair. "We don't need motive?"

"Only in fiction is motive important," Katie dismissed. "We like having it, but not to the point we're fixated on it. Normally motive's pretty clear anyway. All the law needs is Mens Rea and Actus Rea—the criminal act and the intention to do a criminal act. If we have one, or both of those, then we're satisfied."

Well they might be, but Noriko certainly

wasn't. She really truly wanted an answer as to why these men had done what they had. It might not matter in the long run. Whether by sabotage or carelessness, the damage was done regardless. But her curiosity didn't want to let it be. It wanted an answer.

Katie scanned through the rest of the files and nodded, satisfied. "Clearly stated. I don't think I'll have questions, but I'll shoot you an email if I do. Judge will be in court tomorrow, I think I can get this issued in the morning, is that soon enough?"

"Captain didn't give me a timeline," Lizzie explained, "so I'm not sure. I think he just wants these two men off the streets before they can do something else stupid."

"I'm all for that. Lizzie, I release you," Katie intoned in a grand, rolling manner as if a queen was dismissing her subject.

"Ha-ha," Lizzie returned with an exaggerated bow. "Thank you, Katie-sama."

Noriko snorted at this by-play. Lizzie had told her point blank she spoke very little Japanese at all, but she apparently had picked up some to be able to do this back and forth.

Pointing a commanding finger at Noriko, Katie declared, "You I have not released."

Grinning at her, Noriko leaned back in her chair with complete ease. "I wouldn't dream of leaving now. We have things to talk about, I'm sure."

"Absolutely. Let's start with boy bands, shall we?"

23RD MERLIN

KATIE had given Noriko to understand that the law could move very slowly. "Slower than an asthmatic snail" was her actual description. The news came in the next afternoon, just as she started her shift, that the arrest of James Wesson and Henry Landers had already been made. It surprised her, although she was grateful that it had not been the slow process that Katie had warned her about. Perhaps because this case had gotten so much media attention, and it dealt with the destruction of government property, it had been made a higher priority?

If that was the case, then was Goudie done too?

Noriko had grown to like the man. He had been a sort of mentor to her in investigative procedures, and she'd hate to think that he would be shortly leaving. Choosing to do her check in with the captain virtually instead of physically, as was her preference, she did an automatic radio check-in as she made her way to the back conference room.

Somewhat to her surprise, Mike and Cameron were already there. Mike was taking down the multitude of charts, graphs, and diagrams taped all along the walls. Goudie and Cameron were carefully stowing the evidence bags into blue plastic bins and labeling everything as they went. At her entrance, they glanced up and offered casual greetings.

They'd been at this a while as half of the room was already packed. Noriko couldn't help but ask, "Leaving already?"

Goudie paused in his packing to give her a shrug and smile. "I've basically done what I can. I found the reason why the test cell exploded, was able to dissect the actual explosion well enough for trial, and now all that's left is the final report. Wrap-up, strangely enough, always takes as long or longer than the actual investigation."

That seemed weird to her, as she had been under the impression that they still didn't have all of the answers as to what happened that night. "So Wesson and Landers are completely to blame for this?"

Goudie and Mike shared a speaking look but it was Mike that answered, voice a little tired, "We're not sure. I, for one, do not believe they are totally responsible. I know that a ley line surging would supply an unbelievable amount of pressure and electrical charge, but the fail safes on the run line were specifically designed to withstand all of that. I can't help but feel that in order for this to have happened, someone must have disabled at least three fail safes."

"Which means a tech must have been involved," Goudie picked up the explanation, also sounding a little frustrated and down hearted, "as I know from eye witness accounts that Wesson and Landers didn't go near the engine or the run line itself. And it would certainly take more than an hour for them to get in there and do it, which would have been remarked upon. But the problem is, I have no proof that a technician was involved in any way. Or an engineer, for that matter. The only thing that I can prove is that the test cell would not have blown without the aid of that surging ley line."

"I see." It all made sense, and certainly she didn't want to start a witch hunt because of the men's suspicions, but it seemed beyond dangerous to her to go back to work and assume everything was fine. There was still possibly a man on the loose.

Perhaps Mike read her mind as he assured her, "We have reported our suspicions to my bosses already and they're tightening security measures. We'll be very careful moving forward as we build the test cell. None of us wants a repeat of this, after all."

"No, of course not. I hope all of that extra security does the trick." That would have to be good enough. Reality, it seemed, didn't always let you catch all of the bad guys in one fell swoop. Perhaps they would be able to catch whoever else was responsible later on. "It's strange to say this, but this has been a fun learning experience, and

I'll be sorry to see you both go."

"And I'll be a little sad to go," Goudie assured her and extended a hand. "If ever you decide to jump ship, I include you in this, Cameron, come speak to me. Our company would welcome you. You've been very helpful during this investigation and we're always looking for talented, intelligent people."

Beyond flattered at this offer, she accepted his hand and ordered her cheeks firmly to cool down. "Thank you, sir. I'll bear it in mind."

Cameron shook hands with both men, all smiles as usual. "Mr. Goudie, been fun. We're technically on duty, so I need to check in with Cap, but tell me if you need more help."

"I might, to lug all of this into Evidence," Goudie admitted. "But it'll take another two hours at least to log all of this right."

"Yell when you need me, then." Offering a hand to Mike, Cameron said, "Hope we meet again under less dramatic circumstances."

Mike actually chuckled, a low rumble. "I can agree with that. Nice meeting both of you."

With semi-goodbyes said, they left the conference room and retreated back to the office. Once again it was empty, which cinched it for Noriko: no one actually liked sitting at their desks.

Well if Goudie and Mike were already cleaning up, then she could do the same. Noriko went to the main crime board and flicked the timeline into a saved folder on the intranet. Let's see, was there anything else she could put away now? Most of what was laying out, the physical copies, should probably be returned to Evidence.

A chin plopped down on top of her head, two long arms wrapping around her shoulders, a solid and warm chest pressing into her back. Noriko knew without looking exactly who it was and just sighed. "Cameron, what are you doing?"

"You're the perfect chin rest."

That had not at all answered her question. Noriko opened her mouth, intending to tell him off, when she realized that something wasn't quite right. She went still, her senses turning toward him fully. What was it? It was subtle, not at all obvious, but she did manage to put a finger on it. His energy flow wasn't stable. There were little fissures here and there, almost stutters, in the energy flow around him. Cameron, on a day to day basis, had a very consistent flow. It was one of the reasons why it was so easy to work with him. This was highly unusual.

Concerned, she turned within his arms and put a hand to his forehead.

He blinked down at her. "I'm not sick?"

"No, you're not running a fever," she agreed with a slight frown. "But you're not feeling right either."

It was his turn to go still, expression a strange mix so that she couldn't quite read him. "You can tell?" he asked softly.

"Well, it's easy to tell," she returned, not quite sure why she was getting this reaction. Cameron looked almost...surprised wasn't quite the right word, but she couldn't think of a better way to say it. He had not expected for her to pick up on his status. "Your energy flow is amazingly consistent. Of course if it's flickering like this, I'd take notice."

His forehead compressed into a line and for a second it looked like he was close to tears. Cameron brought her in hard and hugged her almost tightly enough to squeeze the breath right out of her. Against her hair he whispered, "You really are the best, Spidey."

Sensing that he really was feeling weak at the moment, and that this wasn't his usual teasing, she hugged him back and let him take what comfort he needed. "The best, you say," she tried teasing, "But you have nothing to compare me to, y'know?"

"Wrong." He curled around her a little more. "I had a partner before."

Noriko stiffened. "You did?" This was the first she'd heard about it.

"Yeah." His energy went on a loopty-loop before settling.

She had the distinct feeling that she had just hit a nerve. "You can tell me about it, if you want? Or if you want to go beat up something in the gym instead, I'll go with you."

A long moment of silence held between them. Maybe he didn't want to do either? Although Noriko wasn't sure what else to offer, as she still didn't know him well enough to guess how he best liked to be comforted.

His voice was so quiet that she missed the first few words. "—in high school, I had a partner. Stephanie. She wasn't my rank, but she was close enough, and we had approval to pair up. We dated."

That in itself wasn't unusual. When you had to work that closely with the opposite sex for days, months, years at a time, then usually a very strong relationship formed. Statistically speaking, almost sixty percent of the partnerships out there were together, either dating or married. The fact that he had come out of high school, out of training, without a partner was what surprised her, as most of those relationships tended to last. Sensing a bad end to this story, she soothed a circle on his back with a flat palm. "And then?"

"She was pitch-hitting for another Dwolcræft who had a project due, in our senior year. I didn't mind, it was just how Stephanie was, but it...took a bad turn. For me, at least. They hooked up. I knew something was wrong, she was spending more time with him than me, but it dragged on for months before I had the nerve to say something. I knew what her answer would be." He blew out a breath and took a half step back, looking down at her. "We split up. It took them over a year to pair me up with you. That's it."

Noriko didn't believe for one second that was all there was to the story. After all, he had been just fine working with her this entire time. So what had set him off today? "For such a talkative guy, you're terrible at telling me the facts. What brought this up today?"

"I got a call from my mom. Stephanie's engaged. She wants me to come to the wedding."

Wait, what? "Your mom does or Stephanie does?"

"Both, I guess."

The words burst uncontrollably from her mouth. "Are they freaking nuts?"

That taut expression he wore eased into a

grin. "You really are the best, Spidey. The way my mom was talking, she was making me feel like a jerk for not wanting to go."

"The girl cheats on you, doesn't have the guts to admit it, forces you into an awkward position, and then invites you to her wedding? A year later? You're not a jerk, she is!" Noriko stabbed a finger toward his wrist. "You can call your mother back and I'll tell her so."

"Naw. No point. I told her I wasn't going. It's just, sometimes y'know, my mom makes me question my sanity. It helps when I have someone else to talk to and see if this is just my mom being mom or if I'm in the wrong."

"You're not in the wrong," Noriko assured him firmly. "And I'm serious, if she calls you again about this, you hand it to me. I'll talk to her."

"Okay." He pulled her back in and rested his chin on her head, but this time his energy flickers died down. In fact, on a strictly power level, he emitted an almost audible hum of contentment. "I gotta say, I'm glad now I didn't stay with her."

"Yeah? Why's that? Because she doesn't have a shred of loyalty in her?"

"That too, but on a work level, she's not your equal. I'm not talking just in terms of power. You read me better than she ever did, and you're far more careful with me than anyone I've partnered up with. I know, when we start working, that I can completely trust myself to you."

Noriko had to blink her eyes rapidly to keep from crying. This unexpected praise hit her straight in the heartstrings. She'd always harbored a doubt that Cameron hadn't tried to find a new partner because she was close to his level and fun to tease, not because he felt any satisfaction in working with her. To hear him say the opposite gave her a thrill of pure happiness.

"Huh." He tilted her head back and put his forehead almost touching hers. "I think I better say stuff like that more often."

A vivid blush stained her cheeks as she belatedly realized that if she could read his energy well enough to see that there was something bothering him, then of course he could return the favor. There would be no way of disguising that spark of pure happiness that had danced around her.

"Spidey...no. Noriko." He tilted his head slightly in a boyish manner, smile shy. "Be my partner always?"

She had to clear her throat twice before she could manage, "Try and get rid of me."

"No way." Grin stretching from ear to ear, he lifted her up in a bear hug.

"*Oof*! Let me down, you idiot."

"No way," he repeated, this time laughing as he said it.

Noriko tried very hard to not smile and sound stern. "We're at work, put me down."

"Giving compliments is appropriate at work," he stated as if it were the most obvious thing in the world.

Noriko tried really hard to stay firm on this. "Hugs are compliments?"

"I'm better at physical demonstrations."

She had to bite her bottom lip to keep from laughing. "That part I believe."

Of course that was the moment that their captain chose to walk in. She couldn't see him, but she heard the resigned sigh. "Powers, what did I say about sexual harassment?"

"It's a compliment," Cameron explained seriously, not budging an inch.

"Uh-huh," their captain intoned, not buying this. "Physical demonstrations are not appropriate at work."

Cameron thought about this quite seriously for about three seconds. "Time for a cool change, brother."

This time, Noriko lost the battle and actually did giggle against his chest.

Her partner blinked down at her. "That was amazingly cute. Do that again."

"Okay," Banderas came and forcefully pulled him off. "*That* is definitely inappropriate. Quit it, Powers."

Noriko waved her captain down. "It's fine, sir. It's just how he rolls."

Banderas gave her a long, evaluating look. "He's sucked you into his pace, hasn't he?"

"Guilty, sir."

Shaking his head, Banderas decided to ignore them. Probably for the sake of his own sanity. "If you two are done being huggy? I've just been informed that we have your midterm test date. You'll be sitting down on the 17th, 10 a.m."

That was just shy of three weeks away. Noriko felt a wave of panic wash over her. Had she studied enough to be prepared for that test?

Cameron's head canted to the side. "So when's the trial date? I mean, if they've already made the arrest, won't trial happen sooner rather than later?"

"Rumor has it about two weeks from now, but we don't have a firm date for that yet. I'll likely have to give testimony, but I doubt the rest of you will. Me, Mike Yockey, and Frank Goudie, we will be the main witnesses for this."

A trial would be another learning experience. Noriko was relieved to hear that she wouldn't be needed for it, though, as she knew absolutely nothing about trial procedure and would prefer to watch one and get the experience before actively taking part.

"So what are we doing today?" Cameron asked. "Preparing evidence for trial?"

"Got it in one. We're not released by Goudie just yet. Let's pack it up neat and tidy so these scum can't repeat their mistakes."

24ᵀᴴ MERLIN

"IT'S SUCH rotten luck," Cameron grumbled. "Why do we have to sit for the midterms *today*?"

"I'm just as irritated about this as you are." Noriko sank back into the seat of the car. Some part of her mind insisted that she try to do some last minute studying on the way to the exam, but she was too agitated to do so. In fact, she was so jittery that it would be better to try and soothe her nerves so she could actually focus on the exam. "Not that I expected them to clear the trial dates with us in advance, but shouldn't we be able to choose our own exam date? Since the proctor has to travel to us anyway."

"You'd think, right?" Her partner slouched even further into his seat, a pout not quite forming on face. "But noooo that's not at all how it works. The proctor chooses our test days, the courts choose the trial days, and despite the fact we did a good chunk of the work finding the culprits, we don't get to see them brought to justice."

The unfairness of the situation rankled her, too. "Although it's still uncertain which technician helped them. Frank Goudie and Mike Yockey were both convinced it would take a tech to sabotage the fail safes." It was Goudie who was investigating that part of things, so Noriko wasn't sure on why he was convinced of it, just that he was.

Cameron spread a palm in an open shrug. "Maybe, maybe not. I mean, you know how the GF runs. Even though we're majoring in a specific field, they encourage us to learn anything and everything. Maybe this pair had been around the Lab long enough to pick up a few things. Maybe someone gave them exact instructions on what to do and how to do it."

There were too many maybes, to her mind. Noriko wasn't entirely convinced that it was a rival company that had hired the pair to sabotage the test in the first place. That seemed like a pat answer that didn't have enough foundation. They hadn't found any communications to either Wesson or Landers and they had been very, very thorough in looking. Well, John and Khanh had, and she trusted their skills. They had found evidence of a pay-off through their expenditures. Well, Katie had mostly found those. So they did have it confirmed that Wesson and Landers were guilty, although they hadn't been able to figure out who their employer was.

And it STILL didn't explain why they had multiple ley lines flare up and go out of control.

She didn't feel for one moment that it was a coincidence the Lab's ley lines had chosen to go ballistic at the same time as the others. "I feel like we missed something."

"If we did, it's not obvious." Cameron rolled his head around on his shoulders, looking suddenly tired and about five years older. "In the movies, when you solve the crime and find the perp, the whole case wraps up in a neat bundle with all the loose ends solved. Why didn't that happen to us?"

"Because the difference between fiction and reality is that fiction has to make sense," she intoned grandly.

Cameron slit open an eye to stare at her. "Quite wise of you."

"Tom Clancy said it first," she admitted.

"Who?"

Was he joking? She stared at him, flabbergasted, for the longest time. No, he really wasn't kidding. "I am absolutely positive you know the man. Author? Wrote *Deep Six, Hunt for Red October*—"

"Oh, him! Sure. Although I didn't realize that was based off a book, but I watched the movie."

"Cameron. Don't you read?"

"Of course. I listen to books all of the time."

That had not been what she asked. At all. Although Noriko supposed that audiobooks did count. "Let me guess. Conspiracy theory books?"

He gave her a shameless grin. "Those are the best kind. They're hilarious."

Yup, she'd had a feeling that would be his answer.

The car braked gently to a stop at a red light.

Noriko glanced out the window, checking to see where they were and how close they were to their testing center. It was being carried out in, of all places, the local library. They had left ten minutes earlier than necessary to give themselves time to find the right room and get settled in before the test, so she wasn't worried about being late.

What she had intended to be a quick glance became a more curious stare. A man stood at the corner, cap low over his eyes, body hunched in, and he was bouncing on his toes in an almost nervous tic. "Cameron. That guy."

Cameron leaned across her to get a good look. "Oh man. He's got 'suspicious' written all over him. Where's one of our brother cops when we need one?"

"I think we better get out and talk to him," Noriko decided. It was a gut feeling but one too strong to ignore.

"What if he's just a nervous kind of guy?" Cameron asked, playing devil's advocate. Even as he spoke the words, he unbuckled his seat belt and hit the 'park' button on the car's navigation system.

"We've got ten minutes, we'll be fine."

"What if he's nervous for a criminal reason?"

"I think the proctor will forgive us." Noriko had a feeling they'd need that forgiveness. She slung her legs out of the car and feigned a smile. "Hi. I'm new in town and not sure if the car is heading the right direction. It's acting a little confused. Are you a resident here?"

The man jerked around, head coming up as he realized that she was addressing him. From five feet away, she could see his face clearly. After a startled moment, she realized that she knew him. His face and name, at least. Robert Hodges, technician, assigned to test cells 2A, 1A, and T3. Now what was he doing here? If she remembered right, he lived in Lancaster, which was a good hour's drive in the other direction from Tehachapi.

He sucked in a startled breath, recognition dawning as he looked at them. Most people, after that split second, would relax and offer a greeting return. Not Hodges. He stumbled back two steps, hands opening and clenching as if searching for something and coming up empty. "Y-you!" he spluttered out, head jerking back and forth as he panned the area. "You're part of something you shouldn't be! Those cities are part of natural selection—they belong in the ocean!"

Um, what?

While she was still trying to wrap her head around this, the man turned sharply on his heel and bolted across the street.

Cameron swore roundly and took off in immediate pursuit. Noriko belatedly sprinted after them. Fortunately, the technician wasn't especially fast, just desperate. She was able to keep up with the chase, although just barely. Also fortunately, all of her physical training meant she had the stamina to talk while she ran, although it made her pant a little in effort. "Why is he running?"

"Guilty people run, that's all I know," Cameron called back to her. "You calling it in?"

"Yes! Catch him!" He had a better chance than she did. Noriko was fast, but Cameron's long legs made him faster. Activating her phone, she pulled up dispatch, then threw the call up to her Bluetooth.

"*911, state your emergency.*"

"Dispatch, we have a runner," Noriko relayed the information as carefully and precisely as she could, trying to remember all the protocols that she had been trained with. "Heading north on West Tehachapi Boulevard. Pursuit is on foot. Arashi and Powers are in pursuit. Could really use a squad car, though."

"*Noriko?*" There was an audible blink through the line. "*It's Cheryl. Why on earth are you chasing a man when you're supposed to sit down for a test this morning?*"

"He looked suspicious, we just pulled over to see if our instincts were right, and he took off?" she offered. Really, she didn't have a better explanation than that. "Can you call the proctor for us? We'll obviously be—" she cut herself off as the man they were chasing dove into an alleyway behind a row of small businesses. "Cheryl, change that, he just went into the alleyway between Tehachapi Boulevard and Mulberry. Now doubling back and heading toward Mill Street."

"*Hold on, I'm dispatching a unit right now. Car 23, are you available?*"

Cheryl must have put her on a conference call or the police equivalent as Noriko heard the cop's response. "*Roger that, Dispatch. Over.*"

"*We have a runner with two GF in pursuit on foot. Currently in an alley between West Tehachapi Boulevard and Mulberry, heading south towards Mill Street. Do you copy, over?*"

"*Copy that, Dispatch, I'm on my way.*"

It was getting harder to run and talk. Noriko had stamina, yes, but not to sprint like this for over a mile in ninety degree weather. Especially not in these boots. How Cameron was managing, that was the real question, as he was running full out in flip flops. Sweat dewed her temples, her breath came shorter and harder, but she didn't dare let up her speed. If she lost them now, the policeman coming to their aid wouldn't know where to go.

Cameron let out a burst of speed, tiring of the chase, and tried to catch hold of the man. At the last possible second, Hodges ducked and rolled, losing his cap in the process. He didn't bend to retrieve it, just changed directions and kept running. Noriko knew he must be tired at this point, but adrenaline and desperation egged him on.

She slowed her own pace just enough to gain enough breath to update, "Suspect now heading down Mill Street. Correction, cutting across toward Pauley Street through a parking lot. Still in pursuit. Car 23, what's your location?"

"On Curry Street and almost at D Street. I'll try to cut him off from the front. Suspect's description?"

"Male in late thirties, brown hair, jeans and black shirt, running like a scared rabbit."

There might have been a chuckle over the mic. *"Copy that."*

Noriko lost some distance because of this exchange, but she didn't have the breath necessary to do a mad enough sprint and catch up. She tried, though, to at least close some of the distance. They crossed over the parking lot, dodging cars as they did, then emptied out again on the sidewalk. It was busier than the street, as this section of town was known for quaint stores that attracted customers who liked to browse. Noriko lost more ground as she bobbed and weaved around people, trying not to run smack into someone.

Fortunately, most of them had the sense to flatten themselves against the building and stay there for a few seconds as Hodges and Cameron came barreling toward them. Noriko's path was half cleared because of this. Hadn't that cop said he was almost there?

Just as the thought crossed her mind, a blue and white squad car flew onto the scene, sirens blaring, lights flashing, and spun into the street to block off their runner. Hodges could hear and see the car coming, but he couldn't do much about the speed with which it approached. He dodged, but it cost him time, as he didn't possess the cat-like agility it would take to vault over the car's hood. Hodges skidded to a semi-halt, reversed directions again, and tried to go back down Pauley Street and for the main boulevard.

Doing this cost him. Cameron put on another burst of speed and launched himself into a flying tackle. Six inches taller, at least thirty pounds heavier, he impacted the slimmer Hodges like a football lineman. They both went down in a tangle of limbs, Hodges taking the brunt of the fall, as he was the one on bottom.

Cameron immediately latched onto the man's arms and jerked them behind his back. The grin on his face was wild with adrenaline and exhilaration.

Noriko skidded to a stop two feet away, dragging in air desperately, now completely soaked along her back and under her arms with sweat. To the still listening Cheryl, she reported, "Dispatch, we have suspect in custody."

"Roger that, suspect is in custody."

From the car came their backup, a face that she recognized, although it took her a moment to remember his name. Conrad, that was it. He was also rather new to the force up here, having only been stationed a year before she and Cameron came in. He still looked it, too, as his dark hair was academy short, uniform perfectly pressed and deep blue. He came out with handcuffs in one hand and the other resting on his gun holster. "Powers, you got him?"

"I got him," Cameron assured him.

"I'll cover you, cuff him."

Didn't anyone wonder what they were arresting him for? Noriko wasn't about to question that, though, not right here at least.

Cameron slapped the cuffs on him before getting off his landing pad and jerking the man up to his feet. Hodges did so with considerable resentment and a glare hot enough to melt steel. "You're one of them," he spat out, "part of this atrocious organization that messes with evolution. You're thwarting nature and progress and you don't even care!"

It sounded like some kind of crazy, cult rhetoric, but it wasn't in the least bit familiar to her. Seriously, what was going on?

As Conrad took over, escorting Hodges into the back of the squad car, Noriko sidled up to stand next to her partner. In a low tone, she asked, "How much you want to bet Hodges was the tech that messed with the fail safes in 2A?"

"I don't take sure bets." Cameron's face reminded her of a gathering storm cloud. "How much you want to bet he knows something about all of these unstable ley lines that are cropping up all over?"

"Not sure I want to bet on that, either." Noriko shook her head. "Cam. I think we better skip taking a midterm today. We need to ride herd on this man and get some answers."

"It's like you read my mind. Call the Cap and tell him."

"No, no, I made the last call. Your turn."

Cameron bent a sideways look on her. "I would like to point out that I went first last time. And I was the one that actually caught the guy."

The first reason was not compelling, but Noriko had to concede defeat on the second one. "Fine, fine, I'll call. Or wait, maybe I should text. He's in court after all."

"Text," Conrad called over to them. "You do not want him in contempt of court."

Excellent point. Text it was.

25TH MERLIN

WHILE Noriko knew that they had two-way mirrors in police stations (mostly because of television shows and mystery movies) she'd never once thought that she would be using one in real life. Neither she nor Cameron were trained interrogators, so they couldn't do the interview with Hodges themselves. Conrad had that pleasure.

Hodges sat at the table, hands cuffed, and looked around with suspicious confusion. There was very little in the room—a table shoved into a corner, two chairs, a waste basket and a box of Kleenex on the table. That was all.

The room she stood in actually connected to four interrogation rooms, and she could choose which window to stand in. There was a listening button next to each, which automatically linked to her Bluetooth when she inserted her ID number. Because of the link, no noise came directly into the room, leaving nothing but the hum of machines as they recorded every visual, every rustle of movement, all to be used in trial later.

Cameron stood uncharacteristically still next to her, watching intently. Seeing him so quiet and serious actually spooked her more than Hodges. That was saying something, as Hodges had gotten progressively creepier the longer he'd been left alone.

It was strange. He just sat there, one leg crossed over another, hands in his lap. He wasn't doing anything provoking or threatening. But the longer she watched, the more convinced she was that this man was no longer in his right mind. His eyes shifted, back and forth, back and forth, and otherwise looked far too calm.

Wouldn't a person normally be worried? Pacing? Upset? Something aside from that unnatural calm.

Conrad waltzed in with his partner, Ben English, at his back. Conrad sat but Ben stayed right in front of the door. Noriko didn't know Ben all that well. She'd basically just met him in passing a few times, so she wasn't sure if that serious look on his face was normal or not. From this angle of the camera, she could see his curly dark hair, a hint of his face, and that was about all.

"Am I under arrest?" Hodges asked as the policemen came in. "I don't understand why I was chased."

Ah-ha, it was about time someone questioned that. Noriko had been waiting for the past hour for someone to ask.

"You were chased because you ran," Conrad

answered forthrightly, as calm and pleasant as if he were chatting with a fellow coworker. "And yes, you are under arrest for now."

"I'm under arrest. For what?"

"We'll get to that." Conrad popped on his holoshades and did a two finger scroll through the file. "But first let me read you your rights."

"Explain why I'm under arrest," Hodges insisted.

"I will, I will," Conrad assured with a waving motion of his hand. "But let me read you your rights first, okay? Just let me get through this, and I'll explain it all for you. That okay?"

Cameron leaned a little her direction and said in a low tone, "This is weird. He was so frantic earlier, when we were asking him simple questions. How come he's calm now?"

"I'm wondering the same thing," she admitted. Although as she spoke, an idea began to form. "It took, what, twenty minutes to bring him here?"

"About that, yeah."

"I think he used that twenty minutes to gather his wits. Maybe he formulated some kind of strategy. He hasn't actually admitted to anything, I mean we basically chased him because he screamed something crazy and ran, so maybe he thinks he can skate out of this if he plays it cool."

"You sure it's not because he's crazy as a bed bug?"

"I am sure of nothing at this point." Her head turned as the door opened.

Banderas strode in, for once not in uniform, but in a very nice dark grey suit and silvery-blue tie. His impression was so different than the rough-and-ready captain she knew that Noriko had to blink twice to get used to this new image.

Cameron let out a low whistle. "You clean up nice, Cap. Your wife dress you this morning?"

"She did," Banderas admitted with a rare smile. "And nearly didn't let me out of the house afterwards. Now, what do we have?"

Noriko hadn't been able to send much in the text, so ran him through a concise summary of events. "And now we're wondering where the crazy man that we were chasing went. He's far too calm now."

Banderas strode to the wall monitor, punched in his ID number, and stood watching intensely for a moment. "Noriko, Cameron, take note: a man that calm in this situation is likely guilty."

"Really?" she stepped back toward the window for another, closer scrutiny.

"Because an innocent man would be upset about being unfairly locked up," Cameron offered.

"Exactly." Banderas put a finger to his lips, hushing them, so that he could listen.

On the other side of the glass Hodges was saying, "I don't understand why they were chasing me."

"If it helps any," Conrad responded, tone still easy and un-pressuring, "they're not quite sure why you ran. They mostly chased after you because you were screaming things and running."

"Running along a street is not a crime."

"Running away from officers of the law that are shouting at you to stop, or trying to jump over my squad car, that is illegal. Obstruction of justice and resisting arrest is what the lawyers like to call it." Conrad shifted forward, his whole vibe friendly. "But we can skip all that, pretend it didn't happen, just answer a few questions for me."

At this promise, Hodges looked the tiniest bit relieved. "Just some questions?"

"Yeah, just a few questions, clear some things up. You know why they stopped to talk to you?"

"No, no idea."

"Well, you're a technician that works out at the Air Force Research Lab, right?"

"Yeah, I sure am."

"The two that stopped you? They are the main investigative team for that explosion. One of them, the girl? Yeah, Noriko's her name. She recognized you. She wanted to stop and talk for a second, as she doesn't get to see the first day of trial for the case. You didn't recognize her?"

Hodges gave a jerky shake of the head. "No. Why would I?"

Noriko frowned at that. "But I did meet him. The night of the explosion, he was there."

"He was part of the cleanup crew that last day, too," Cameron recalled. "Although he was mostly on the 1A site, but we did cross paths quite a few times."

Why would he lie about something so easily disproved?

"Really?" Conrad didn't sound doubting, it was more like a verbal shrug. "Okay. You said something to her. What was that all about?"

"I don't believe," Hodges said carefully, as if picking his way through a minefield, "that the cities off the coast should be kept afloat."

"Huh. First time I've heard that. Why do you

think so?"

Not getting a negative reaction, Hodges seemed encouraged, and he had more enthusiasm as he explained, "It's going against the natural order of things. Look, we have evidence that the earth was all one big landmass at one time, right?"

"Sure, sure."

"And they all broke apart, and drifted outwards because of the pressure of tectonic plates and diverging lines, and they eventually became what they looked like today. We consider this to be its natural state, as it's an evolution of how things worked out. California itself is a collaboration of seven different landmasses all shoved together, held in place by converging lines and tectonic pressure."

That was news to Noriko. She looked to her captain and Cameron, both California natives, and asked, "Really?"

"He's correct," Banderas answered without looking at her. "It's something every child in California learns in high school."

So this was common knowledge in this state? Wait, was that why California was so earthquake prone? Because it literally had multiple gigantic fault lines where all of these different landmasses were being shoved together? What a terrifying thought.

Hodges was really on a roll now. "It stands to reason that these separate landmasses can't stay in the same place forever. The tectonic plates will shift, the convergent lines will fall out of sync with each other, and everything will move in response. That's exactly why Los Angeles and Santa Barbara broke apart from the mainland." Pointing a finger empathically toward the ground, he declared, "It was natural. They weren't a part of the North American continent to begin with. They were doomed from the start to eventually fall away from the mainland and return to the ocean."

"What about the people that live in those cities?"

"They need to leave. They can leave, it's not like their lives hang on living there anyway. If they don't want to drown, they can move to some other area of the country and let nature take its destined path."

The problem with his words was that he was almost convincing. Noriko was stunned by his logic, the way that he so clearly and calmly laid out the facts, without once considering what the consequences would be. Just abandon two of the largest cities in the United States? Granted, their country had a lot of unused land, but that was because a good section of it was desert and not usable. Where did he expect all of those millions of people to go?

"Certifiable, this one," Banderas stated firmly.

Cameron blew out a low breath, rocking back and forth on the balls of his feet. "Oh man. Like, I don't even know how to respond to what he's saying."

"You two were right to stop and talk to him. Chasing him down was also a good decision. This man might not be criminally culpable for anything, but he definitely needs mental help. Although honestly I think he was part of the 2A explosion." Seeing their looks, he explained with a slight shrug, "An innocent man will tell you what he was doing. A liar will spin a story and then try to sell you on it. Like he's doing."

Conrad didn't bat an eye at any of this. "Okay. So you really think that we should stop sending all of that energy toward the generators, just shut them down, let nature take its course."

"Absolutely, I truly do."

"Okay, man, I gotcha. Can we switch topics a little? I have a few questions about the night of the explosion. I know you went over it a dozen times already, just answer two questions. That okay?"

Hodges looked put upon but had the sense to not say 'no' to a cop. "Sure, what are your questions?"

"You were assigned to the test cell that blew up. And we know you were there the night of the test. Did you see either Wesson or Landers near the engine? Or near the big tanks nearby?"

"I don't really recall seeing them there."

"So they were there, and you were all prepping for the test that night, but you didn't see them at all?"

"I don't remember seeing them."

Banderas had taken on the role of teacher and explained quickly, "A man that won't give you a straight 'yes' or 'no' is trying to hide something."

"Why do you think you didn't see them? I mean, in those bright red jackets, they're hard to miss."

Hodges responded so quickly his words almost ran into each other. "I was inside the test cell. Inside, where the engine was sitting."

"So you couldn't see anyone? The engine was blocking your view or something?"

"Yeah, must have been because of that. I couldn't see anyone because of where I was."

Noriko hissed out a breath. That was not what Hodges had declared in his verbal report, or his written one. "He said in his initial interviews that he was working 1A that night more than 2A and only came over to help for a half hour before the test."

"And he wasn't anywhere near the run tanks or engines." Cameron had a sharkish smile on his face. "Cap, can we pull him into the trial based on this?"

"You bet we can." Banderas gave an approving nod. "Chappell's good at this. In focusing on one thing, he's making Hodges admit to being there, and contradicting his own story."

Conrad didn't let any signs of victory show up on his face. "Well, that makes sense, you can't see around that huge engine. I mean, how big is that thing? Several hundred tons?"

"Huge, I know that much, and the test cell isn't exactly small either." Hodges actually smiled, as if he were perfectly at ease and knew that he was going to walk out soon. "You can see why I miss a lot, when I'm up there prepping for a test."

"So what all do you do? To prepare for a test?"

"Well, we check all of the lines, make sure they're airtight. Then we check and double check the fail safes. Takes a couple of guys to do that. We have a whole checklist of things to do, sometimes it changes depending on what type of engine we've got in there."

"So you did business as usual with the 2A engine? Nothing unusual or different there?"

"No, just the same 'ole, same 'ole."

Conrad turned to his partner and asked, "You getting all of this, Ben?"

"Sure am," Ben assured him, hands just busy typing up something on a holo keyboard that only he could see.

"To sum up," Conrad started ticking points off on his fingers, "you were actually there near the engine on the night of the test, you personally handled the fail safes, and you were there for most of the prep time before the test fired. Is that right?"

Hodges must have realized his goof as his eyes shifted away and the relaxed posture went abruptly rigid. "Well, I didn't mean to say that, just that I was there part of the time. I was at 1A part of the time, too."

"Sure, sure, didn't mean to say differently. So, last question for you." Conrad's easy smile went stiff. "What was the reason? Corporate sabotage or does your belief in natural progression play into it?"

Hodges shifted in his chair, one leg coming up behind the other so that his ankle hooked behind his knee.

"Ahhh," Banderas cried in soft victory. "He's got him."

Wait, what? Noriko didn't see how this change in body positioning meant something.

"Captain, please share with the class," Cameron drawled.

"It's a sign of constraint when they do that,"

Banderas answered, his whole body leaning forward in anticipation. "Hodges is holding something back."

When Conrad didn't get an answer, he pushed. "Did you not understand my question?"

"I don't understand," Hodges denied, nervously scratching at the palms of his hands.

"We think the reason why Wesson and Landers sabotaged the test cell ley lines was because they were paid to do so. Because of corporate sabotage. At least, there's evidence that they have more money than they should from their spending habits."

Hodges' head jerked back in surprise. "There is?"

Noriko was very glad that Katie had found that, as it was what cinched their case against Wesson and Landers. Although it did beg the question: Just how thorough was her research for trial? And how much power did that woman wield, that she could get their bank statements?

"Is that why you helped them?" Conrad pressed. "Because you were paid to do so by some corporation?"

Hodges lost his cool. He slammed backwards in his chair, ramming into the wall. "I want a lawyer."

"Okay, man, that's fine. You're not going to answer my question?"

"I want a lawyer!" Hodges screamed, eyes wild.

Banderas gave a satisfied smile, like a glutton after putting away a feast. "I do love it when they lawyer up. It means we have the man dead to rights. Makes Conrad's and Ben's lives a little harder, though." Turning, he smiled at them, in the most jovial mood that he'd ever displayed. "Excellent work, you two. I will make sure this goes on your records. Also, I'll talk to the proctor for you and get you out of trouble there. You caught the one person we needed to find for this case to come to a close, they can't blame you for skipping a test."

Knowing proctors as she did...Noriko was not convinced. They tended to hold grudges.

A call beeped in and Banderas tapped his Bluetooth. "Banderas." All coloring wiped out of his face in an instant. "WHAT?!"

Noriko did not like that response. It meant something had gone very, very wrong. Internally, she started praying: *Please not another berserk ley line, please oh please.*

Banderas gestured for them to follow even as he hung up the call, burst out of the room and sprinted down the hallway.

"What's happened?" Noriko demanded, hot on his heels.

"The main generator in Tehachapi just went off-line and sent power surging through the main ley line in town," Banderas snapped over his shoulder. As he ran, he slapped a hand against a large red button near their office doors, sending an alarm blaring. "I need everyone on hand, MOVE!"

26TH MERLIN

NORIKO piled into the van so quickly she nearly did a nose dive for the floor and only just caught herself on the bench. Her team poured in like a tsunami wave, but, even still, Jack had the van in motion before the back door was properly closed. The van tires squealed as they went on two wheels out of the parking lot and raced for the mountains.

As they went through the town, Noriko couldn't help but notice that there wasn't a single building that had its lights on. A blackout? "Was the power surge bad enough to knock everything in town offline? Or..." They left the main part of town, opening up her view past buildings and to the mountains that surrounded the town.

Noriko's eyes went to the windmills that were spread out like a carpet of needles on top of the mountains. Not a single one moved. The full impact of what she was seeing made her stomach sink and then twist into a Gordian knot. If no power was being generated, not from the windmills, not from the ley lines, then there was literally nothing being sent to the coast. "This is not good."

"This is in fact a horrible, terrible, no good, very bad day," was Cameron's flat take. "To quote one of my favorite storybooks. Now. Cap, we got a plan?"

Banderas didn't rattle off an answer but instead looked at the two of them steadily. "You told me your max is 78 kilomerlins before, but is that your absolute max?"

Somehow, Cameron managed to smile as if nothing were wrong and shrug. "Nope."

"So what is your max?"

"Well, Cap, depends. How long you want me working? The 78 KMs I can do for about three hours, or I can top out at 80 KMs for one hour. Your call, boss."

Again, Banderas didn't respond immediately, but instead look at Noriko. His eyes demanded confirmation.

"I can keep up with him, sir," she assured him. She'd likely collapse on the spot doing it, but she COULD do it.

"They really, truly didn't rank either one of you right," Lars whispered, as much to himself as to anyone else.

Banderas pulled up a map of the generator on his holoshades and then threw it to theirs. Noriko put hers on to see it. They called it a generator, but, in fact, there were five—four smaller ones and a large receiving generator that was a connecting hub for all four. They looked small on the diagram, but she knew from the scale that they were in fact huge—two stories each with 300-foot diameters.

Jack turned from the phone call he had been on and reported, "Generators are offline but only because they did an emergency shutdown. No damage to any of the units."

Their captain's eyes closed and his mouth moved in a silent prayer of thanks. "I wasn't sure what we were going to do if any of them were damaged. Right now, we have far too much power lashing about to put it back into a ley line, the generators are the only other safe place for it to go. Alright, people, here's the situation: we have nearly a megamerlin or more power surging through the two main ley lines that run along the foot of the mountains."

Noriko thought she'd been nervous before, but this news made her borderline panicky. A megamerlin?! It would take the dozen teams stationed in Tehachapi working for hours before they could parse that energy level down to where it was supposed to be! And they might not have that time. Odds were something would burn out or explode before they could get there.

"Charlie and I are heading for the north ley line, we'll batten it down so it's no longer surging. Lars, Lizzie, you're working with us. At my signal, they'll turn one generator back on—funnel every bit of power you can into it, but don't blow us up in the process. Comprende?"

"Si, El Capitan," Lars joked, smile beyond strained.

"Good. Cameron, I understand you hang out

with Noriko's friends, you ever work with them?"

"Just little things, Cap, like the climbing trick."

"Good, so you have some experience. I'm pulling another partnership from the Team Dawnflight. For this, you need people you know. Sam and Teddy will be with you. They'll work to batten the line down and keep the power from surging into the generator while you feed merlins into it."

"Roger that." Cameron looked to Noriko, manner confident, or trying to look that way. It was the tension in his shoulders that spoiled it. "At least we get to work with friends this time around."

"I'll take any silver lining I can get right now." Noriko sent a quick text to both of them that read: *Heard we're partnering up with you. You on your way?*

She got a reply almost immediately from Sam: *ETA looks like we're a minute behind you. Which way we playing this? Who's catcher, who's batter?*

You're catcher, we're batter. Although baseball terminology seemed beyond strange to use in this situation, Noriko wasn't arguing the point now.

Kk.

Some part of her mind that still operated logically reminded her that in her gear bag was a certain present she needed to use. Digging it out, she took off radio band, phone, and Bluetooth and dropped them all into the protective box before clamping it shut. Glancing up, she caught Jack's eyes and reported, "I won't have any equipment on me during this."

"Afraid of frying it?" he asked, almost rhetorically as he didn't wait for a response. "Good idea. I know John and Khanh will appreciate the thought. We'll coordinate with you through Cameron."

The van jumped a little as it sped over a speedbump, then again, jostling its passengers. Noriko paid it little heed as the most overwhelming sense of power washed over her skin, making it prickle and crawl. It felt like a thousand fairies with needles were stabbing all over. The previous experiences were nothing compared to this.

They skidded to a halt, Lars hit the van door hard enough to make it bounce, and they all tumbled out. Noriko was at that point glad she had skipped lunch, as if she'd had anything in her stomach, she would have lost it. Her feet were barely on the ground and it was so statically charged with energy that it gave her vertigo.

Cameron grabbed her around the shoulders in a vise-like grip, a shield snapping up around them as he did so, keeping the worst of the power at bay. Glancing up, she found that he was just as white and shaken as she felt.

"Thanks," she gasped.

"Take advantage while you can," was his only response. He was already leading them both toward the generator just in front of them.

Noriko stumbled along with him, trying to get her bearings as they moved. From here, she couldn't see more than two generators. They were large enough that they blocked her view of anything else. The concrete all around the base was already cracking in large fissures from the pressure, and there was a hint of scorch marks.

As they half-jogged forward, electricity jumped from one transformer to another, arcing like lightning, although fortunately it didn't shoot away from the transformers. The sizzle and pop of the electricity made her jump and a painful tingling raced along her skin.

Banderas was shouting at Jack as he ran forward, "I thought these things were shut down!"

"They're supposed to be, I'm on it!" Jack shouted back, racing for the far left side, where the control room was supposed to be.

The ley lines were completely exposed to the air, power coming out of them in visual waves, like a heat wave off a desert floor but far more sinister and dangerous. The air held that charge that felt like mild electrocution, Noriko's skin stinging at the sensation. If she had smelled her hair melting, it wouldn't have surprised her. There was sand kicked up in the air too, hovering like dust motes, only far more thickly. It obstructed the line of sight in every direction, although of course it was worse right next the lines. The closer she got, the more she saw that the edges of the open ley line were melting.

Cameron stopped five feet from the edge and looked to her with a maniacal grin. "Ready?"

"Max-max or max?" she double checked, and prayed that he wouldn't say what she knew he would.

"Max-max."

Yeah, she knew that would be his answer. Gulping, she chose to sit seiza style again rather than risk falling over later.

"Dying request, Spidey."

"Shoot."

"Warn me before you collapse."

She'd think he was joking if the situation wasn't this dire. "You do the same. Alright, ready?"

"Ready."

"Three, two, one, go!" So saying, she drew power heavily from the ley line and sent it to him. Because of the emergency of the situation she couldn't hone the power as she normally did before sending it on, so it was half-raw and must have felt very prickly to him. Cameron didn't even flinch, just took it all on.

Her immediate focus had once again been on the ley line out of control, but of course for one to be out of control, another would have to be robbed of all strength. Cameron immediately diverted the power she gave him into that drained line. It went from nearly nonexistent to glowing ever so slightly as it was revitalized.

From the other side of the line, Banderas and Charlotte did the same thing, although being Level 5s they didn't have the ability to handle as much power.

Another van in GF red screeched up, and people poured out of it. Noriko nearly wept at seeing Sam and Teddy racing her direction. Also, being Level 4s, they would be able to handle power like she and Cameron could, and the more power that was put back in place, the better.

Sam grasped her shoulder briefly in greeting but wasted no time on words. She glanced at Teddy, who gave her a nod, and then she started transferring power into the drained line as her brother fed it to her. "I've got damage control," she informed Cameron in a professional, clipped voice. "Batter up!"

"Cap, generator's okay?" Cameron checked.

"Only the one right next to us."

Cameron didn't need another nudge. He promptly turned his attention to the generator to his immediate left and started pouring power into it. It whirred to life, making a distinct hum that was almost subterranean in its volume.

Even as she fed her partner power, she wondered about the other four. Were they only temporarily offline? One of them at least had damage to it, from those sparking transformers. Were the others as well? There was no way in heaven that a single generator could take on the load of the other four.

Jack came sprinting up although he stopped ten feet away, a prudent measure as he had no means of defending himself from a power overload. "LA dispatch has called! They've lost six inches already and the backup generators are threatening to overheat. What do I tell them?"

"We're feeding power into a generator now," Banderas relayed crisply. "They should be seeing it shortly. Jack, what about the others?"

"Generator 3 is offline until we can repair it, but the others are functioning."

"Cameron," the captain jerked his chin to indicate the generator next to them, "get this one. I'll focus on the other one."

"Got it, Cap."

Noriko kept feeding power, kept up the

insane wash of merlins and transferred them to her partner, and tried not to either pass out or lose focus. She caught Teddy's eye once and he looked just as overwhelmed as she felt, but also just as determined.

The tsunami of power that greeted them slowly dissipated as it was either fed into a generator or returned to the other ley line. It felt like years, decades, for this to happen. Without a watch or phone on her, Noriko couldn't begin to tell how long they actually worked. Streams of sweat poured from her temples, under her arms, and down along her spine.

Two more teams poured in, all of them joining in the efforts, and then two partners focused on burying the exposed ley line and replacing the broken cement. Noriko counted it as a victory as she watched this happen, because if they had the manpower to spare to do that, then the situation wasn't nearly as dangerous as before.

Jack tapped her shoulder and then pulled her gently to her feet. "Up you go. You're done."

"Stick a fork in me, that kind of done?" Cameron gasped. He had his hands braced against his knees, sucking in air with ragged pulls.

"More like 'you're done in,'" Jack corrected dryly. "Either way, to the van, both of you. Get checked by medical. I don't want you collapsing."

If they could be released, then the situation really had improved drastically. Noriko looked around blearily as she stumbled for their van. As she watched, Sam and Teddy were also pulled away and sent toward the medics. More vans and ambulances were arriving to help, but it was more like stabilization and cleanup now. The hard part, the emergency surges, were all gone.

She felt like crying in relief.

The medics gave them a quick once over, ordered them to rest and drink lots of liquids, then shooed them away. Noriko retreated to the van only to find that Banderas was already there, propped up in the doorway as was his wont, with Charlotte collapsed on the van floor.

Noriko meant for a greeting, but what came out of her mouth was, "How long were we at it?"

"An hour and a half by my reckoning." Banderas gave them both a thumbs up. "Good work, both of you. I got another call from L.A. dispatch. The crisis is averted. They haven't gotten the city back up to its normal sea depth, but they're no longer sinking, which I consider good enough for the moment."

So did she. Beyond relieved, she crawled into the van and plopped onto the bench. Then she toppled straight to the side, not caring that she wound up in a half-contorted position.

"Cap, I gotta tell you, another scene like this and I'll start demanding hazard pay." Cameron was only half-joking.

"This is not normal," Banderas assured him darkly. "In fact, it's so abnormal that I feel sorry for both of you coming on when you did. Six months ago we were so peaceful that we were actually playing games half the shift because there was nothing to do."

They had said in her welcome packet that Tehachapi was a very quiet place. Noriko just hadn't believed it after that first week. "So who's doing this?"

"Not sure," Banderas admitted. There was a slight smile on his face that spoke of feral intentions. "But that man Hodges that you two caught earlier today? Some of the things he was saying suggests that he might know something about this. I think I'll have a little chat with him tomorrow about it."

"Don't do it without us," Cameron requested. "This is one interrogation I don't want to miss."

27ᵀᴴ MERLIN

MERCY (or at least their captain) had more compassion on the two newest members of Pathmaker, as they were able to attend the last day of trial this time without a test interfering. Noriko hadn't been sure of the dress code for court, but everyone else was wearing their GF uniforms, so that's what she wore as well. It turned out to be the right choice as every GF member that wasn't on duty was in attendance. Half the courtroom was a sea of red because of that.

Hodges's cool did not return after that first interview and he had basically crumpled under the cross-interrogation of the prosecuting attorney. He had admitted to being paid to tamper with the fail safes, along with Wesson and Landers, but he was adamant that it was not corporate sabotage. "They" had asked him to do it, and so he had.

No matter what he was threatened with, however, he wouldn't name his employer.

Whatever or whoever they were, they scared him more than jail time could.

Noriko had watched him carefully, as had everyone else in the room, and he had been terrified up there. Also terribly alone, as no one would come in and speak for him even as a character witness. Wesson and Landers were slightly better off as it was Hodges that had paid them and acted as messenger boy. They were clueless as to who it was that wanted the test cell destroyed, they had assumed what everyone else had—it was some corporation or rival company that wanted the engine destroyed. To hear that they were part of some conspiracy group with its own agenda had been a complete shock to them.

Cameron fidgeted on the bench beside her. "What is taking so long?"

"The jury has only been out ten minutes," she drawled, poking idly at her phone.

"What's there to deliberate?" he grumbled, more to himself than to her. "All three of them were basically oozing guilt."

That part was very true.

"What are you doing?" he asked, leaning over her shoulder.

"Refreshing my email."

"For what?" As soon as the question was out of his mouth he went, "Ahhh. Test results come out today. I forgot."

Noriko bent a look at him. "You forgot. Seriously?"

"What? I was more interested in how the trial would go."

Why was this uncaring man her partner again?

"Aren't you the tiniest bit worried about your test scores?"

"Naw, I passed, that's all I care about."

She decided on the spot that if he got anything above a C, she would murder him. Just for his attitude alone.

The jury filed back in, and the court room went abruptly silent. It took a few minutes for all dozen members to be seated, and then the judge turned to them and asked, "Jury, have you reached a verdict?"

The jury foreman stood. "We have, your honor. We judge all three defendants guilty on all accounts."

Noriko let out a breath she wasn't aware she'd been holding. The evidence had been good, but some of it was circumstantial, and they only had Hodges' confession to even prove he was part of the whole debacle.

"Let the defendants rise." The judge waited for all three men to stand before intoning, "Lance Hodges, you have been charged with the purposeful destruction of government property, resisting arrest, conspiracy to cause explosions, and multiple cases of aggravated assault. For all of these you have been found guilty and will be punished to the full extent of the law. This court sentences you to twenty-five years without parole."

No one quite dared to openly cheer, but every person in the room made their own version of a happy noise. Hodges seemed too numb at this point, as he didn't even react, just stood there with his head hanging.

"James Wesson and Henry Landers, you are also charged with the purposeful destruction of government property, conspiracy to cause explosions, and multiple cases of aggravated assault. The additional charges from the Gældorcræft Forces of failure to enforce safety codes, failure to protect ley lines protected under governmental regulations, and the violation of preserving the civilian laws you are sworn to uphold are also laid against you. For all of these you have been found guilty and are hereby sentenced to life in prison without parole."

Wesson let out a strangled cry and dropped his head into his hands. Landers kept shaking his head over and over, but no sound emerged.

Noriko watched their reactions and wondered: had they really thought they could get by with it? They'd sworn something as sacred as the Hippocratic Oath when entering the Force, had they forgotten that? Because of what they could do, the damage they could inflict, they were held to a much higher standard than any civilian worker would be. Had they chosen to ignore that in their greed?

"The Case of State v. Wesson, Landers, and Hodges is now dismissed." The judge hit the sound block with her wooden gavel and stood.

The bailiff called out, "All rise."

Everyone promptly did just that, but they ignored the judge as she retreated back into her chambers. They were too busy rehashing the event to each other.

Noriko found it far too noisy in the room and so was one of the first to escape out into the hall. Finding it narrow and also full of people, she retreated further outside and onto the front steps. Cameron was right behind her.

"Oh hey. Our test results are in."

Immediately she put her holoshades on. "Email, open. Message from Proctor Center, open." Her eyes scanned the results and she let out a little happy dance. Straight A's, as expected of herself.

"Sweet," Cameron whistled.

That tone. That tone suggested she might have to murder him. Slowly pivoting about, she asked suspiciously, "What did you get?"

"A's. You?"

"Why does a person who doesn't care about his grades get A's?"

"Naw, I care," he assured her.

That was exactly the same tone he used when he was answering a question honestly but also trying to rile her up at the same time. Not able to take it anymore, she hopped up, hooked an elbow behind his neck, and started rubbing at his head vigorously.

"Ouch, hey, Spidey, quit!" He laughed and squirmed and managed to win free after about five seconds. "What was that for?"

"Because you irritate me," she shot back.

Cameron shook his head, laughter lingering on his face as he headed down the short stair to the sidewalk. "Haru's right, you're prickly on the strangest things."

Wait, what? "Haru? When did Haru say that?"

"Oh, we're texting buddies. Have been for a while."

Why was he saying that in such a nonchalant way?! How in the world had he even gotten her brother's number to begin with? Noriko wanted to ask, dearly wanted to ask, but she could tell that Cameron was teasing and just waiting for her to pounce on him to strangle answers out of his cryptic little throat. And she was loath to give him that satisfaction.

Since the beginning of their partnership, Noriko had been constantly thrown off-balance by him, not sure how to respond to Cameron. Even as she was laughing at his silly jokes, she was groaning at the same time. This was a beautiful opportunity to get a little revenge for feeling constantly off center. "You know, the captain told me the first day you arrived that if I didn't like you, he'd reassign you to someone else."

Cameron tripped over thin air. "He did?!"

"It wasn't the only time he said it, either." Seeing that Cameron actually was worried about this, she let him squirm for a full three seconds before admitting, "But I did decide to tell him that I wasn't interested in changing partners. So I guess I've already passed the point of no return on becoming crazy."

There was a smile on his face, but worry still in his eyes. "Glad to hear you want to stick with me, but you need to tell the cap, right? Soon?"

"And close all my escape routes?" Tsking him, she skipped ahead.

"Spiiiiidey!" he whined, stretching out his long legs and easily catching up with her. "Don't be mean."

Teasing her work partner was quite fun, really.

Why hadn't she tried this earlier? Teasing was the only way to survive with a jokester like Cameron, that was obvious, and she was ashamed of herself for not trying it sooner. "It's alright, Cam, I'll tell him," she soothed.

"Soon," Cameron demanded.

Now he definitely wasn't teasing. Her heart warmed when she realized he really, truly didn't want to have any partner other than her. Pivoting about, she walked backwards for a few feet, a grin on her face. "Soon," she agreed easily.

"I don't trust that smirk you're wearing. Today, Spidey."

"But we're only a few hours away from end of shift, I might not be able to catch him today," she protested innocently.

"Emails. Texts. Phone calls. Pick one."

He really wasn't going to let go of this, was he? "Shouldn't something like this be said in person?"

Wrong response. Cameron lunged forward, catching her around the waist so that he could snatch her phone off her wrist. With his prey caught, he double tapped the screen to wake it up. "Here. I'll text him for you."

Noriko struggled in vain to get her phone back, but of course he was not only taller than her by several inches, his arms were ridiculously long. With him holding it high above his head, she had no chance of reaching it, even if she did hop up. "Cameron. Give that back!"

"Almost done," he assured her cheerfully.

That was what she was afraid of. Alright, time to fight dirty. Switching tactics, she startled tickling his ribs. Cameron immediately doubled over, squirming and trying to get away from her. Not that it worked. She'd survived five siblings: she knew how to win a tickle fight. In no time, she had Cameron on the ground and was able to put a knee into his stomach, grab his arm, and wrestle her phone free of his reach. "Ha!" she crowed in victory.

"Too late," Cameron panted, flat on his back and not minding a bit that she was literally sitting on top of him. "Already sent."

"You rat," she growled, pulling up the messenger app and hoping that she could rescind the message. No luck, it was already delivered. Snapping it back onto her wrist, she glared down at him. "Harmony Cameron Powers, you have the patience of a water flea."

"I had a feeling," Banderas said from nearby, "That it wasn't you who sent me that message, Noriko."

Scrambling upwards, she landed an elbow in Cameron's chest, making him go "Oomph." Not stopping, she got to her feet and whirled around, finding her captain just in front of their designated van. The rest of their team waited behind him, badly hiding their amusement at the situation. Clearing her throat, Noriko belatedly realized that tickling Cameron into submission in front of one of the main doors of a courthouse might have been a bad call.

Not fazed at all by the embarrassment of the situation, Cameron rolled to his feet in a smooth motion. "It's okay, sir, she meant every word. She was just a little shy about telling you."

Banderas arched his brows in a noncommittal manner. "That right."

"What I *said* was," Noriko punctuated this by poking Cameron hard in the ribs, "that it was more appropriate to tell you in person. Sir."

"Now that I believe." Their captain's unreadable expression eased into a more gentle smile. "So, Noriko, do you feel like you're alright where you are?"

She gave him a thumbs up. "I've found his tickle spots. I'm good."

Cameron didn't seem the least bit worried about this. In fact, he started laughing. Squinting at him, she asked suspiciously, "Are you a masochist?"

"Nope. There's only one thing in the world I'm scared of." He gave her an impish grin.

Oh this was going to be good. Noriko waved him on. "Let's hear it. What's that?"

"That I'll get put in Slytherin."

Despite herself, she choked on a laugh. Banderas, she saw, rolled his eyes to the heavens as if to ask how he'd gotten stuck with this idiot. She assured him, "He's crazy, but I finally have a handle on his particular brand of craziness. No worries, Cap."

"Glad to hear it." Shaking his head, Banderas did the safe thing and went to a different topic. "I've decided to have the two of you retested."

Cameron pointed toward himself. "Us? Why?"

"I saw you handle 80 KMs for nearly two hours straight and you're asking me that question?" Banderas gave him an exasperated look, the same one that parents reserved for their children when they asked a stupid question. "You're getting retested, you and Noriko; there is absolutely no way under the sun that you're Level 4. I do not believe it."

Noriko had rather hoped that she could ignore tests for another two months until finals, but if her captain was insisting, then she only had one response. "Yes, sir."

"Good." Banderas gestured them to the van. "Load up, people. We're done for the day."

ABOUT THE AUTHOR

Over thirty years ago, in the hills of Tennessee, a nice, unsuspecting young couple had their first child. Their home has since then been slowly turned into a library as their daughter consistently brought books home over the years.

No one was surprised when she grew up, went to college, and got her Bachelor's in English. Despite the fact that she has a degree, and looks like a mature young woman, she's never grown out of her love for dragons, fairies and other fantastical creatures. With school done, she's ready to start her career, hopefully by blending two of her loves: books and fantasy.

Her website can be found here: http://www.honorraconteur.com.